ADMISSION

Also by Julie Buxbaum

Tell Me Three Things

What to Say Next

Hope and Other Punch Lines

ADMISSION

Julie Buxbaum

DELACORTE PRESS

Text copyright © 2020 by Julie R. Buxbaum Inc.
Jacket art copyright © 2020 by Shutterstock

All rights reserved. Published in the United States by Delacorte Press, an imprint of Random House Children's Books, a division of Penguin Random House LLC, New York.

Delacorte Press is a registered trademark and the colophon is a trademark of Penguin Random House LLC.

Visit us on the Web! GetUnderlined.com

Educators and librarians, for a variety of teaching tools, visit us at RHTeachersLibrarians.com

Library of Congress Cataloging-in-Publication Data
Names: Buxbaum, Julie, author.
Title: Admission / Julie Buxbaum.
Description: First edition. | New York : Delacorte Press, [2020] | Audience: Ages 12 up. | Summary: "An affluent teen who thinks she is headed off to the college of her dreams must reckon with the truth and possibly her own guilt when her mother is arrested in a college admissions bribery scandal"— Provided by publisher.
Identifiers: LCCN 2019058571 (print) | LCCN 2019058572 (ebook) | ISBN 978-1-9848-9362-8 (hardcover) | ISBN 978-1-9848-9364-2 (ebook)
Subjects: CYAC: Universities and colleges—Admission—Fiction. | Parent and child—Fiction. | Scandals—Fiction.
Classification: LCC PZ7.1.B897 Ad 2020 (print) | LCC PZ7.1.B897 (ebook) | DDC [Fic]—dc23

The text of this book is set in 11-point Berling.
Interior design by Trish Parcell

Printed in the United States of America
10 9 8 7 6 5 4 3 2 1
First Edition

For Halee Hochman: my first friend and my first phone call should I ever need to dispose of a body.

Jerry, just remember . . . it's not a lie if you believe it.

–George Costanza, *Seinfeld*

CHAPTER ONE

Now

My younger sister, Isla, will claim that she heard the footsteps before the doorbell rang, like a swelling movie score. *On. The. Count. Of. Three.* That she knew then what was to come. The guns, the hard metal handcuffs, the cameras, the headlines, the conversion from human being into meme.

The everything being over, just like that.

I don't believe her.

Isla has also sworn that she had a dream about an earthquake the night before the big one in Thailand last fall, that she suspected Beyoncé was going to drop that surprise album, that three years ago she predicted everyone would grow tired of cupcakes and start eating macaroons instead. Which is to say that Isla likes to be the first to know stuff, to take credit for willing into being that which is incapable of being willed. I am always the last to know. Maybe this is the biggest difference between us, how comfortable we are anticipating that which can't be anticipated, how prepared we are for that for which we can't prepare.

I am not ready. The apocalypse shouldn't arrive when you're in flip-flops or wearing sweatpants that have your high school's acronym (WVHS) spread along your backside. At least, this wasn't how I'd always pictured the end: I'd expected to need a stash of batteries and a flashlight and canisters of water, none of which would have helped make this moment any easier.

I certainly didn't expect hungry paparazzi with cameras slung around their necks.

I hear the doorbell, which triggers a Pavlovian burst of joy. The doorbell usually announces the arrival of something good: cosmetics I ordered from Sephora, a swag box from the studio that my mother will pass on to me and Isla; less often and less exciting but still plausible, a script sent in a rush from her agents, which may mean a new shooting location for my mom and a family adventure. Vancouver or Atlanta. Last time, Scotland. Once, luckily, New Zealand.

But it's 6:30 a.m. on a Monday, a school day, too early for UPS, too early for anything, really, except coffee. It's still dark and foggy, the world cruelly indifferent to the fact that I am not, nor will I ever be, a morning person. When LA has not yet become the city I love, full of glitter and grit, and is instead a sleepy and quiet town. My toenails are painted in alternating cardinal and gold, a detail that will be dissected by the tabloids later. They match my brand-new oversized Southern California College sweatshirt. This last item, I will, of course, end up regretting even more than my polish or the letters on my butt, a convenient way for my idiocy to be memorialized.

I'll be honest, since there's no other way left to be: There's a whole lot I will end up regretting.

But before I swing the door open, I'm still blissfully unaware of what's on the other side. In my uncaffeinated haze, I imagine a cardboard box on the stoop: the teal eye shadow palette I impulse-ordered last night to beta test for prom. Later, when all I have is time, when the hours stretch long and lonely, I will realize this first instinct made no sense at all. I didn't pay for overnight shipping.

When the chime fades, there's a hard knock and an "Open up," and I wonder what's the UPS guy's problem.

"Coming," I yell back, and then, "Relax, dude."

My dog, Fluffernutter, thinks I'm talking to her, and so she lies down at my feet and rolls over to expose her belly. I take a second to give her a quick rub. When I tally my long list of mistakes later, this will not be one of them. Fluffernutter, ever loyal, gave me one more moment of ignorance, an extra second in the before.

Another knock, so I scoop up the dog, kiss the top of her curly brown head, and then open the door with a "Hold your horses."

When we watch this moment on TMZ, and then again on CNN and MSNBC, and even for a dark minute on Fox News, my face is blurred because I'm only seventeen and still a minor. Afterward, Isla will turn to me and say, "'Hold your horses'? Really?" and I will shrug, like *Who cares?* though she will be right and again I will be wrong: This will turn out to be another thing that makes me look bad in the court of public opinion, if not a real court one day.

You don't say *Hold your horses* to the FBI.

The relief of my blurred-out face is short-lived. My picture will soon be splashed across magazines and newspapers and most indelible of all, the Internet, images borrowed from my mom's old Instagram posts and therefore legally considered public domain.

On the porch, seven men spread out in a line, all wearing black bulletproof vests, lettered like my pants (though theirs say FBI, not WVHS, of course), guns pointed in that way you see on television procedurals. Two-handed grips. Serious faces.

This must be some sort of joke, I think.

My mother's fiftieth birthday is coming up, though she has so far refused to acknowledge it, partly because according to IMDB and Wikipedia, she's only forty-five. The only reasonable explanation for the scene in front of me that I can conjure up on such short notice is this: It's a gag. These men are strippers. As soon as my mom makes her grand entrance, cheesy techno music will start blaring and they'll all do that one-piece tear-off. A choreographed move down the line, like Rockettes. Aunt Candy, my mother's best friend, is exactly the sort of person who would think sending FBI strippers to your door at 6:30 a.m. is hilarious. When she had a colonoscopy last spring, she blew up the black-and-white picture of her poop-flecked insides, had it expensively framed, and sent it to us as a Christmas present with a card that said, *Now you know me inside and out.* My mom hung the photo in the guesthouse bathroom, and if you didn't know any better, you'd think it was a modern art masterpiece and not what it really is: proof that Aunt Candy is literally full of crap.

"Can I help you?" I ask, smiling despite the hour. Because it's still funny, this before-moment, when I think that I'll get to see these semi-handsome muscley men undress and dance. When I still believe they're carrying toy guns and not semiautomatic assault rifles. When my default was friendly, not defensive.

"We're here for Ms. Joy Fields," they say, and at the exact same minute, I hear my mom exclaim in a panic: "You weren't supposed to answer the door."

My mother, Joy Fields—who you probably already know as Missy, the surrogate for the two gay dads on the long-running aughts CBS sitcom *My Dad, My Pops, and Me*, or more recently as the queen in *Blood Moon*, the royal vampire show on the CW—is an actress, and therefore, I don't react when I hear her nervous voice behind me. She's won six People's Choice Awards, she can weep on command, and sometimes she speaks with a British accent just for fun.

Which is to say, my mother can be a little dramatic.

Then again, as the world will learn mere minutes from now, I can be a little oblivious.

"What's going on?" I ask.

"Go get your father," she says, and she puts her arm out straight across my chest, like she does in the car when she has to stop short. A reflex to protect me. Her hair drips water onto her shoulders, and when I see she's not wearing any makeup, that she's run here straight from the shower and hasn't even stopped for undereye concealer, it hits me, finally: This is not a practical joke. This is real.

"Just give me a minute to get dressed first," my mom says to the man in front of her, like she knows exactly what's going on, like she's not surprised that they are here, only that they are here this early, slightly ahead of schedule.

"Ma'am," the guy in the center says, in a surprisingly mild voice, and he does a hand signal thing to the others that obviously means *Put down your guns*, which they do, all at once, as synchronized as Rockettes, a bizarre version of my original imagining. I feel a sudden relaxation in my body; at some level I must have known that these were actual weapons, with bullets, and that they were pointed, if not quite directly at me, then close enough. "Someone can bring your clothes later, no problem. Please hold out your wrists. I have a warrant for your arrest. You have the right to remain silent. . . ."

I don't hear all of it, though I can guess what he says, because I live on this planet and have therefore seen *Law & Order*. Isla, who despite being one year younger is always one step ahead, must have been standing here at least part of the time, because she's the one who fetches Dad. He comes running in his pajamas—a T-shirt we bought him as a joke last Christmas that says *Master of the Universe* (the tabloids will have fun with that too) and fancy pajama pants from Fred Segal, crisp and paisley. He has a phone glued to his ear. I can't imagine who he could be calling.

Not 911.

The cops are already here.

My mother is led to a waiting car, and they do the hand-on-the-head thing while she ducks into her seat, and for a second, before I remember what's happening, even though they are gentle, I wince. My mom hates anyone, other than her stylist, touching her hair. She's convinced she's thinning at the back ever since an unflattering paparazzo shot of her scalp, exposed on a windy day, was featured on the cover of *Star* with the headline INSIDE "MISSY'S" CANCER SCARE!

Thirty seconds later, my phone beeps in my pocket and a *New York Times* alert reports what I've witnessed in real time.

The headline: JOY FIELDS, SITCOM STAR, ARRESTED ON MULTIPLE FRAUD CHARGES IN COUNTRYWIDE COLLEGE ADMISSIONS SCANDAL.

And that's when I know: This is all my fault.

CHAPTER TWO

Then

"Listen, I realize it's not your fault you've been body snatched," Shola, my best friend and partner in crime, says. It's a Sunday morning, only three weeks into senior year, and I sit studying for the SAT at the dining table, refusing to put away the books to go swimming. Before now, it's always been the other way around. Shola, fastidious and focused, me the one begging her to go outside and play. "But who are you and what have you done with my best friend?"

Last spring, Shola managed to get a 1560 on the SAT without a $500-an-hour tutor, and then to see what would happen, took the ACT and walked away with a 34. So she can put her feet up, which she is doing now, literally, on the chair next to mine. If she weren't my best friend and my favorite person in the world, I might hate her just a little.

"Be supportive of Nerd Chloe," I say.

Beyond the sliding glass doors, the pool's bright blue water ripples, a rectangular oasis with chaise lounges scattered around, like wheel spokes. A big woven basket sits full of Turkish towels, all rolled and at the ready. It's a crime against humanity that I am stuck inside deciphering math equations.

"Please never refer to yourself in the third person ever again. It's icky." Shola turns back to reading a romance novel, because even though I have to study and she doesn't, she prefers hanging out here rather than at her own house, which isn't a house but a small apartment with only two bedrooms over in West Adams. She shares bunk beds with her three brothers and sisters. "Come on. I'll even let you have the unicorn float this time."

Shola, at five foot eleven, is the shortest in her family, but sometimes when we stand next to each other, I have to crane my neck to make eye contact. This is only one of the many ways in which I feel small next to her. Shola is Nigerian American and beautiful, and she recently dyed her short hair platinum blond, like a young Grace Jones, because she has no fear. Sometimes it's confusing to be best friends with someone so effortlessly cool. We met in seventh grade, before either of us noticed how much better she was at everything, and it's an unspoken tenet of our friendship not to dwell on my relative mediocrity.

Instead, we've gone the much healthier route of my celebrating her accomplishments like they are my own. Her wins are my wins. To be jealous of Shola would be to miss the point entirely.

"Pancakes, ladies?" My mom glides into the room wearing a pristine red gingham apron I've never seen before, red short-shorts, and matching four-inch red stilettos, and holds out a giant stack of pancakes plated on a red ceramic platter.

Shola and I grab a few from a red rubber spatula and as she pirouettes back out, my mom stage-whispers: "I swear I put on five pounds just from the smell."

"*Marie Claire* profile," I say to Shola before she can ask. Shola already knows that my mother is not the type to make pancakes on an ordinary Sunday morning because: carbs. Not to mention my mom doesn't usually color-coordinate her clothing with our kitchen utensils. In fact, this might be the first time I've seen her play sexy homemaker, though she does bake a lot of holiday cookies in Christmas movies on the Hallmark channel. In those, though, she's always forced to wear plaid and cutesy Santa hats.

Readers of women's magazines would be devastated to learn that unlike her party line—"I love nothin' more than a burger and fries"—originally coined in a string of McDonald's commercials in which my mother smiles while digging into a Big Mac, the real way my mom keeps so thin is, spoiler alert, by the time-tested method of not eating, a fast metabolism, religious exercise, and, to leave no room for error, a frightening amount of self-shaming.

My mom spins and does Pilates and works out with a personal trainer named Raj, who she pays to yell in her face and to push her so hard she sometimes pukes. As she likes to say, *Fans don't want to know how the sausage is really made.* The truth is that fans don't want to know that the body they celebrate as beautiful may in fact be the product of a clinical disorder.

True story: Despite the fact that McDonald's residuals, at least in part, paid for this house, I wasn't allowed to step foot into one. Isla and I only went once I had my own driver's license, a tiny act of rebellion and curiosity that ended up giving both of us diarrhea.

Perhaps my parents have taken *too much* care with our digestive systems.

"One of those 'at home with Joy Fields' things. Carrie came early to mix the batter, so all my mom had to do was ladle it onto the pan in front of the reporter," I explain to Shola. Carrie is my mother's assistant and one of the many magical people who keep our lives running smoothly.

"Your family is so weird," Shola says with affection and a full mouth.

"Can you take this test for me? Please. I'll be your best friend," I joke, though if there were a way for Shola to impersonate me—short and white, with boring brown hair and boring brown eyes, I wouldn't say no. In fact, I wouldn't mind borrowing Shola's transcript too, since I've somehow slipped into the bottom half of our class. We go to Wood Valley, which is not only the best private school in Los Angeles, but is widely considered to be one of the best schools on the planet. When I first got in for seventh grade, my parents would adopt a self-congratulatory tone when talking to their friends, as if this spot at a middle and high school would alone be enough to secure me a particular kind of life, though I still have no idea what that life is supposed to look like.

Exactly like theirs, I think, but with a fancypants degree.

"Don't worry. Even if you end up in clown college, I'll still love you." Shola pinches my nose and makes a *boop* sound.

"At least someone will," Isla says as she walks in from

11

the butler's pantry, holding a racket in one hand and a six-hundred-page Dickens novel in the other. She's wearing a short white tennis skirt and a high ponytail, which means she's heading to the club with Dad. She looks like an advertisement for milk. Or Princeton.

"Where's Isla? Is she upstairs solving the energy crisis and brokering world peace again?" my dad asks, wandering in from the other door in his golf clothes. "It's almost tee time."

We are always like this, even without the benefit of an audience. All quips and separate entrances from side doors. A mediocre sitcom come to life.

"Nope, that was yesterday," Isla says, and for no reason at all other than this is who we are, when I catch her eye, I scratch my face with my extended middle finger. In response, she slowly winds up hers and then pretends to use it to apply lipstick.

My dad doesn't even blink.

"Your family is so weird," Shola says again after Isla walks out, not in anger so much as boredom. This is how Isla and I show each other love—with idiotic takedowns and clever ways of giving each other the finger (my personal favorite is blowing mine like a harmonica). It's the inversion of my relationship with Shola—I don't celebrate my sister's many accomplishments as my own, or she mine (if I had any), even though you'd think it would be easier with your own family.

But it's not. It's harder.

My dad walks over to me, grabs my head, and sniffs it like I'm an infant. He looks at the pancakes longingly.

"I told your mom she should have told the *Marie Claire* lady: 'Do you expect your male interviewees to make god-damn breakfast?' I don't think so, but she said Paloma would fire her as a client if she said that," my dad says.

"Paloma can suck it," I say, and my dad gives me a high five. We're united in our hatred for Paloma, my mother's publicist. If we are actors in a sitcom come to life, she's our director. Such is the power of Paloma that at last year's Emmy party, she made our family wear coordinating beige outfits and pose on a red carpet in front of a wind machine, so if you google me, what pops up is a deranged version of a Kardashian Christmas card.

"My mother would wash your mouth out with soap if she heard the way you talk, Mr. Bellinger," Shola says.

"A boy can dream," my dad says.

Shola once told me, "Your dad is super hot. He talks like he knows what he's doing in all the things, Chloe. All the things."

I think about this a lot, in that strange way a random detail can get lodged in the brain. Not about my dad's attractiveness or prowess, of course, which is gross and will never be mentioned again, but I wonder at the casual ease with which he moves through the world and convinces everyone he's got this. That heady combination of white male privilege and substantial wealth that inspires restaurant hostesses to give him the best table, makes investors hand over their money, and generally forces the world to bend to his will.

Though I've inherited the white privilege and I guess, eventually, some of the money, I do not got this. On any front. If I were one day given my own fragrance line, it would be named, in that sexy breathy whisper of perfume commercials, *Indecision*.

"Shola, how many times have I told you to call me Richard?" my dad asks.

"Approximately eleventy billion," she says.

"Call me Richard," my dad says.

"Eleventy billion and one," Shola says, and not for the first time, I wonder what she really thinks of my family. *Weird* seems too small, too limiting a word, like she's intentionally being vague.

I might pick these two words instead: *lovingly deranged*.

"This one's quick." My father taps his nose and grins at Shola. "You should give some SAT tips to Chlo. God knows she could use all the help she can get."

Later, after Shola has gone home to tutor the Littles, what she calls her twin brother and sister, who, in the sixth grade are already taller than me, my mother plops down on the couch. She has traded her apron for a crisp white pajama set with navy blue piping, and she looks like she's in an ad for expensive linens. I again have my SAT book open, though my hair is wet from an afternoon swim.

"How'd it go?" I ask, and my mom leans her head back against the tufted velvet and sighs. Her blond hair spreads out like spilled water. Whenever people meet her, they can't help staring, and not only because she's famous. They stare because she's flawless. Even in LA, where we have a ridiculous number of pretty people, she's a Monet in a room full of Bob Ross paintings. All are pleasing to the eye, but a Monet demands you stop and linger. You take a piece of its beauty with you in your mind when you go.

I've always wanted to ask but have never gathered up the nerve: *What's it like to look like you? How does it feel to walk around with that kind of power?*

Looks-wise, I take after my father. My features add up to a perfectly normal, albeit bland, face. I'm like the art you find on the walls of a hotel room, a photograph of a familiar local landmark designed to blend into the background.

To be clear: I'm not complaining. I learned long ago that there are worse things than being unnoticeable.

"It's the same interview for twenty years. They ask me how I'm like Missy in real life, and I say, 'Actually I'm nothing like her,' and then I try to pivot to promote the new show, though no one actually wants to hear about the new show. Paloma said the pancakes were a mistake."

She puts her arm around me and brings me in closer for a snuggle. We're a touchy-feely family. Not a day goes by when my parents don't say *I love you*, and often, before bed, they'll swing by my room to tuck me in even though I'm seventeen and supposed to be too old for that. I realize that if I'm going to rebel—beyond that sacrilegious trip to McDonald's—I should do it now. I'm supposed to want to ink my arms with tattoos and dabble in recreational drugs and dream of living a life free from my parental overloads.

But Hudson, my half brother, who's ten years older and the product of my dad's first marriage, has ruined all of these things for me. He's tatted out, more ink than skin, and more than a dabbler on the pharmaceutical front, and I don't think he's ever listened to a word my mom and dad have said.

He and I share a little DNA, and not much else.

My parents' worst nightmare—and to be fair, maybe mine, too—is that I turn out like Hudson, who didn't go to college and instead goes to rehab on the regular.

My mom taps the SAT book.

"So what was your last score?"

"About the same," I say, and my eyes fill and I fidget with my wet head. This is a lie: My score seems to be going down, not up. "I swear I'm studying as much as I can. I really am."

Here's what I want to say instead: *It turns out I'm stupider than we thought and I'm sorry.*

"Aunt Candy says she knows a guy who can help."

"Another tutor?" I try to keep the whine out of my voice. Senior year has barely started, but between Mandarin five days a week and my volunteer work at the Reading and Resource Center, on top of studying and homework, I'm already burned out. I would cut down my volunteer hours, but it's the only extracurricular activity I actually enjoy. Cesar, my first-grade little buddy, is my favorite person in the world after Shola, and I refuse to let him down.

"Not a tutor. An admissions consultant."

"That's what Mrs. Oh is for. I thought Wood Valley doesn't like us to hire privately." Last week, I had my first meeting of the year with the Wood Valley college counselor, Mrs. Oh. She patted my hand, like she was a doctor about to tell me I had only three weeks to live, and said, "Honey, I

16

think this application list has too many reach schools. With your numbers, we need to be more realistic."

Then she asked me what I was hoping to get out of my college experience. I couldn't tell her the truth. That I'm looking forward to fraternity parties and football games and if it doesn't happen before, a not-so-traumatic loss of my virginity.

"This guy is supposed to be the absolute best. He's based in New York, but he's flying in to LA to meet with us. He'll come up with a list of schools, he'll help us with our applications, and he'll edit our essays. He advocates behind the scenes." I don't comment on my mom's creepy use of the words *us* and *ours* like she is applying too.

"Aunt Candy says you'll love him. He helped Philo get into Yale." Aunt Candy is not really my aunt; she's been my mom's best friend for the last thirty years, since they met doing off-off-Broadway in New York. Candy quit acting when she married a hedge fund billionaire and moved into a town house on the upper east side of Manhattan. Now when anyone asks her what she does, Aunt Candy calls herself a "philanthropist" and likes to joke that her wrists get tired from writing so many checks.

I blame Aunt Candy for the fact that no matter how much I complain about my lack of aptitude when it comes to foreign languages, my parents won't let me quit taking Mandarin. A few Christmases ago, when we were all vacationing at her house in Mystique, she casually mentioned that Philo was fluent. Not a week later, Isla and I both had a private tutor.

If my mother's gifts are her ability to mesmerize people

with her looks and to elevate bad TV dialogue, Candy's is her unerring confidence and the fact she always *knows a guy*.

Actually, not *a* guy. *The* guy.

"Seriously? This is a done deal?"

"What?" My mom drops a kiss on the center part in my hair and smooths my flyaways with her hands. "It can't hurt."

CHAPTER THREE

Now

Isla and I sit in stunned silence as my father paces and shouts into his cell phone.

"No, this isn't like the time we bailed Hudson out for that ounce. These are felony charges. She could go to *jail.*" My dad's voice breaks, and Isla and I both involuntarily shiver. My brain had not gone there yet. Apparently, neither had all-knowing Isla's.

I don't know who he's talking to. Aunt Candy, maybe, or perhaps Aunt Candy's husband, Charles, who probably keeps a team of lawyers on retainer. My mom always says that it's impossible that anyone could have gotten as rich as Charles has by doing everything on the full up and up. I've always assumed that was sour grapes on my mom's part—as cushy as my mom's life is, Aunt Candy's is significantly, outrageously cushier. Even with my mediocre math skills, I know a billion dollars is, after all, a *thousand* million—but maybe she's right.

"I know," my dad says. "I know."

Isla and I watch him, our eyes moving back and forth as he crosses the room. This feels only slightly better than watching CNN, which we've consumed for three hours straight already, injecting their endless, breathless coverage of what they are calling the "college admissions scandal" straight into our eyeballs. The footage played on a loop: my mom ducking into that cop car and being driven away, the tie of her robe flapping out the door, like a broken hand waving goodbye.

I turned off my cell phone—the hate texts and the morning show requests started almost immediately—so I can't call Shola or Levi. Then again, I can't imagine what my friends could say that would make me feel better at this point: *Sorry your life has turned into an episode of* Breaking Bad?

"I'm heading over to the courthouse. The top guy from Dinnison and Cromswell is meeting me there. And my banker is standing by for bail."

Bail. That's a word we've only ever used in relation to Hudson, and even then, as far as I know, only once or twice. Plus, Hudson has always faced state charges; my mother has, apparently, been arrested for federal crimes. I don't know what the difference is, but from the way my dad's voice pitches up, frantic, I gather federal is way worse.

My dad crosses the room, steps over my outstretched legs. Isla's been glaring at me on and off all morning. What she wants to say but with uncharacteristic self-control hasn't said yet: *If you weren't such an idiot, none of this ever would have happened.*

Isla has ranked in the top five of her class since she started at Wood Valley. Whenever I was studying for the SATs and struggling with a question, she'd glance over my shoulder and say, "Duh, it's C." When she wasn't looking, I'd check the answer key in the back. She was always right.

"They say likely anywhere up to a mil. When we first heard, I called around yesterday. But I don't know. We didn't expect this. There were guns. Semis, I think. What does it matter? We should sue them. Emotional distress. Child endangerment. Violation of privacy. I mean, Chloe, her whole life is ruin—" My dad freezes, suddenly remembering I'm in the room. But I'm not following what he's saying. I'm stuck at "I called around yesterday."

CNN has informed us that there is a two-hundred-page criminal complaint publicly available online. So much for privacy. I haven't found the courage to click on it yet, but I bet Isla has.

According to the *New York Times*, forty-five people have been arrested alongside my mother. From what I can gather, the charges are conspiracy to commit mail fraud and conspiracy to commit honest services fraud.

I have no idea what any of these words mean when they are put together in that order.

But I do know that my mother is being accused of fixing my SAT score and paying bribes to get me into SCC.

My idiocy is right out there, in the open, for the whole world to see.

As I watch my dad stride one more time, back and forth, my stomach revolts.

I sprint to the bathroom and throw up.

CHAPTER FOUR

Then

We sit in a circle in English 4. Mrs. Pollack thinks this formation encourages discussion, that if we see each other's faces, we're more likely to say what we're thinking out loud. Instead, it makes me queasy. I've long wanted to raise my hand and tell her that if she really wanted an intense conversation, we should hold class via text.

Today, a month into senior year, we're talking about *Crime and Punishment*, which of course Shola loved and I hated, or at least I hated the first fifty pages enough not to read beyond them.

"So Fyodor Dostoyevsky—and this is in real life, not in *C&P*, remember—is about to be executed, is mere seconds away from being shot in the head, and instead ends up being sent to a labor camp in Siberia for four years. Now, what is four years? Let's unpack this." Though we are less than a month into the school year, we already know that *unpack* is Mrs. Pollack's favorite word. Shola and I count, and she once used it thirty-two times in forty-five minutes. "Four years is how long you will spend in high school. Imagine, for a moment, that instead of lounging around in this lofty bastion of privilege and entitlement, you were serving time at a prison camp in Siberia."

"Samesies!" Levi shouts, and the room dissolves into laugher. Axl and Simon both fist-bump him, and he looks over at me, as if to make sure I registered the joke. I smile, and catching his eye feels like the most delicious kind of panic.

I've had an intense, debilitating crush on Levi since seventh grade, and I've been relegated to the friend zone for just as long. Which is totally fine. We can't get everything we want. Deprivation builds character.

Levi and I hang out sometimes and text constantly— about school, about our existential crises, and of course about all the girls he likes, because life is cruel and though this may not be a Siberian labor camp, high school has its own indignities. Shola's convinced that Levi is just as in love with me as I am with him, but as my ride-or-die, it's her job to feed my ego when the rest of the world craps on it.

I do the same for her, because even though Shola is the best person on earth, high school isn't a place known for recognizing out-of-the-ordinary greatness or for celebrating true nonconformity. They only seem to like the intentionally cultivated, Instagram-friendly kind. Shola's literally too cool for school.

Levi, on the other hand, has found his venue here at Wood Valley. I'm not the only girl who watches wistfully as he walks down the hallway. He's half Indian, half white, and has unruly brown hair and big brown eyes and a grin that spreads so deliberately and sensually, it feels like he's unzipping a zipper. He's president of our class, is a National Merit Scholar, and takes five APs on top of playing two sports. But sometimes he rubs his eyes with his fists, like babies do when they're tired, and it is so cute and guileless that I die a little. I suspect he knows how I feel, has always known, and I also suspect that he likes to stoke my crush, because it's fun being on his end of its unrequitedness. I don't blame him.

"What do you think, Chloe?" Mrs. Pollack asks, but I've been off in Levi land, so I have no idea what she's talking about.

My face flushes hot.

"Um, what was the question?" I hate being caught out in class. It's embarrassing enough when our tests get handed back and I have to flatten my palm over my inevitable B minus so that no one else sees.

"*Crime and Punishment*. We know from history that Dostoyevsky is rejecting Russian nihilism," she says. She's trying to help me out here but it's not working. I have no idea what nihilism is. "This is a deeply moral novel about a murderer. Amazing, right? How he garners our sympathy—or is it empathy?—despite the fact that from almost the very beginning, we know Raskolnikov's capable of monstrous things. We don't have to like him. People forget that about novels. It's not our job to like our main character. It's our job to try to understand them. Let's be honest, most people are deeply unlikeable."

"Yeah, totally," I say, but I'm not sure I agree. Sure, when I turn on the news, I see that our government is filled with truly disgusting people, but that doesn't seem to apply to my daily existence. Am I deeply unlikeable? What would happen if I wrote a book about my life? It's hard to imagine anyone caring about the life and times of Chloe Berringer. There are no dead bodies, no deep dark secrets, no real intrigue. I have, thus far, murdered approximately zero people. Most of the plot would consist of me eating fro-yo with Shola and making sad doe eyes at a boy who doesn't like me.

Poor little rich girl in unrequited love.

Even I can hear the orchestra of the tiniest violins.

"Right," Levi jumps in, and my appreciation for him rescuing me almost supersedes my embarrassment. "It's because we get to watch his slow descent into crossing a sacred moral boundary. Also, I think there's simply the benefit as a reader of being in his head and having access to his innermost thoughts. He may be a deeply flawed person, but we see, at the end of the day, he's still a person. Just like us."

A few months ago, *Us Weekly* ran a photo of my mom at the Whole Foods salad bar in their "Celebrities: They're Just Like Us!" section. In the picture, she looks impossibly glamorous despite wearing head-to-toe spandex and wielding tongs to dish out baby spinach.

My guess is that Paloma staged the picture. That it was orchestrated perfection. A gaslighting of sorts, because I doubt that a single woman who saw that photo came to the same conclusion as the headline: that Joy Fields was "just like her."

"How does it feel to be forced to see a murderer as a person?" Mrs. Pollack asks Levi, and I realize with relief that

I'm off the hook. I keep writing anyway so it looks like I'm listening.

I scribble down: *Criminals: They're Just Like Us!*

"Taking it again?" Levi asks after class, nodding at my SAT prep book, which I carry around with me everywhere, tucked under my arm, exactly the same way they made us hold the robot baby for an entire month for health class last year.

"You know," I say noncommittally. I haven't mentioned to Levi that I'm living in a never-ending loop of SAT hysteria. He obviously has Isla's and Shola's test-taking superpowers. He too was one and done.

"I can help if you want. I weirdly love standardized tests."

"You would," I say, and nudge him in the shoulder, in that flirty-not-flirty way we've perfected that suggests either an easy friendship or a loaded one. "I have a tutor already, but thanks."

The SAT would be a perfect excuse to hang out with Levi alone; too bad studying with him is my worst nightmare. My class ranking isn't a secret—people generally know how everyone else does here—but you can chalk bad grades up to laziness or lack of interest in the material. My kind of SAT and ACT scores would make him think I was never smart enough to be at Wood Valley in the first place.

"You going to Xander's party this weekend?" Shola asks Levi, since she knows that I'm desperate to know if he'll be there.

"Yup," Levi says, and I can't tell if I'm imagining the

eagerness in his voice when he adds: "You're coming too, right, Chloe?"

"We'll be there," I say, super casual, and I'm impressed with my play-it-cool delivery. Maybe Xander's party will be the thing that helps us cross over that delicate line, and we'll start flirting for real, and become more than friends, and kiss, and then go to prom in the spring and then Levi, my first real crush, could transform into my first real everything else.

"Cool," he says, and double taps my shoulder with his fist, the same hand he uses to rub his eyes, and I feel that zing that always happens whenever he touches me. "Later."

After he walks away, Shola puts her hands on her hips like Wonder Woman.

"He's either into you or he's a jerk," she declares, and I ready myself for what Shola calls "real talk," which I've learned is a euphemism for brutal honesty. "He knows you like him. He flirts with you all the time. He's either toying with you, which would make him a jerk, or he actually likes you. And I don't think he's a jerk."

She holds out her palms to me, like a shrug emoji, as if to say *I rest my case*. Shola's life goal is to be this country's first black woman chief justice of the Supreme Court, a double first, and because she is Shola, I have no doubt she'll make that sort of herstory. I look forward to my mother one day playing a lawyer in the biopic of Shola's rise to fame.

My life goal, on the other hand, is way more modest, like an inversion of those people who say if they had a genie they'd wish for more wishes. My life goal is to have an actual life goal, to feel about something the sort of excitement and passion Shola seems to feel about the law, because I realize partying on a yacht with Rihanna shouldn't count.

"I get that I'm not everyone's cup of tea," I say. Shola looks me up and down, a steady sweep of evaluation, as if running a tally in her head of my pros and cons. Like we haven't spent every day together for the last five years.

"We really need to work on your self-esteem," she says.

CHAPTER FIVE

Now

I stare in the mirror, as if I can find answers on my face, but there are none. I crawl back to my spot on the couch and lie there wide-awake even though it's 5:30 a.m. Thanks to CNN, I've been able to track my parents, so I know they're finally on their way home. My dad met a lawyer at the courthouse yesterday afternoon, and a judge granted my mother's release contingent on her posting $250,000 in bail. That number rolls around in my head, familiar, an echo: *a quarter of a million dollars.*

The paparazzi are staked out in front of the house, so my parents' arrival as they make their way up the walk is accompanied by a series of loud clicks, and "What do you have to say?" and "Will you plead guilty?" and other questions to which I too would like to know the answers.

Once they are inside, my dad closes the door and puts his back up against it, like people do in horror movies. He rubs his cheeks a few times, slaps them as if to wake up, and then, without another word to me or to my mother, takes the stairs two at a time and disappears into their bedroom, slamming the door shut behind him.

I stand up and stare at my mother. She's both familiar and foreign. Although it would have been impossible for her to have lost any real weight in the not quite twenty-four hours since I last saw her, she's pale and looks somehow too thin. A plastic bag dangles from her wrist, her bathrobe stuffed inside, as she's changed into the fleece pullover and jeans my dad must have brought to the courthouse. Her hair hangs limp around her face, the first time I've seen it air-dried in as long as I can remember.

I've occasionally caught my mother lifting the skin around her jawline and then letting it drop when she thinks no one is looking. In this unforgiving morning light, cold and sharp, I see what she's been worried about: midlife jowls. Her face spilling off into a frown.

"Mom," I say. I don't know if I want to scream or cry, if I'm supposed to comfort her or she's supposed to comfort me. I don't understand how this is our real life, how we managed to screw everything up this much.

I keep my voice low. Isla is sleeping. She ended our joint vigil when we got the text that my mom had been granted bail.

"Processing will take a few hours. They won't be home until crazy late," she'd said, and like with everything else with my little sister, I wanted to ask *How do you know that?* Not for the first time, I thought about how Isla must have been given a manual at birth called *How the World Works*, and that someone had forgotten to slip me a copy. "Things are going to be a mess tomorrow. And for the foreseeable future. You should get some sleep, Chlo."

She said this in her resigned, martyr-like Isla way, like she's forty and not sixteen, and like she was born into this family against her better judgment.

"I'm going to wait up," I said.

"Suit yourself." Isla went upstairs and left me alone on this couch to wait for this moment, when I would again face my mother. You would have thought in all those hours I'd lain here staring at the ceiling, I'd have figured out how I felt or what I wanted to say.

Now that I see her, I feel only one thing: the sense of the world righting itself. Like that moment on a flight when the fasten seat belt light dings off, and you think, *This will probably not be the day I die after all.*

"Mommy," I say, a word I don't ordinarily use that makes me think of my childhood—fairy wings and birthday parties and the unfolding of endless free afternoons. She's been Mom for a long time.

"Are you okay?" I ask, at that exact same moment my mom says: "You all right, baby?"

I nod and she nods, and then she opens her arms wide. I think, *I'll be angry tomorrow.* I think, *I'll never forgive her.* I think, *Maybe tomorrow I'll gather the courage to ask, What have we done?* But thinking is different from feeling, and at this moment there's no space inside for any of it.

I'm too filled up. No room at the inn.

I want my mommy.

I burrow into her outstretched arms and rest my face in her neck.

We both cry.

CHAPTER SIX

Then

I hadn't planned on drinking at Xander's party, but Levi handed me a cup and I took it and started sipping. I was nervous, and now I'm not—*thank you, beer that tastes alarmingly like urine*—and for the first time, talking to him is almost as easy as it is to text. Levi puts the flat of his hand on my exposed back and his fingers spread like a starfish.

This silk tank top, which I borrowed from my mother, knows what it's doing.

I hope he can't feel my pimples.

Shola is off somewhere with Mateo, a guy from Brentwood Country Day she's been crushing on, and I wonder if they've disappeared into one of the bedrooms upstairs. We've been to many identical parties here before, down to the playlist blasting from the backyard speakers, the same groups of kids holding red plastic cups, the same listless carrots-and-celery platter that someone, though I have no idea who—Xander? His Carrie equivalent?—has laid out on the kitchen table. Xander has rich absentee parents who keep a fully stocked bar and spend most of their time, for reasons unexplained, in Monaco. I imagine they are unaware of how many and how often teenagers traipse across their lawn and puke in their bushes.

Xander loves to cultivate the sense that he's a budding Hugh Hefner, so he presides over his parties in silk robes and randomly screams directions like "Down it!" or "Take it all off!" from the second-floor deck. Whenever we come here, I get a propulsive form of déjà vu, the feeling that not only have I been in this same moment before, but also that I will never not be. Which, come to think of it, is how I feel about high school generally. Like I'm in stasis, which is, so far, my favorite SAT word, at least in its secondary definition of a *stoppage of flow*, because it describes how I feel studying for the test.

Levi and I play beer pong on the patio against Simon and Axl, who are not twins or even brothers but who somehow have always felt interchangeable to me, in much the way that this party feels interchangeable with its previous itera-tions. This is because Simon and Axl are inseparable, and because they're both floppy-haired, wiry white boys who golf. I know exactly what they will look like in twenty years, how far their hairlines will recede and their guts will extend, and how soon they'll molt into Republicans for tax reasons, so the now of them feels temporary. It's totally unnecessary to tell them apart.

"Cheaters," Axl yells after he chugs his beer for the bil-lionth time and then raises his arms in victory, even though technically he lost.

"How could we possibly cheat? You saw her throw the

ball," Levi says, and I giggle, and just like that, I've morphed into the scantily clad girl at the party talking to Levi, the one who, in parties past, used to make me burn with jealousy and on occasion go home and cry.

"Turns out Chloe over here has impeccable hand-eye coordination when under the influence."

"I do," I say. "Maybe I should put that on my college applications? *Can't math, but kills at beer pong.*"

"You used *math* as a verb," Levi says, and I think, with sudden clarity, *We're both drunk.* The college counselor is coming tomorrow morning, but it's too late to undrink that beer.

"Sure did," I say, and Levi high-fives me. "We should turn more nouns into verbs. Like we're beer ponging."

"You're verbing."

"And we're bantering," I say, and then realize I've said the quiet part out loud. I've always wanted to banter like they do in rom-coms, and now that I'm actually doing it, I'm hyperaware that it's as much fun as it looks.

"*Banter* is already a noun and a verb," he says.

"Stop technicaliting." Levi's eyes sparkle and he throws an arm around my shoulders in mock apology, and it feels like the opposite of stasis. Like we are actually moving along, and he might actually kiss me. Like all the hours I've spent counseling him about other girls, or all the times he said things like *Man, Chloe, you are such a good friend,* never happened.

And then, as I turn to Levi, wondering if my lips are chapped or if my breath is tangy or if he'll make that move I've long fantasized about and pull me toward him—I'm suddenly blinded, and my eyes burn with a searing pain.

"Score!" Simon yells. He's landed the ball in the cup right in front of me and doused my entire face in beer. I'm sure the mascara I lovingly applied earlier is quickly laying tracks on my cheeks.

"*Score:* also both a verb and a noun," Levi says before gallantly jogging away to find me a paper towel.

What I'm thinking about while I sit with my parents across from Dr. Wilson in our living room the next morning is not college.

I am thinking about the fact that I did not score.

There was no kiss.

I left the party at 11:45, and as we said goodbye, Levi drew me into one of his usual friendly bear hugs, and I wondered if my hair stank of beer. That was it. We're still friends. Flirtier friends who banter, maybe. But still just friends.

Or, to turn it into a verb: We friend hard.

I consider pouring myself a cup of coffee from the elegant tray set out on the table but then wonder if that might make me throw up. If I vomit on the expensive college counselor, my parents will never forgive me. Just this morning, my mom told me we are "so lucky that Dr. Wilson is willing to meet with us." But a few days ago, I overheard her telling Carrie to arrange his first-class flights from New York and two nights at the Four Seasons Beverly Hills and to issue him his check in advance, so I'm pretty sure his coming has nothing to do with luck.

He hasn't asked me a single question, so I've been able to marinate in my hangover, which is a new unfamiliar, unpleasant feeling—a stew of nausea and regret. The good news is I don't need to be in top form. We're already fifteen minutes into this meeting and I've only said seven words— *It's nice to meet you, Dr. Wilson*—none of which is true.

When I met with Mrs. Oh, our counselor at school, she asked straight out: "Tell me, who is Chloe Wynn Berringer?" like it actually mattered. When I stammered an incoherent response, she followed up by asking specifics about academics—my grades, the subjects I liked best and why, my extracurriculars, what I was considering as an essay topic, what I might want to major in. Then she got more personal. She wanted to know my favorite food. My hobbies. The best thing that's ever happened to me. The worst.

"My grandma died a few years ago," I said, because I couldn't think of anything else; nothing bad has ever really happened to me. My dad's mother lived on the other side of the country and was one of those old people who thought her age allowed her to say whatever mean thought crossed her mind without worrying about the consequences. On the rare occasions we saw her, she'd make comments like *Joy, it's a shame Chloe didn't get your nose* or *Chloe, dear, remember: a moment on the lips is a lifetime on the hips. Self-control is essential, darling. If you don't work on it, you'll turn into Hudson.* Her dying was sadder in theory than in actuality. Isla and I didn't go to the funeral because we had *Hamilton* tickets, which, in retrospect, was not our finest moment. "I guess I could squeeze an essay out of it."

"I think the admissions people are tired of kids exploiting their dead grandparents," Mrs. Oh said with a laugh, and her honesty made me like her. "Don't worry. You'll come up with something. I have faith in you."

Since then, I've been scribbling ideas in a notebook. Sometimes I think about writing about Hudson and what it's like to have a half brother who's an addict—the sudden tightness in my dad's face when his name pops up on his phone, like this might be *the call;* the way my stomach falls too—and then I remember that I can't. It could be leaked to a tabloid in six seconds flat.

"As we discussed on the phone, it's time to get Chloe an accommodation because of her learning issues," Dr. Wilson says, looking at my parents, his attention so focused, I feel like a piece of the furniture, human clutter.

"What learning issues?" I interrupt, and both my parents shush me, as if I'm a little kid and not an almost-adult, here to maturely discuss my college options.

"ADHD is probably most apt," Dr. Wilson says, continuing to ignore me as if I weren't the one to have asked the question he is answering. *Attention deficit hyperactivity disorder?* I haven't been diagnosed with ADHD or any other acronym. True, I don't have the best attention span in the world—the idea of reading all of *Crime and Punishment* felt very much like I'd committed a crime and that book was, in fact, my punishment—but I think that's true for most teenagers. The only notable exception might be Shola.

My problem isn't my attention span. It's that for me the stuff we learn in school is boring and irrelevant. I don't care if some made-up Russian dude from a gazillion years ago murders a greedy old lady and then feels bad about it for five hundred pages. Classics are overrated, unless we're talking *Pride and Prejudice* film adaptations.

I know I can focus when I'm interested. I once watched every episode of *The Good Place* in almost a single binge, and I basically mainlined the Fyre Festival documentaries. Also, after watching the shows *and* listening to the podcasts, I have very strong feelings about freeing Adnan Syed and locking up Elizabeth Holmes.

"Once we get that accommodation, she'll have unlimited testing time, which I think will help her elevate her score," Dr. Wilson continues, again with the *she*s and the *her*s as if I'm not even here. "She can take that accommodation to college, which will make the next four years way easier. It can really make the difference between getting As and flunking out."

I don't like Dr. Wilson and how he talks about a possible learning disability accommodation as if it's this season's must-have accessory, like an A.P.C. weekender bag. I once read an article about people pretending to have disabled children so that they could skip the lines at Disney World, and I thought, *Who would do that?* Now I wonder if the answer is us. *We* would do that.

Dr. Wilson is wearing a white linen shirt tucked into slim-fitting khaki pants, with shiny brown loafers. His hair is combed over a bald spot, as if he thinks he can fool us about what's under his sweep. I imagine him doing the same thing with my application, maneuvering some kind of comb-over of my bad grades.

He must be in his midforties, and I wonder what would

make someone want to spend his life helping teenagers like me get into college. It seems like a really sad way to make a buck. Though I guess it's a large buck, if the way my parents have rolled out the red carpet is any indication. "I'll help you with that paperwork. We're late, of course, but I think we can make it work."

"That would also help explain away her grades, right?" my mom asks. Apparently, she too has forgotten I'm in the room, and like with anything Aunt Candy recommends, she not only eats up this stuff, she also seems eager for more.

I don't want unlimited testing time.

Time isn't the problem. Not being able to figure out the answers is.

"Mom," I say. "I don't have ADHD. I mean, I'm not a genius, obviously. I know I'm not as book smart as Isla. But I don't have, like, a problem?"

My voice turns this into a question, which pisses me off. It sounds like I'm not sure. For the record, I wouldn't be ashamed if I did have an issue; I'd be thrilled if some legitimately prescribed Adderall was the solution to my GPA. But I'm not fooled by their broken logic. Some kids, by definition, have to be in the middle or the back of the class rankings. We can't all use learning disabilities to explain away our performance.

I know I can't.

I also realize I used the words *book smart* as if to carve out some wiggle room for myself. Like I have some other kind of yet-to-be identified intelligence. I can't imagine I'll ever be great at school—and let's be honest, "street smart" is off the table since I was raised in Beverly Hills. Still, surely there's something I'm good at that will come in handy in adult life.

I mean, Isla's a genius, but she's also a moron. She once wore a Canadian tuxedo to school with Tevas.

Dr. Wilson knows nothing about me, beyond my transcript and SAT scores. How can he make a diagnosis? Is he even a real doctor?

"Chloe, maybe you should go wait in the playroom," my dad says. The playroom is what we always call our den, even though it's been Lego- and toy-free since Isla was ten. For the first time, the word, which used to feel cute, chafes.

"Are you serious?" I ask my dad.

"This is all very common," Dr. Wilson says, finally turning to look at me, and he smiles. It's not quite creepy in the way it often is when middle-aged men smile at teenage girls, like they're the Big Bad Wolf and they want to eat you whole. Shola calls that the Perv Grin. His is simultaneously condescending and menacing. "I would bet at least forty percent of the kids in your class got an accommodation for their tests."

"I don't know a single person who got an accommodation," I say, hating the stubborn edge to my voice. I assume Dr. Wilson already thinks I'm spoiled. No need to play into that perception.

Privileged is the word I'd use instead, but maybe that's equally obnoxious. It's its own kind of cop-out.

"Of course no one goes around telling people. Not that anyone should be embarrassed—it's all perfectly legit—but you know how teenagers are. They like to keep this stuff on the DL, as you kids say."

No one says that, I think.

"Why should those other kids have an advantage that you don't?" Dr. Wilson asks. Clearly he has dealt with a lot of wealthy parents, because there is no quicker way to fire mine up than to suggest someone else is getting something that I'm not. That's how Isla and I ended up with a private meditation teacher and etiquette lessons and kidnapping insurance. That's how I ended up at Wood Valley in the first place. All my parents needed to hear was that it was the "best school in Los Angeles."

No one stopped to think whether it was the best school *for me*.

"Shola didn't get an accommodation," I say, and Dr. Wilson glances at my parents with an unspoken *Help me here*.

"That you know of," my dad says.

"Dad!"

"Also she's black," my dad says, with a knowing look to Dr. Wilson. "She'll get in wherever she applies."

"Dad!" I say again, this time louder. I know it's hard having a stupid kid, but that doesn't give him an excuse to be a racist jerk.

"What? I'm progressive. You know that. I think Shola's great. And we need diversity. But let's not pretend it doesn't give her a leg up."

"Or maybe she'll get into every school she applies to because Shola's third in our class and a National Merit Scholar. And a genius."

"Maybe this one should think about pre-law," Dr. Wilson says, and laughs, an attempt to lighten the atmosphere. I wonder if he even remembers my name.

"We're getting off track here, sweetheart," my mom says, and her performative tone—slightly louder than the moment calls for—makes clear I've lost this fight, not that I'm sure what we're even fighting about. It's the voice my mother used to use on Lil' Missy, the seven-year-old kid on *My Dad, My Pops, and Me*, in the beginning of each episode, when she'd misbehave adorably. It's the voice she uses when we are out in public and I'm embarrassing her. "This is not about Shola, whom we love, of course, and who I hope gets into any college she wants. This is about you, darling, and us doing our jobs as parents to make sure you don't get left behind."

I have no response to this. I want to ask her what she means by *left behind*. There are, in fact, many colleges that will accept me even if I don't get my scores up. Not the kinds of schools my parents will want to flaunt with license-plate frames or brag about at dinner parties or drop into interviews on the *Tonight Show*. Still, Mrs. Oh gave me a long list of safeties, none of which we bothered to visit this summer but all of which are perfectly respectable schools where I imagine I'll learn whatever it is you are supposed to learn at college to prepare yourself for adulthood.

"We didn't pay six years of Wood Valley tuition, plus make God knows how many donations, for you to go to some no-name place," my dad says. "This shouldn't be that hard. You *deserve* this."

"I mean, look at Philo. He got into Yale, and he's truly an idiot, not to mention a criminal," my mom says, which is true. Aunt Candy's son got kicked out of Andover for dealing coke his sophomore year.

"Not when I got through with him," Dr. Wilson says, tapping his coffee cup against my mother's, like a fist bump. "If you read his application, you'd have thought the kid belonged in Mensa."

"What's Mensa?" I ask, even though I know perfectly well what Mensa is. Isla has been a member for years, because she's ridiculous like that. I think about how this meeting will go for her next year, when she's applying to colleges. Will Dr. Wilson suggest ADHD again so she has enough time to ensure a perfect score? To iron out any chance of minor human error? Probably not.

"Chloe," my mother says with a defeated exhale. "Please just stop."

"Sorry," I say.

CHAPTER SEVEN

Now

"You know Dad could go to jail too," Isla says without apology, waking me up from a deep sleep by sitting on my bed. The horror of yesterday seeps back in slowly. I tell myself that it can't be that bad. This is a blip in what has been my otherwise seminormal existence. My mom's home now, safe, and she'll get the charges dropped like she did for Hudson a few years ago. Life will resume.

I reach past Isla for my phone and turn it on. I have three hundred twenty-six text messages and a full inbox of voice mails from various news outlets. The *Today* show, *The View*, even *Dateline*.

Apparently, this will not blow over. Blips do not involve being grilled by famous morning talk-show hosts.

"What do you mean Dad could go to jail too?" I ask. I swat at my eyes, which feel goopy and swollen, a reminder that I cried myself to sleep last night.

"Too, as in also. As in Mom might go to jail, and Dad might go too. What do you think I mean?"

"I think you're getting ahead of yourself. Mom's not going to jail. Neither is Dad." I sit up, yawn, smile at my sister as if she is blowing this out of proportion. I pat her hand, and she pulls away.

"Have you even read the complaint?"

"No one is going to jail," I repeat, avoiding her question, because no, I have not yet read the complaint. It's two hundred terrifying pages long. According to the *New York Times*, the vast majority of it deals with the charges against the forty-five other people who've also been caught up in Dr. Wilson's shenanigans. All of their kids are waking up today, like me, with their whole worlds shattered. I wish I could talk to them and ask, *What do we do?* Isla is not blowing this out of proportion. It's just that she's usually impossible to scare or to ruffle, always calm and collected, and so I will take this single opportunity for a role reversal. I'll rise to the challenge. "Everything is going to be okay."

"Stop playing stupid, Chloe."

"I'm not. You're freaking out."

"Wake the hell up. Read the complaint. Find out what we're dealing with here. The only reason why they haven't pressed charges against Dad yet is because they don't have as much clear-cut evidence against him. But there's a ton on Mom. Apparently, there is a phone call between Mom and Wilson—"

"Dr. Wilson," I correct.

"Oh my God! Fine. Dr. Wilson. That call was wiretapped. Dad wasn't there that day, so for now, at least, he's in the clear. According to this legal blog I was reading last night, the prosecution will likely put pressure on Mom to plead guilty by offering not to charge Dad," Isla says. She looks tired, and it occurs to me that when she went upstairs last night, it wasn't to sleep. It was to research in private.

I wonder if Isla went to bed at all.

Of course, Isla would have been trying to find a way to help, unlike me, who spent most of last night weeping on the couch and staring at the ceiling. It hadn't even occurred to me that I could be useful.

"You're not a lawyer," I say. It's not fair that I'm angry at her. If anything, it should be the other way around. She has every right to be mad at me. I didn't only blow up my reputation, but probably hers too. She's in her junior year, on the cusp of this process.

Still, her competence feels cutting.

"You don't actually know how any of this works," I say.

"Do you think this is a game, Chloe? This is serious." My sister looks like a mini replica of our mom, but unlike our mother, who clawed her way up out of a blue-collar life to Hollywood using her looks, Isla will never have to rely on her appearance.

"I was the one who had guns pointed at her. I realize this is serious."

"You need to get a lawyer too. Someone separate from Mom's—to represent only you."

"What?" I ask. "Why?"

"Come on, the dumb act might fool Mom and Dad, but it doesn't fool me. I wouldn't count on it fooling a jury either. You've never been a good actress."

"Stop talking in code, Isla," I say, feeling the icy cold of panic infiltrate my veins. I was tired before, but that fog has

46

been wiped clean. Now I'm alert, conscious that I'm blinking too much and too hard. I don't want to hire my own lawyer. Even the thought of it makes me feel like I might be sick again.

I can't do this.

Honestly, I don't even understand how my mom broke the law. Shady is different from illegal.

"Why would I need my own lawyer?" I ask.

"You want to go to jail because you were stupid enough to cheat on the SATs? And then pretended to be a champion pole vaulter to get into SCC? I mean, pole vaulting? Seriously? I don't think you guys could have picked a more ridiculous sport if you tried."

"I didn't know," I say, fighting the tears that are gathering behind my eyes. I wrap my arms around my body and squeeze tight, but it gives me no real comfort. I wish I could hug Isla, but we haven't hugged since we were kids. Our family has that weird pairing thing: my mom and I are on one team, my dad and Isla on the other. Which isn't to say that this division is hostile—we love each other; we're a family, after all—but this is how things usually shake out. I would never spend an afternoon with my dad at the club playing organized sports. Isla would never spend an afternoon with my mom at the spa, sweating in a sauna. It's an interest/personality alignment issue. "I didn't know about any of this."

"It doesn't matter. You need to protect yourself. You can be charged as a coconspirator." I stare at my sister, who has always been a complicated package. Freckled nose, tiny ears on the outside, and combustible, tightly wound inside. She always plays the long game, takes the hardest route out. Once, she insisted on making all of us a three-course meal entirely from scratch, even the bread, a process that took a whole week. This was not born from some real passion for cooking. She wanted to prove to herself that she could do it. In other words, she's made of the same stuff that makes people do bizarre, exhausting crap like triathlons.

"I didn't know," I say again, and hate that my voice is shaking. That my face is already wet again. "They can't charge me if I didn't know."

"Really? Is that how the law works? You say you're innocent and so they believe you?"

"Whatever, Judge Judy," I say, using my sheet to wipe under my eyes. I take a deep breath, try to sound like I'm in control, like everything is fine. "Listen, it's going to be okay. I'm not going to jail. And neither is Mom. There has to be some sort of mistake."

I'm not sure what sort of mistake I mean. There hasn't been a mistake. Not really. They say the devil is in the details. When I took the SAT the last time, my score went up by 240 points. If it's true what the newspaper reports—that I applied to SCC as a pole vaulter, that somewhere along the line, Dr. Wilson changed my application and my parents paid off a coach to vouch for me and make a space—then that's not a mistake. That's a lie.

And apparently, a crime.

That's news to me.

Maybe what I mean is not that there's been a mistake so much as there's been an *overreaction*. *The View* called. Why would *The View* be interested in this? In *me*?

My little sister, who is not so little, is wearing flannel pajamas covered in cartoon bunny rabbits and her night retainer. I'm older and wiser, if only by a year. It's my job to rein in her anxiety.

I grab her hand and squeeze.

She pulls away.

"I'll get you a list of lawyers," she says, and marches out of the room.

CHAPTER EIGHT

Then

"So, to be clear: You're going to go on torturing yourself and me about Levi Haas forever?" Shola asks. Today she's wearing a vintage TLC T-shirt, cutoff jean shorts, and knee-high black Dr. Martens, the sort of amazing outfit that makes me proud to know her but makes the rest of our classmates shake their heads. I'm wearing a short '80s babydoll dress I inherited from the "casual lunch/beach" section of my mom's closet, which makes no one do anything. Shola and I often talk about our school's aesthetic, how we haven't quite yet figured out the line between what makes people admire your bravery with your style choices and what ignites irrational anger at them.

We are sharing a cup of fro-yo on the bench outside the auditorium, as we do most afternoons after school before I head to Mandarin or to see Cesar. If you asked me my single most favorite thing about Wood Valley, besides Shola, of course, I'd say it was the self-dispensing yogurt machine.

That chocolate-and-vanilla swirl is almost worth the $50k a year my parents pay in tuition.

"Yup."

"Both of you need to grow a pair," Shola says, and pauses, as if reconsidering. "Of ovaries."

"Did you say I need to grow a pair of ovaries?" I ask.

"I did. The language of courage should not only belong to men." Lola fist-bumps me, and I grin.

"We can do better than ovaries. How about: *You need to grow a vagina?*"

"*A vulva.*"

"You need to learn to shed your lining," I say.

"Nailed it," Shola says.

It's been a month since beer pong, and though I feel like things have shifted between Levi and me—he often waits for me after classes, he finds excuses to touch me, he hasn't mentioned another girl in a while—we've made zero progress. I need to learn the language of courage and kiss him first.

None of this passive, *please kiss me* nonsense.

"I hear that Xander's parents are away again."

"I wish my parents lived in Monaco."

"Stop complaining. You have the best parents in the world," Shola says, and I'm about to reflexively disagree when I realize that my parents, though far from perfect, are still pretty kickass. My mom, in particular. When I first got my period, she lay on the floor of the bathroom to give me real-time instructions on how to use a tampon. Later, I did the same for Shola, since her mom left her a box of maxipads in her backpack and explained nothing. "My dad is super pissed because I didn't help out with the church barbecue last weekend. I had gotten up early to finish that big physics project and I was tired and he was like, 'We don't do lazy in this family.'" Shola puts on a heavy Nigerian accent whenever she imitates her parents, and it's always stern and menacing and disapproving. In reality, Shola's parents are as warm and friendly as she is, and on the rare occasions we hang out at their apartment, they treat me like I'm an interesting, exotic pet that needs to be fed. Shola has a ton of friends in her neighborhood, who she sees outside of school when she's not hanging out with me, and though I know all about their secret lives and I've seen pictures on her phone—a squad of beautiful black girls—I've only met them in person a few times.

"My mom's on my case too. I'm taking the SAT again this weekend," I say.

"Here?"

"Nope. Some testing center in West Hollywood. They had more availability or something. I don't know. My parents set it up."

This is a half-lie. My accommodation came through, and apparently, there was some sort of conflict with the dates available for extra time at Wood Valley. I'm relieved. My test-taking juju hasn't been great at school. Maybe sitting it somewhere new will help.

I guess it turns out I do officially have ADHD, though when I asked for an Adderall prescription my mother suggested I dot my wrists with ylang-ylang instead. I haven't told Shola, because I suspect she'll think the diagnosis is nonsense, and knowing her, she won't be shy in telling me so. As it is, she thinks my family is ridiculous and over the top, and I guess we are, if you are Shola. I mean, the first time I showed her my mom's closet, which to be fair is like a museum with ever-changing exhibits, she dropped to her knees and started genuflecting.

It's not like there's anything I can do about the testing accommodation, even if I share Shola's suspicions. I don't let myself dwell on it too much, anyway, because I don't like the way it makes me feel something uncomfortable and un-familiar: an uncertainty about my parents' judgment.

According to the SAT board, I'm allowed a full two days for the test, though my mom says it's okay if I finish in one. I tell myself the extra time won't make a difference one way or another, so I shouldn't stress too much about *why* they gave it to me.

"Just remember, if they were testing for awesomeness, you'd get a sixteen hundred," Shola says.

"Who's paying you to be president of my fan club?" I ask, and rest my head on her shoulder, which is about half a foot higher than mine and therefore at a perfect angle.

"Why do you assume everything comes down to money?" Shola jokes. When we met on the first day of seventh grade, Shola walked up to me and said, "Everyone here seems super weird to me, and you look like you're probably weird too, but maybe slightly less so, which I think means we should be friends." She was wearing a T-shirt that said NERD, in all caps, like she wanted to shout the word. I said, "Define *weird*." And she said, without missing a beat, "Did I say *weird*? I meant *rich*."

I'm not going to lie—my first thought at the time was: Do I look different from everyone else? Once we were close enough for me to ask her why she picked me without her judging me for wanting to know, Shola would confess that it was my slouch. I didn't walk around like I thought I already owned the world, even though it turned out I was as privileged as everyone else at Wood Valley.

After being her best friend for five years, I'm deeply grateful for my terrible posture.

"Just kidding. It's your parents. Yup, they're totally paying me," Shola says. And then we both burst out laughing.

On Friday night, I get into bed early, with Fluffernutter tucked under my arm for extra comfort, but I can't sleep. I'm too nervous. My tutor, Linda, told me not to worry, that *what will be will be*, and these words were so disconcertingly out of character, they freaked me out more.

I guess even she has given up on me.

Linda wears blazers and dainty shirts that have little bows that tie at the neck and basic pumps. She's widely considered the best tutor in Los Angeles, and there's a waiting list to work with her. In fact, sometimes we have our sessions over FaceTime, because she's busy tutoring the children of oligarchs in places like Dubai. She calls pants "slacks" and I bet she's never had much fun, not even on the private jets her clients arrange for her. When the air hostess offers her a glass of champagne, I'd put money on her responding with something prim like "No thank you. I'm on the clock."

She's complimented me exactly once since we started

working together over a year ago, and that was to tell me she appreciated that I always showed up with sharpened pencils.

I don't think Linda likes me very much, which, fair enough. I bring down her stats. Despite all my studying, my score rose a measly ten points on my last practice exam, which, by the way, was untimed.

I'm so screwed.

My phone dings with a text, and I scoop it up, greedy for the distraction. I do a little shimmy when I see Levi's name.

> **Levi:** Shola says you're taking the SAT tomorrow. GOOD LUCK!!!
>
> **Me:** Thanks. Need more than luck. I need a miracle.
>
> **Levi:** Nah, you'll do great. You're a smartypants. You always give such good advice. Speaking of which . . .

We've been down this road enough times that I recognize the pattern. This is how it always starts: Levi drops the *I like so-and-so* bomb and then asks me what to do about it, like it's fun for me to be his personal relationship consultant.

I always help out, because I'm a self-defeating masochist.

I can't do this tonight, though. I need my beauty rest. The goddamn SATs, the Academy Awards of the high school experience, are tomorrow. I even canceled on Cesar, my reading buddy, this afternoon, and I *never* cancel on Cesar. That little dude and I are halfway through Harry Potter.

I'm about to say something to Levi like *Going to bed, talk later*—but his next text beats me to it.

> **Levi:** There's this girl who've I've known forever . . .
>
> **Me:** I'm tired. Can I give good advice tomorrow?
>
> **Levi:** I promise it'll be quick.
>
> **Me:** You realize I'm no expert, right?
>
> **Levi:** You totally are, especially with this one. So, anyhow, I've known her forever and she's amazing and well, things have been different between us lately. In a good way.
>
> **Levi:** But I'm worried about ruining our friendship.
>
> **Levi:** What do I do?

My mouth goes dry and I fold over. Fluffernutter pushes her head into my stomach to make sure I'm okay. He can't be talking about me, right? I mean, we've known each other forever, or at least since seventh. There's been a noticeable shift in the air between us lately, or at least I think there has, and if we were to hook up, I'd be worried about ruining our friendship too. I mean, not *that* worried, because friendship was always my second choice, but still. I get it. I mean, who would he ask for breakup advice when he got bored of me?

I totally guided him through ghosting on Sophie. And Evianna. And Blue. And Rain.

This might be it. For real this time.

I decide that I can't assume, which, as Isla likes to say, *makes an ass out of u and me.* Isla always says dumb-smart stuff like that, which is why I hate-love her.

> **Me:** I don't know. I need more information.

> **Levi:** Well, she kills at beer pong and turns nouns into verbs and she gives good advice and she's fun and awesome and she's . . .

I hold my breath. I wait through three rounds of ellipses, and then disappearing ellipses, and then ellipses appearing again. So many ellipses. Are you kidding me?

> **Levi:** taking the SAT tomorrow.

My stomach falls out. Me. He's talking about me. I think. Just to be sure, I write back.

> **Me:** Tell her

More ellipses.

> **Levi:** I just did

I fall asleep that night, way too late, grinning and hugging my phone, like it's actually Levi and not an electronic device that translates his thoughts into words on a screen. My mom would be mad, since she's constantly harping on about blue light disrupting sleep and the radiation giving us cancer.

No matter what happens tomorrow, even if I sit for my unlimited time and still manage to bomb the SAT again, Levi Haas, *Levi Haas*, likes me.

CHAPTER NINE

Now

After Isla leaves my room to play Nancy Drew girl detective, I realize I need to talk to Shola. What are best friends for, if not for when the FBI comes pounding on your door? How many times have we joked about the fact that when the time comes, we'll always be there to help each other bury a dead body?

My corpse-in-the-trunk moment has arrived.

I scroll through my phone and realize the messages are from numbers I don't recognize. Every single one of them, without exception, seems to be a hate text.

Deep breaths. No one would ever say this stuff to my face. When I eventually go back to school—though I have no idea when that will be, as it went without discussion that Isla and I were staying home today—people will be, if not exactly nice, then at least civil. I will not get assaulted in the parking lot.

Have I been doxxed somewhere?

Hope your mom rots in jail

Die of AIDS cheater bitch

Spoiled See You Next Tuesday

You too stupid to live

entitled rich idiot

I deserved that spot so much more than you

"Isla!" I scream, because I don't know what else to do. Deep breathing is a scam. I feel like I'm getting stabbed in the brain by my phone.

I need Shola. She'll know, for example, how so many strangers have my cell number. When I dial her, it goes straight to voice mail.

"Delete all your social media accounts," Isla yells back from her bedroom. "Carrie'll get us new phone numbers later today. Ignore them."

"You're getting texts too?" I ask. It hadn't occurred to me that Isla, who had nothing to do with any of this, whose only crime is being my sister, would also be targeted. Will everyone forget about this by next year, when it's her turn to apply?

"Just shut down those accounts. The lawyer told Dad to tell us yesterday but he forgot," Isla shouts. "And then turn off your phone."

"He forgot?" I ask, as if that's inconceivable, even though it makes total sense. My online life was no one's priority yesterday, not even mine.

Instead of listening to Isla, I open Instagram, and as I've been doing for the last week since I was accepted, I check in on the SCC Class of 2024 page. Before, I'd scroll through looking for a potential roommate, or potential friends, or to marinate in the idea that it was official: I was going to a kickass school.

Today, clicking over is a very bad idea. I need to learn to listen to my little sister.

Photos lifted from my account are posted everywhere with comments that are as cruel as the texts.

You better not come bitch or we'll be waiting for you
Screw her and screw her mom and screw SCC
I hope she rushes and then dies of alcohol poisoning

There's a meme with a picture of my face Photoshopped onto a cartoon water polo player, a ball being smashed into my face, even though I apparently applied as a pole vaulter, not a water polo player.

Two totally different things.

Apparently, it was Ignacius Smith Wollingham, IV, a name I've only recently learned, who was the one who applied to Yale as a pretend water polo player.

There are a bunch of gifs of my mother on *My Dad, My Pops, and Me*, mostly from the episode when she's arrested for trying to break into her own house. But in another one of the memes, my mom's in stirrups giving birth in the pilot, but instead of baby Lil' Missy, out comes out an emoji poo with a name tag that reads: *Chloe Berringer, dumbass p.o.s.*

"Chloe," Isla yells from the next room. "Seriously, stop looking. Shut it all down."

I have no idea how she knows through the wall what I'm doing. Maybe she does have second sight.

I keep reading. No one is supportive. Not a single person even suggests the possibility that I did not know.

No one says *Hey, leave her alone. She's only a kid.*

The world has decided I'm a spoiled, entitled lying bitch—*bitch* is the word used most often—which makes me wonder idly what the boys who've been caught up in this are being called. Did the rest of my fellow scandalees also wake up feeling scared and heartbroken and blindsided, but also like they're officially the stupidest person in America?

The meme doesn't hurt so much as feels like confirmation: I am a piece of shit.

This is not news to me. I had thought I had done a good job of hiding it, that's all. But I guess that's what a dumbass p.o.s. *would* think.

And then that's when I see it, a new text from Levi. My pulse stutters, and I feel a sickening dread. I don't want to read it and fillet my own already filleted heart.

Levi: I mean, Chlo . . . seriously?

I write back immediately:

Me: It's not how it looks

He doesn't make me wait. I thank God for small blessings.

Levi: I need a beat to process

Me: Levi, let me explain

Levi: I need time. I'm so . . .

Levi: Never mind

Me: Please

I wait a minute, but the little *Delivered* never appears under my message. I retype and resend. Again, no delivery confirmation. There's only one explanation: Levi, without even giving me an opportunity to explain, has blocked me. I tell myself this is temporary—I take him at his word; he needs time—and still a loud, flushing sound, like the suction roar of an airplane bathroom, fills the empty space in my head.

I deactivate all my accounts, as I should have done fifteen minutes ago. I feel a pang of nostalgia and loss as the pictures that have chronicled my life—mostly shots of Shola and me making silly faces in front of LA's many Instagrammable walls, or smiling big as we are about to dig into red velvet cupcakes—all disappear.

My life as I know it is officially over.

Delete. Delete. Delete.

Flush.

I scan through my texts one last time before powering the phone off. Just to double-check.

But no. I was right the first time.

There isn't a single word from Shola.

CHAPTER TEN

Then

I take the SAT at a nondescript building in West Hollywood next to a marijuana dispensary advertising THC gummies. A bald man with a long, unkempt brown beard, a tie-dyed Phish T-shirt, and Birkenstocks meets us at the door and introduces himself as "Proctor Dan." He's friendly and warm, less taskmaster and more stoner camp counselor, and he moves his coffee mug to his armpit to shake both my and my mother's hands. I guess an accommodation doesn't only guarantee more time, but a chiller vibe all around.

He doesn't ask me for ID, even though I have it ready. Once we reach the classroom where I will take the test, my mom hands me a lunch sack and grabs my cheeks, eyes shiny, like it's the first day of kindergarten.

"I had Cristof pack lots of extra protein to keep your energy up," my mom says. "Just do your best. That's all I ask."

Cristof is our chef, who I've never actually met, though I eat his food almost every night. He cooks three mornings a week in our kitchen, while I'm at school, and then leaves his food behind in our fridge in glass containers—my mom says Cristof is anti-plastic for hormonal reasons, not environmental ones—all of which have adorable chalkboard labels that list the ingredients. Sometimes Isla and I write back notes: *Please ignore Mom. More real food. Less salad. Thanks!*

"Okay," I say, because that's the only word I can get out. I'm too nervous to talk. I think about Levi, hoping the excitement of last night's revelation will counteract today's nauseating fear, but it does the opposite. I feel like my entire body is on sensory overload.

I notice Proctor Dan's exposed toes, which sprout hairs at fixed intervals, like a doll's scalp.

"You'll do great, honey. I know it." My mom is, as usual, way more confident than the occasion calls for, as if enthusiasm alone is all I need to understand complex mathematical equations. I realize with a start that this is the exact tone I use with Cesar whenever he catches on a word he doesn't know when reading, and it makes me wonder, for the first time, if we all turn into our mothers one day.

"Let's get this party started," Proctor Dan says, and drumrolls the desk.

"Can I stay?" my mom asks, looking around the room for a chair.

"Mom! Get out," I say, and I cringe because I sound like a tween on a Disney show. Since she hired Dr. Wilson, my mom's become obsessive about this college admissions process, and she's driving me bananas. I usually like the feeling of my mom being invested in my life, but with the applications, the tenor feels different.

Did my mom really think she could sit in on my test?

Next, she's going to want to pitch in when I don't know the answers.

"Sorry. It'll be hours. I'll text as soon as I'm finished. Promise," I say. "Go shopping or something. What will be will be." I echo Linda, who is in Hong Kong and sent me a text this morning reminding me to fill in an answer for every question, even if I have to guess.

"Okay, sweet pea," my mom says kindly, as if she's unbothered by my initial outburst, or maybe she's in public mode, that tone shift that happens whenever we leave the house. Who knows what tabloid connections Proctor Dan might have? We are in LA, after all.

"Sorry again," I mutter. "I'm nervous."

"Me too," she says, and kisses my cheek, and only later, after she leaves, will I wonder what she has to be nervous about. She already got into college.

About two hours later, I'm working my way through the third section of the exam while Proctor Dan sits behind a desk and noisily reads a newspaper. Each time he turns a page, the crinkling disrupts my focus. Couldn't he read the news on his phone like everyone else?

The "math, no calculator" section is the part that always trips me up the most. I see Linda's floating head on FaceTime: *First identify the kind of question.* Okay. This is what they call "passport to advanced math." Now what? The equation—numbers and letters and symbols I don't understand—swims on the page. My heart pounds, loud and arrhythmic, and my chest tightens. I wonder about the mechanics of the human body. If my blood can break free of my throbbing veins and drown me. I put my head down on the desk and close my eyes to stop the undulating.

I try some of the box breathing I learned from my meditation teacher. In for four, hold for four, out for four. Or something like that. Even that information has been wiped clean.

"You okay?" Proctor Dan asks, but I don't answer. My body is slick with sweat, and I have the adrenaline shakes that always precede my puking.

I cannot throw up on the SAT. How do they even score an exam that's drenched in vomit? No. Not going to happen. I'm better than this. I box breathe some more. I channel Isla, Shola too, their coolness under pressure. Their shared ability to stuff the fear away, into a pocket that can't be reached.

"Chloe?"

I nod, though my head is still down. I lift one hand, a single finger, as if to say as politely as possible without words *Give me a second, please.*

"It's okay. We have unlimited time here. Take as much as you need. No rush," he says, so calm, I wonder if maybe he has a stash of those gummies from next door. Clearly he's talked hundreds of students like me through panic attacks. I wonder why I couldn't have had Proctor Dan the two previous times I took the test. I didn't freak out then like I am now—mostly because I didn't know how badly I'd bombed until I got back my score—but I could have used the general support. Maybe I needed this accommodation after all. "Just skip what you don't know, and you can always go back to it later. Not a prob."

I lift my head and wipe my forehead with my sleeve. Sniff at my wrist, where my mom rubbed some lavender essential oil she bought off Goop to relax me. The question rearranges itself into a normal-looking equation. Still, no amount of time or essence from the Provençal region is going to give me the answer. The SAT is written in a language I don't speak.

"I'm all right," I say. "Thank you so much."

"That's what I'm here for. Want to stop and have a snack?" Proctor Dan throws a peanut in the air and catches it in his mouth. He has an array of food laid out in front of him. Trail mix, chips, Doritos, even Fig Newtons. *The munchies*, I think.

He tips a container of sour cream and onion Pringles toward me, and I reach in and grab a couple. I open my lunch bag and take out apple slices and a small glass tub of homemade almond butter. I offer him some in return.

"Nice. Brain food," he says.

Obviously, this is how everyone should take the SAT. With a kind, likely high dude like Proctor Dan suggesting you take a beat and share some snacks. With extra time to breathe through your fear and the perfect pick-me-up prepared by Chef Cristof.

The whole thing is way more humane.

My mom takes me out for ice cream after the test. We go to Scoops, the same place we used to go after doctor checkups when I was little, the reward for getting shots. She doesn't eat any, of course, not even a sample, but I get a double to self-medicate. We sit outside at the picnic tables, and I tip my head back as if to absorb the healing powers of the sun. The test took me six hours, and despite my snack breaks and lunch, I feel undernourished and vitamin D deficient. As if the testing center spun and baked me via its fluorescent lights, like a rotisserie chicken at the supermarket.

"So how'd it go?" my mom asks. I admire her restraint. She waited a whole forty-five minutes—until I had a treat in my hands—before starting her interrogation.

I want to shrug off the question. I don't want to tell her the truth: It was a disaster.

"I was reading about this school the other day: Colorado Mountain College?" I tell her instead. "I bet they don't ask for the SATs. They have an adventuring program."

"I have no idea what that is."

"Me neither," I admit, and take a giant bite of mint chocolate chip. I can sense an ice cream mustache forming on my upper lip. I'm feeling childish and churlish, so I leave it. "But I like being outside and adventure and Colorado. I'd probably get to snowboard a lot."

"Sure sounds like a good way to pick a college," she says. My mother went to Rutgers University in New Jersey, which is a state school. She paid for it with money she won in beauty pageants during high school and earned waitressing in Manhattan. During her college years, my mom lived on ramen, and the way she tells it, she would have gotten rickets if she didn't occasionally get taken on dates to fancy restaurants. She would order filet mignon and steamed broccoli and sneak bread into her purse when the guy went to the bathroom. My mom is proud of her scrappy rise to fame, as she should be. A million girls like her show up in LA every day trying to make it. Most head back home a year or two later. My mom, on the other hand, had a steady income acting on television by the age of twenty-three.

"The test didn't go well," I say eventually, when what I really mean is *I bombed. I guessed on more than half of the questions.* According to Mrs. Oh, colleges take your best scores. I've sat through enough practice tests to know this is not going to be it.

"I'm sure you're not giving yourself enough credit. I bet you did better than you think," my mom says.

"Nope." I lick my ice cream, fight back the tears. It's a test. Nothing more, nothing less. Shola reminds me all the time that a score is only a score. It says nothing about the real me: how I'm a good friend and a good daughter and a good citizen, even if I'm a crappy student. Every Christmas, my reading buddy Cesar's mom bakes me cookies, and last year's card read *Thank you for taking such good care of my little boy. He talks about you all the time, like you're his big sister for real.*

I remind myself that Levi called me *amazing* less than twenty-four hours ago. I try to hold on to that boost, but it's already slipping. He texted me this morning: *BREAK A LEG SUNSHINE!!!!* and I wrote back, *Pls take it for me* with fifteen prayer hand emojis, and he wrote back, *Wish i could babe.*

He's never called me *babe* before. I like it.

"You'll see. I have a good feeling," my mom says.

"Whatever."

"Don't be so negative."

"Mom!"

"What? It's the Rule of Attraction. Negativity attracts negativity. You should make a vision board. Put SCC right in the middle." I've long thought my mom's woo-woo-ness must come from her being in entertainment. When you've been as fortunate as she's been on that front—regular roles on not one but two long-running television series—you turn to mystical forces to explain it. I mean, she's a great actress in the sitcom world, don't get me wrong, but so are a lot of people. It helps to attribute your success, at least in part, to a positive attitude, to some unseen way you're more deserving. It's an atheist's prosperity gospel.

"I'm not going to SCC," I say.

"What's wrong with SCC? It's down the road. We'd be able to see you all the time. Carrie could even pick up your laundry."

"Nothing's wrong with it. It's an amazing school. But I'm not getting in there. Mrs. Oh put it in the 'likely out of reach' category, and that was before today. She said all the schools we visited over the summer were out of reach."

"Mrs. Oh doesn't know everything, Chloe."

"You and Dad need to be more realistic," I say, my voice catching. I hate disappointing my parents, who have both worked so hard to give me this big, beautiful, privileged life. I will not cry about the SAT. I have my entire adult life ahead of me, and I have been nothing but lucky.

This is nothing. A blip. A minor fail.

I remind myself that their love is not conditional on a score.

"Don't say that," my mom says, and the hopeful look in her eyes breaks something in me. "I want what's best for you. That's all."

"I'm sorry I'm not super academic like Isla. I wish reading comprehension didn't feel like hieroglyphics. But that doesn't mean I'm destined to be, like, a terrible failure at everything!" I scream this last bit. I've subconsciously opted for yelling over crying, a code-switch defense mechanism, and then I remember we're in public. When we walked into the ice cream shop, Oville was blasting on the speakers and the scooper, a girl wearing a Bruins hat with a name tag that read JESSIE and who felt vaguely familiar from Wood Valley— was she a senior when I was a freshman?—immediately recognized my mother. When it came time to pay, she said, "When I was little, my mom and I used to love to watch you on *My Dad, My Pops, and Me* together, so it's on the house," and then she asked my mother to autograph a napkin. Before we even left, she whipped out her cell phone and said, "Ethan, you will never believe who just walked in here. . . ."

I squeeze my eyes shut and then open them again. Fortunately, no one is nearby. Still, I know I should be more careful. Last thing I need is some tabloid cover announcing MISSY'S REAL-LIFE KID'S OUT OF CONTROL BEHAVIOR ISSUES.

"Darling, trust me. It'll be fine. I know you think I'm wacky but let's make a vision board together tonight. We'll put a 1600 on it and the SCC logo and maybe some dorm room decor ideas. It will help. I promise."

"Okay," I say, because the vision board thing came originally from Aunt Candy, who, after seeing the idea on *Oprah* a million years ago, put a picture of Steve Jobs on her own board and the next day met Uncle Charles, a billionaire, who, unlike Jobs at the time, had a full head of hair. Since then, my mom swears by the method. She thinks it's how she landed the *Blood Moon* role.

Really, she got the role because of nostalgia. The millennials who grew up watching her on *My Dad* wanted to see her play the immortal queen mother of a prince vampire. If she can't be their actual mom, they want to see her continue to play one on TV.

Also, it helps that she doesn't age.

I wipe my eyes with a napkin.

"I got you, kid. You never have to worry about a thing," my mom says, and pulls me in for a hug. And that's when I hear the telltale click of the camera. I look up.

The ice cream scooper puts down her iPhone.

"I'm sorry. I never do this, I swear. Last week, Ariana Grande was here and I didn't even blink, even though I knew my stepbrother would be mad that I didn't get a selfie. It's just that my mom used to love Missy. She was a book person, not a TV person, but there was something about *My Dad*," she says, with an apologetic smile, and then realizing she's accidentally said too much, she wipes at her eyes, which I notice are wet.

My mom makes strangers cry with joy.

"Sorry," she says again, and then she slips back inside as quietly as she came out, taking the photograph of my mother and me, still with my ice cream mustache, with her.

CHAPTER ELEVEN

Now

Isla and I don't go to school on Wednesday either, because no one tells us we should. I've barely seen my parents since they returned from court. They're too busy with the lawyers, who've come wearing frowns and dark suits and have camped out in the living room with their laptops and their cell phones. They run extension cords across the rug, and my mom, who would normally freak out about possible ridges, doesn't say a word.

Carrie keeps ordering in food, so the kitchen table is covered first with sandwiches, and then later in the day with sushi platters. She doesn't take the time to make either spread aesthetically pleasing. I finally meet Cristof, who keeps making healthy meals for our family, though they go uneaten in the fridge, their little labels hanging off forlornly. He's decidedly less French than I imagined—it turns out he's from St. Louis, his name is really Christopher, and like everyone else in LA, he's an aspiring actor. Clean cooking is his side hustle.

Paloma, my mom's publicist, paces around the house—long, angry strides back and forth—with her AirPods in her ears, and she shouts nonsensical, highly detailed expletives at random. I have no idea who's on the other end of her tirades, or why she thinks they have *their heads so far up their own butts that they're coming out their nostrils* and *could they listen for once in their tiny miserable insignificant little minuscule pissant lives*. But apparently, these mystery callers are not cooperating.

I consider going to the backyard to get away from the madness but am stopped by the sign Paloma posted on the playroom doors. WARNING: STAY INSIDE! PAPARAZZI HAVE TELEPHOTOS/LADDERS.

"Here's the list of lawyers," Isla says, when she finds me hiding out in Dad's office picking at a muffin. I'm tired of my room, which is covered in pictures of me and Shola, and more recently Levi, too, our smiling faces like an advertisement for my former life. "Trust me. Call them. I'd start with the first guy. I wanted to find you a woman, but beggars can't be choosers."

"Who's going to pay?"

"You are."

I laugh. I heard my dad tell my mom last night that the lawyers they hired are costing a thousand dollars an hour. Last I counted, there were at least six lawyers downstairs. "I'm serious. You're going to pay out of your trust fund. It's important this is separate from Mom and Dad."

"I won't have access to any of that money until I'm eighteen, and then only like a tiny portion of it."

"Talk to the lawyer. He'll help you figure it out."

"Do you really think this is necessary?" I ask.

"Look around. What do you think?" Isla asks, and motions to the chaos beyond the office doors. The air is ripe with tension. I catch a glimpse of Paloma going by, and I wonder if she's hiding a Fitbit clipped to her bra; maybe she's trying to get her steps in. "By the way, don't freak, but Hudson is coming over."

"Why?" The very last thing we need is for my half brother to show up high out of his mind and to put on a show for the paparazzi. Even worse, depending on whether my dad is still giving him money—he was supposed to have cut him off because a therapist told him it was enabling—Hudson might be desperate enough to sell a story. I feel sorry for my brother—his mom, Sage, my dad's first wife, was an addict too, years ago, so he's genetically predisposed—but my empathy for him doesn't mean I want him anywhere near here. Not to mention, my dad does not have the bandwidth to deal with Hudson. None of us does.

"Hud says he wants to give moral support. I told Dad to tell him we moved," Isla says.

"Did Dad laugh?"

"Nope," she says. "But in all fairness, I wasn't totally joking."

Isla leaves, probably to go do homework or, you know, find the legal loophole that will save my mother. Before I lose my courage, I dial the first number on the list. Carrie decided yesterday that it was too complicated to change our chips, so instead she bought both Isla and me brand-new iPhones. Normally, I'd be excited by this—I'll wipe my old one and give it to Cesar's mom—but every time I look at the shiny new cell, which is empty of all contacts and texts and photos, I feel lonely. Nothing has carried over. Not even my apps.

"Jaberowski, Lowe, and Stein," a receptionist answers. "Mr. Lowe's office."

"Hi, may I speak to Mr. Lowe, please?" I ask this in as confident a tone as I can muster. My voice comes out tinny and young, a child asking for permission. I hate talking on the phone. If I could manage to hire a lawyer over text or email, I totally would.

"I'll see if Mr. Lowe is available. Who may I say is calling?"

"Umm, Chloe Berringer? Umm, Joy Fields's daughter."

I hear an audible gasp from the secretary, followed by an: "One moment, please." Apparently, she too must get the *New York Times* news alerts.

"Chloe," a man says warmly, less than twenty seconds later. "I'm so glad you reached out. I've been worried about you."

"Hi," I say, because I'm not sure what to say to this. I've never met Mr. Lowe. I don't even know how he found his way onto Isla's list, or why she put him at the top. I have no idea why it would have occurred to him to worry about me.

"I assume you're calling because you've found yourself in a little spot of bother." *That's one way to put it,* I think. *Spot of bother.*

"I guess so? I mean yes. My mom has. And my sister said I should call you in case, I don't know, I could be in trouble too?"

"You have a smart sister," Mr. Lowe says, and I'm glad we're on the phone so he can't see me roll my eyes so hard

I almost sprain them. "Given the nature of the allegations against your mother, and potentially your father, you absolutely need to have your own separate counsel." This is the second time I've heard the word *separate* and it still makes me uncomfortable. A surge of loneliness bubbles up in the back of my throat, and I swallow it down. I think of the corner of my mom's robe hanging out of the FBI car, waving goodbye to our old life.

"I . . . I . . . This is all a little overwhelming. Am I . . . I mean, if I didn't know anything, can I still be in trouble?" I ask. "I mean, I didn't know. I only knew—"

"Stop!" he says sharply, and then catches himself. "Chloe, I don't want to hear anything about what you did or did not know, do you understand?"

"Yes," I say, though I'm not sure I do.

"There'll be time to iron that all out later. In some cases, it's better for lawyers to know less, not more. How about we set up an in-person meeting for later today? I'll come to you, since I imagine you can't leave your house."

"No, the paparazzi are here. Also, I'm not sure how I'll pay you. I have a trust fund, but—"

"We can worry about that part later too. Until I get there with a retainer agreement, I only need you to do one thing. Can you do one thing for me, Chloe?" He's talking to me like I'm a little kid, as if he too thinks I'm clearly the stupidest person in America. I'd be annoyed except for the fact that I want the hand-holding. I'm terrified.

"Okay."

"Don't talk to anyone—not your mom or your dad or

even your sister—about the case or anything that's happened. Not a single word."

"I can't talk to my family?" I glance at the picture of the four of us in Bora-Bora that sits on my dad's desk. Isla's in the middle, grinning without front teeth and wearing bright orange wonder wings. I'm next to her, holding up a hairy coconut and drinking out of a giant straw. My mom, in a string bikini, stands behind us, my dad's arm around her shoulders, his abs more chiseled than they are now.

We look so happy. A perfect family.

"Of course you can talk to them. You can say 'good morning.' You can say 'I love you.' But you can't discuss college or these allegations or anything that happened. What you knew or did not know. Nothing. Do you understand me?"

"Yes."

"Also, don't talk to your mom's lawyers or the FBI. They might want to interview you."

"The FBI?" I can't keep the panic out of my voice. I think of their guns, long and precise, and I think about *Law & Order* again, which I like to watch late at night, when I can't sleep. I imagine sitting at a table in a small room, trying not to get manipulated into a game of good-cop/bad-cop.

I am in so over my head.

"Chloe, listen, you are central to this case. You do not talk to anyone, do you hear me, anyone, without my say-so. If the FBI asks to speak to you, you say, 'I need my lawyer, Kenneth Lowe,' and then they'll have to call me."

"Right. Got it." I want to ask *Can I talk to Shola?* but then I remember that apparently she's not talking to me. If she were, she would have texted or called. She would have returned my dozens of voice mails. She would have found a way to say *I'm here, Chlo.*

I think about the word *separate,* how it conjures up that movie about the guy who becomes untethered from the International Space Station and is left floating alone in the infinite universe talking to himself.

"Not a word to anyone, understand?" Kenneth asks again.

"Sure," I say, and mime zipping my lips. And then I feel like a moron all over again, *a dumbass p.o.s.,* because we're on the phone.

He can't see me.

CHAPTER TWELVE

Then

"Will you be one of my backups?" Cesar asks. I can tell he's nervous because he doesn't look at me. I'm used to his brain zipping around so fast I can't always keep up, so at first I have no idea what he's talking about. Sometimes I'll think he's telling a story about the playground at school, and then all of a sudden, a talking porcupine starts shooting bullets from their wrists, and I'll realize he's transitioned to some show he recently watched or a dream he had.

We're hanging out at the Reading and Resource Center, where I've been volunteering with Cesar for four years, five afternoons a week, since he was three. What started as school-required community service has become a big, essential part of my life, the place I go to decompress and relax, and the only place where just being me is more than enough. Cesar's assigned as my "little buddy," which means in addition to helping him with his homework, reading to and with him, and, of course, playing, I'm occasionally allowed to take him on field trips if I get permission from his mom in advance.

"Backup for what?" I ask. Of course I'll be Cesar's backup, regardless of context, because I love this kid like he's my little brother. Sometimes he tells me stories about other kids making fun of him—for not knowing about *Minecraft* or sucking at kickball—and it takes all my willpower not to drive over to his school and destroy some first graders.

"You know, in case anything happens and I need, like, more adults," Cesar says. He has a giant gap where his two front teeth used to be, a dark bowl cut, and no concept of personal space. When we read together on the big over-stuffed chairs, he likes to hurl himself onto my lap, like he's doing gymnastics. He often farts out loud, and then giggles his contagious giggle, and for a minute, he turns me seven too, and farting becomes the funniest thing in the world.

"Anything happens?" I ask. I do not reflexively correct him. Do not say what I am thinking, that I'm not, by any measure, an adult. Because to Cesar I am. When we first started hanging out together, I asked him how old he thought I was. He guessed fifty. "What do you mean?"

"Like, you know, if my mom has to go away or some-thing." My heart sinks. By necessity, Cesar's been taught to talk in code, even with me. His mom is a refugee from El Salvador, and though no one has told me outright, it's pretty clear she's undocumented. A lot of the parents of kids at the Center are.

"Your mom's not going anywhere," I say, and then realize that I shouldn't make promises I can't keep. Cesar and his mom live with a daily fear I can't even begin to contemplate, a fear I don't even try on for size while I'm here and then leave behind. Rita, the head of RRC, told me recently that many of the moms, even the immigrants here legally, have started forgoing free lunches at school and SNAP benefits for their kids because they're scared they'll be targeted by ICE and deported if they use government resources. It's horrifying to think about the level of terror they must feel to be giving up needed meals for toddlers.

I've learned to compartmentalize my time with Cesar and to not think in comparative terms when I learn horrible stuff like that. Otherwise, I wouldn't be able to go back home to my normal life, to comfort and Cristof-prepped meals. Instead, I do what I can to help—volunteer my time, bring bulk snacks from Costco, encourage my parents to donate to the RRC. No good can come from my dwelling on the giant divide between Cesar's life and mine.

"Don't worry. I wouldn't stay in your house with you or anything. My mom said that wouldn't be possible. I asked. I was like, *But Chlo has a screening room!* But she wants me to keep seeing you, no matter what. She says you'll make sure I go to college one day." I almost laugh—I should not be responsible for helping anyone get into college. The only reason why I'm able to help Cesar with his homework is because he's only in first grade. Still, I'm all in. "So what do you think?"

He is staring at me, waiting for my answer. I sweep the hair out of his eyes.

"Of course. I'm like a bad rash, little dude." I blink back tears, flash him my biggest smile to hide how both honored and heartbroken I am. Cesar should be thinking about Legos and, just on the night before it, his spelling test, and even maybe those little jerks who tease him. He should not be worrying about losing his only parent or counting his people for the long run.

"I don't know what that means."

"It means you couldn't get rid of me if you tried." I resist the urge to pull him into my lap. I don't want to frighten him with my affection.

"I had a bad rash once," Cesar says, looking up at me, his eyebrow tented, like in a cartoon. "But it went away after like two weeks."

"You look beautiful," Levi says when he picks me up the Friday night after the SATs in his new Prius, and I blush. We do not usually say things like this to each other. Our move from good friends to something else has been slow and steady at school, and I wish we could stay like this, on the cusp. Luxuriate in the potential before I inevitably screw it up or he realizes that this was all a mistake.

That I'm a mistake.

Every night this week, we've texted late into the night, and twice I've fallen asleep holding my phone and woken with a circle on my cheek from my PopSocket. I liked the indentation, like physical proof I've been struck by Cupid's arrow.

My mom helped me get dressed tonight. She wanted me to wear her bandage dress, which is red and so tight I'd have to choose between sitting and breathing. What if we're going some place casual like In-N-Out? I'd be forced to order a Double-Double in something once worn to the Emmys. I opted instead for my favorite ripped jeans and a peasant blouse—a step up from school, a step down from trying-too-hard.

Levi calling me *beautiful* feels like a stretch—at least in the ways in which my mom is synonymous with the word—but I feel . . . attractive under his gaze. I feel *seen*. Maybe like with the word *smart*, I can find a more expansive view of the word *beautiful* so that it can somehow include me too.

"Thanks," I say, and of course I ruin the moment by playfully punching his shoulder despite the fact that this is not a locker room and we are not teammates. Still, I don't know how to take the compliment, how to fold it up like the notes that used to get passed around in sixth grade—*Do you like me? Y or N*—and keep it in my pocket like a good-luck charm. I should have stepped on my tippy-toes and kissed him on the cheek. I should have grabbed his hand. I should have smiled back.

He's wearing a blue cashmere sweater and khaki pants, and I realize that in the five years we've known each other, I've mostly seen him in jeans or athletic shorts. He's stepped things up a notch too. He smells like that expensive candle my mom likes to burn in our living room, an almond woodsmoke, and it makes me want to lick it right off his neck.

Levi Haas.

Once we are settled in the car, Levi puts on music, a guy and a guitar, acoustic and relaxed, and I wish Shola could telepathically tell me who's playing since music is one more thing she knows and cares more about than I do. I worry this is one more test in my life that I will not pass.

"So where are we going?" I ask.

He takes his hand from the steering wheel and puts it next to mine on my seat. His pinky touches my pinky, and the enormous thrill of it, from this smallest of touches, surprises me. My insides tremble. What happens when he touches me for real? I don't know if I'll survive it.

"It's a surprise."

"Give me a hint," I say.

"Nope."

"Do you know how hard it was to get dressed not knowing where we're going?"

"I think you did just fine," Levi says, and his fingers move to the hole in my jeans, right at the thigh. He draws a circle, and I swear, for a second, I leave my body. I'm a puddle on the floor. I've never had a real boyfriend before, never had anyone casually reach out for me like that, like my thigh is also his thigh for the taking. The entire ripped jeans trend now makes sense to me.

I've kissed a few guys, but always at parties, always not-quite-sober kisses, the kind that happen on a dance floor in front of other people and lead nowhere, certainly not upstairs to the empty rooms at Xander's house, where the doors lock and the sheets are changed by a daily maid service.

For five whole years I've fantasized about kissing Levi. I've thought about doing all the things my classmates seem to get to do to each other in those rooms, or in their own bedrooms, or in their cars, and the thought that some limited version of that might happen tonight, *will likely happen*, is hard for me to wrap my mind around. What if I'm a bad kisser? What if being that close to my face, where Levi can see my pores, where he can see my distinct tangy human-ness up close, turns him off? Or even worse, what if we don't even make it to the kissing? What if we go to a restaurant and sit across from each other at a table and he discovers that I have nothing interesting to say?

We're merging onto the freeway, heading west, and he takes back his hands to concentrate on the road. I like that he's careful and cautious. In lab, he always wears his goggles and gloves, and moves slowly with the pipettes. In seventh grade, our math teacher gave us one of those trick quizzes where he buried in the instructions to not answer a single question, a lesson in reading the fine print. Levi was the only kid in the whole class who passed.

"So tell me, how do you feel about sand generally?" Levi asks.

"I'm pro-sand. Especially in large quantities spread out across the coastline."

"Cool. I'm pro-sand too. I can't remember: Do you surf?"

"Oh crap. We're not surfing, are we?" I ask. I spent an hour blow-drying my hair. Getting it wet was not an option I'd considered.

"Nope. Was curious. I don't surf and it always feels like it hurts my Cali cred. But I'm scared of sharks."

"Seriously?"

"Dead serious. They eat people's limbs. I don't under-stand how anyone could *not* be afraid of sharks," Levi says.

If he had asked me to guess, I would have said Levi was afraid of nothing. Levi seems deliberate, not anxious, like

87

reading the fine print keeps him from experiencing fear. He does not need to expand the definitions of words so that they one day include him.

"Well, they're not what I'm *most* afraid of, but I'd say sharks are in my top ten." He exits onto the PCH. We're headed to Malibu and I feel myself relax, maybe because I can picture our destination, the white sand and the setting sun, a postcard place where only good things can happen. Our conversation is flowing. It seems silly that I was ever worried. I've never had any trouble talking to Levi. The trouble has always been my feelings *while* talking to him.

"What're the other nine?"

"You really want me to list my biggest fears?" Levi asks, and a smile spreads across his face, a withholding, a reminder that with Levi the ratio of what he thinks and what he says out loud is way lower—or is it higher?—than mine. But then, I say everything I think. Shola calls me *FDB*, Full Disclosure Berringer, for a reason. I think it's because I'm naturally lazy—it takes work to filter your thoughts before you say them aloud.

"I'll do it if you do it."

"Well, sharks, obviously. So, nine, small spaces. I'm claustrophobic, for real. Eight, that spinning ride at Magic Mountain where you stick to the walls, which is probably related to number nine. Seven, dying," he says.

"Only number seven? I feel like that's most people's number one."

"Definitely seven. The inevitability, and some near misses we won't get into, somehow make it less scary."

"You've put a lot of thought into this," I say. I know I

won't be able to rattle off my own fears as easily when it's my turn.

"What else am I supposed to do late at night when I can't sleep?" Levi asks, and I try to picture his bedroom, a place I've never been. What color is his comforter? Does he have posters on the walls? Are they of athletes or rock stars or, God forbid, inspirational quotes? I imagine leftover Lego model sets from childhood, a few debate team trophies, and a stuffed animal that he still sleeps with, like I do with Funny Bunny. I bet he has a Harvard pennant hanging above his bed, the thing that keeps him motivated in that fifth hour of the daily grind of homework when he goes for the extra credit. I wonder if he has an illicit Adderall prescription. Maybe he also got extra time on the SATs, but then I remember he was there, a few rows back, the first time I took the test.

"Watch *Law & Order.* Works like a charm. I hear that *chick-chick* sound and I'm out."

"I'll have to try that."

"So, number six?" I ask.

"Six, rats. Five, black holes. Four, cats."

"You are *not* afraid of cats," I say, and grin at him, and he flashes one back, like a gift.

"I hate them, and that hate commingles with fear. Also, I'm super allergic, so they could actually kill me."

"Kittens too?"

"Kittens *are* cats, Chlo."

"I'm starting to think you're secretly a wuss."

"Oh, not so secretly. Where was I? Three. Getting shot at school."

"That's dark."

"That's America. Number two, losing my mom or dad or, God forbid, both, and then my number one biggest fear— drumroll, please . . ." I tap out a beat on his dash and look over at him. He's staring out the windshield. I've always liked his profile—strong and hard-jawed, a profile worthy of a Roman statue. "Disappointing my parents."

"Really?"

"Yeah, and I realize it's super messed up. Like losing them should come before disappointing them, but for me, if I'm honest, it really doesn't."

"I get that," I say, because I do. I mean, my own list is totally different: I'm not afraid of rats or kittens or small spaces, and I love a good Gravitron. I'm not even sure I know what a black hole is or if it is something to be afraid of. But I do worry about my parents, about their inevitable disappointment and embarrassment, because I will not one day rise, like they have both risen from the ashes of their past.

I do not come from ash.

Rising for me involves a different sort of calculus.

A vision board is not going to get me into a top-tier school, and so very soon, there will be a reckoning. A moment when my mom will have to admit to Aunt Candy that despite the wizardry of Dr. Wilson, I'm still going to clown college.

We are off to the side of the PCH, and Levi pulls into a parking spot in one of those lots right up against the beach. He takes my hand and holds it properly in his.

"Your turn," he says. Our fingers lock into place, and my mind goes blank. I turn to face him, and I look into his eyes, which are brown like mine, but a more interesting brown. With depth and flecks of gold and a burning black center. Curious eyes.

"I don't know," I say, and before I need to be clever and come up with my own list, which if I was going to be honest—and despite my full-disclosure tendencies, I wasn't going to be—would be topped with *I like you too much*, Levi leans across the seat and kisses me.

CHAPTER THIRTEEN

Now

My new lawyer, Mr. Lowe, shakes my hand and insists I call him Kenny, which is a kid's name on a cartoon, not a professional's. He comes armed with a legal pad but nothing else—no laptops like the legal team my parents have assembled—and asks to borrow a pen, since he left his in the car. I think of Linda, my SAT tutor, and how she complimented me on always remembering my pencils.

This is not a reassuring start.

We're meeting in my dad's office—and I've told Kenny nothing more than my birthday—when shouting erupts in the living room.

"Are you kidding me? No. Just no!" my mom screams, hysteria in her voice, and so Kenny flips over his pad and we both get up to see what's happening. My mom's lawyers are assembled in a row on the couch, and despite their suits, they look like seventh graders waiting to get yelled at by the high school principal. Paloma stands near the fireplace, and for once the buds are out of her ears. She hugs a clipboard, and something about the way she holds it like a shield reminds me of the FBI's bulletproof vests. I feel a deep unsettling in my bones.

My father runs into the room at the same moment we do, though he comes from the kitchen and he's double-fisting pastries. Apparently, we're all turning to carbs in this time of crisis. Isla claimed she saw my mother eating a bagel with cream cheese yesterday, and not the Tofutti stuff, but *strawberry* flavored. An actual bagel with what my mom would call, with disgust, "sugar-cheese." But I won't believe that until I see it with my own eyes.

"What's wrong? What's happening?" my dad asks me, and then looks over at Kenny. "Who's he?"

"My lawyer," I say, and my dad nods at me, like this is completely reasonable, the fact that I have my own legal counsel. "Isla's idea."

"Smart," he says.

My mom sits on her knees in the middle of the living room, her hands in her hair. This can't be about the case, because everyone keeps saying we need to wait, that these things move slowly—we're still months, maybe even years, away from any potential trial. I know things are dire, but I find myself unsympathetic. At the moment, I have little patience for her theatrics or her self-pity.

"Joy, what's happening? Are you okay?" my dad asks, approaching her slowly, hands at his sides.

"They fired me," she says, and looks to my father, like he's the only person in the room. Unlike what many of my classmates seem to report about their own moms and dads (or moms and moms and dads and dads), my parents are, after twenty years of marriage, still solid. They bicker, obviously: My mom wishes my dad exercised more, my dad wishes my mom would look at her phone less, and they both think the other works too much. But most of the time, they truly seem like best friends in love. They kiss and go out on dates, and sometimes, late at night, I can hear them laughing as they stream a silly movie on the projector screen in their bedroom. I'd find it all icky, except I've seen the flip side with friends—weekends in different houses, testifying in court about who you want to live with, fights over child support payments—so I feel grateful that I've never once worried my parents would get divorced. Until now, we've been immune to that kind of misfortune.

"They all fired me. *Blood Moon*. That Biogurt commercial that was going to run in Japan. My agent said even Lifetime is shelving that ripped-from-the-headlines-murder-y thing. Twenty years of steady work, and poof! It's all gone."

"What about the—" My dad looks at the assembled lawyers and remembers that the resurrection of *My Dad, My Pops, and Me* by Netflix is still a carefully guarded industry secret. They haven't announced to the trades yet.

"They're writing Missy off. It's over," my mom says, and dissolves into tears all over again, which is how my mother cries, both in real life and onscreen. In discrete outbursts. My dad takes her into his arms and she clutches his shirt, twisting it in her fingers, the same way she did to her television husband on *Blood Moon* when he drank the potion that would reverse his immortality.

"Don't worry. We can turn this around," Paloma offers,

and as much as I've always resented how much of a hand she's had in our lives, how there have been so few public family moments that haven't been in some way curated or manufactured by Paloma, I can't help but admire her fearlessness. I'd be too scared to interrupt this performance. "The crisis folks are landing tonight. They've already sent over their initial plans. We'll get through this. I promise."

"Listen to Paloma. She's never steered us wrong," my dad says, though I catch his eye over my mom's head and I know we're both thinking of that time not too long ago when Paloma suggested that my mother not dispute some tabloid cancer rumors, even though she was perfectly healthy. *Why not garner some temporary goodwill in the run-up to the reunion? I'm not saying lie; I'm saying do the* I ask for privacy during this difficult time *thing and we'll tip off some paparazzi to take a picture of you with a head wrap.*

That was one step too far, even for my mom—you don't tempt the gods with fake cancer, which would be like pinning it to a vision board. But as we sit here with seven lawyers and my mother facing actual prison time, I start to think about all the small moral compromises we've made over the years. Not this college admissions stuff. I'm thinking of the million tiny fibs we told without blinking: how we aged my mother down five years, how we pretend she makes and eats pancakes for interviews, how we gush about my mom and Hudson's closeness despite their being step-related.

We've long assumed the actual truth isn't relevant.

That's a publicist's job, after all. To misdirect the public, allow them to believe we are better people than we actually are. I think of that photograph in my dad's office again. That it is, or was, us too. I think about how far we've strayed from that image of perfection.

"Right," my mom says, gathering herself and standing up. She nods at the line of lawyers, suddenly businesslike, as if her outburst never happened, as if she can erase it from our minds, *Men in Black* style. She has switched modes, like a director has yelled from off-set, *This time try it strong and proud*. "The crisis folks will fix this."

"Reputation rehabilitation. They do it all the time," Paloma says. "Look at Martha Stewart. She had a reality show with Snoop Dogg."

My mother winces. She resents Martha Stewart because back in the early aughts, Martha's postarrest exclusive *People* magazine interview bumped my mom's long-in-the-works Missy cover story. I wonder, idly, if my mother will get her own cover now.

Is this the cycle of celebrity life?

Kenny leans down to whisper in my ear, "Don't worry. We can hire crisis PR for you too."

"No way," I say. I'm tired of the petty lies and the spin. I never wanted to be part of the sort of family who fakes a disability to be first on Space Mountain. "I don't want one."

"Google yourself," he says. "Then we'll talk."

CHAPTER FOURTEEN

Then

I come home with sand in my hair and lips bruised from too much kissing. I'm what would come up if you did a Google Images search for the word *tousled*. But actually, there's no such thing as too much kissing. That's what I learned tonight. Not when you're with the guy you've had a crush on for half your life and he takes you to a beach in Malibu to eat cheese and baguette on a picnic blanket while you watch the sun dip below the corners of the earth. My hands smell like Brie—Levi forgot a knife, so we resorted to using our fingers—and salt and boy hair wax, and if I could choose a night to live forever and ever, on repeat, it would no doubt be this one.

We didn't do more than kiss. Levi didn't even fumble for my bra clasp. It was like we mutually agreed without saying so that this was the beginning of something real and neither of us was in any rush. We'd have plenty of time for all that later.

I head to the kitchen to get a glass of water—that much

kissing, apparently, makes you thirsty—while simultaneously texting Shola (*Omg, Omg, OMG, OMG!!!!!!*), so I
jump when I see my mom sitting at the banquette in the
corner in the dark. Her hair is pulled back with a silk wrap
so her blowout doesn't get ruined, her face is bare, and she's
wearing one of my old Wood Valley sweatshirts with matching sweatpants. The blue under her eyes is bright despite
the fact that she's had the blood vessels shrunk with a laser,
and I decide this is my favorite of her looks, even though it
doesn't appear in the book her stylist made. If I were to label
it, I'd call it *Home*. Or maybe *Mom*.

"You scared me!" I say, hand to my chest, a senseless reflex, as if my cupped palm alone could keep my heart inside
my body. "Were you waiting up?"

"Your dad went to bed early, and I couldn't sleep. I
thought I'd hear how it all went." My mom has a glass of
white wine in front of her, and she sips from it. She's not
much of a drinker, because alcohol has calories, though she
claims she likes the ritual. The unwinding that happens
when your fingers wrap around a stem.

I glance at the clock. It's 11:57.

"Three minutes till curfew."

My mom taps the bench, and I pour myself some water
and sit down beside her, so close our arms touch. I'm actually bursting to talk about what happened.

"I wasn't watching the clock. I trust you. So?" my mom
asks, and I rest my head on her shoulder, grinning. "That
good, huh?"

"Amazing," I say. "Best night of my life."

My mom smiles too, and I watch as my joy fills her up

like a balloon. My happiness is her happiness. This is one of those things about parenthood, or perhaps only mother-hood, I don't understand. I mean, I get why she'd be happy for me, but she's not happy *for* me. She's happy *because of* me. This feels not unlike one of those SAT logic games, the *who ends up with what at the end of the day when everything is dished out* in a long series of hypotheticals, though I imagine happiness is not finite or tangible. It's a feeling, not pizza slices.

"Tell me everything," she says, so I do, or most of it, any-way. There are a few details I save, because I guess that's part of growing up. Allowing some bits of ourselves to not be shared with our parents. I don't tell her that when he drew my body closer to his, I shuddered with joy.

I tell her about the kissing, though, because my mom, between television seasons, used to make her living making movies about magical kisses at Christmastime, and now, be-tween television seasons, makes movies about magical kisses at Christmastime, though instead of playing the woman get-ting kissed, she plays her mom. Which is to say, she'll know exactly what I'm talking about.

"It was so great, I'm not even worried about whether he'll still be into me tomorrow."

"Of course he'll still be into you. What's there not to like?"

"Mom," I say.

"Okay, fine. I'm biased. You are my favorite person in the world." My mom says this all the time, though she says the same thing to Isla.

"What about Dad?" I follow our script.

"A very, very close second," she says, pinching her fingers together, as she always does. Do all families have these sorts of inside jokes? I wonder. Once, when Isla was about four, she sat up in the middle of the night, and apropos of nothing screamed, "Lizard breath!" And so even now, every so often, one of us will shout "Lizard breath!" at random and we'll crack up.

"*Levi Haas*, Mom," I say, because I still can't quite believe what has happened tonight. How much my life has transformed. "Levi. Haas."

"I bet he's sitting in his kitchen right this minute with his mom saying *Chloe. Berringer.*"

"I don't think so."

"Well, then that's only because his mom isn't as cool as I am. Not because he's not thinking it."

"His mom is definitely not as cool as you are." Levi's mom looks like the kind of wide-hipped and frizzy-haired mother who packs lunches and chaperones field trips. She doesn't tell stories about the time when she was twenty-two and she almost had sex with Mick Jagger at a club in New York. To be fair, neither does my mother, but that's because Aunt Candy tells them for her. Apparently, Mick passed out on her halfway through, and my mom had to yell for a security guard to help lift him off. Afterward my mom looked Candy straight in the eye and said, "I can't get no satisfaction," and then the two of them laughed so hard they cried.

I don't want to make assumptions about Levi's mom, but I'm 99 percent sure she's never even come close to sleeping with a rock star.

"Next time you speak to Levi, let him know that if he decides to break my little girl's heart, I will break his legs," my mom says, and ruffles my hair.

"I'm sure Aunt Candy knows a guy."

"We don't need a guy for that. I'd do it myself. Don't forget, I take kickboxing."

"You do have serious biceps," I say, and I glance at my mother.

"I would kill for you and your sister. With my bare hands if I had to."

"Don't be creepy," I say.

"I'm serious. I'd do anything for you, sweet pea."

"Please don't, you know, resort to murder, though."

"You never know," she says, and flexes her arm muscles.

Shola: OMG

Me: OMG

Shola: OMG OMG OMG

Me: RIGHT? Right. I think I might be in love. Like for real.

Shola: I don't know. Let's not get ahead of ourselves

Me: The way he looked at me. I mean I've never had anyone look at me like that

Shola: Remember Liam, that senior when we were freshman? He used to look at me like that

Me: I totally forgot about him. Remind me what happened there?

Shola: He went to college, never to be heard from again, and with a girlfriend no less. But hot damn, the way he used to glance at me across the cafeteria. So . . . yum

Me: Who knew looking could be even sexier than kissing? I mean the kissing was great too, don't get me wrong. But there's something about that look, like right before the kiss . . .

Shola: You are going to be insufferable for a while

Me: YUP

Shola: I'm so happy for you

Me: Thanks

Shola: I bet you are dying to send me a string of ridiculous emojis

Me: YUP

Shola: I'll make an exception to my no-emoji rule, just this once

Me: You are a true friend

Shola: I know. You're lucky to have me

Me: I am

Shola: I'm going to miss you next year. Is it too early to get weepy about graduation?

Me: We have nine months!

Shola: I've already graduated in my mind tho. Putting my apps in

Me: Noooo college talk

Shola: Okay, only Levi talk

Me: Thank you. Did I tell you he's afraid of cats?

Shola: You did not

Me: Did I tell you I think I'm in love?

Shola: You are the worst

Me: I am but you love me anyway

Shola: We can't help who we love, my friend

CHAPTER FIFTEEN

Now

Hudson poses for the paparazzi on the lawn. He puts his hands on his waist and looks off into the distance like Superman, and he follows that up by arching his back and holding up a pretend microphone, *Mamma Mia!* style. Paloma rushes outside and wrangles him into the house to get him away from the hungry camera clicks.

He's done his damage already, though.

Here's what the gossip sites will say: we're not taking this seriously, we assume we're above the law, this is another example of our gross entitlement and privilege.

If Hudson has a superpower, it's that he can always manage to make everything worse. I always feel the need to at least partially cleave myself from Hudson, to use that isolating *half.* I tell myself that I wouldn't attach this qualifier if I liked him, but it's hard to like addicts. My dad claims that when I was little, I was Hudson obsessed, that as a toddler I followed him everywhere. Now I can't imagine choosing to be in the same room as him.

"Are you kidding me? Do not talk to the media. Do not make silly poses. Do not give them anything," my father says.

"Come on. I was having a little fun." Hudson sticks out his tongue at Isla. He and Isla have always gotten along, even though they couldn't be more opposite. She's a consummate rule follower. Once Isla and I were the only people in a movie theater, and still she made us sit in our assigned seats. Hudson, on the other hand, ingests illegal substances for breakfast.

But Isla never uses the word *half*, even though it's accurate. And when she won her class's academic award last fall, she invited Hudson to the ceremony, even at the risk of him showing up high and embarrassing us. In the end, he didn't come, which is the way it is with Hudson—we all know better than to count on him for anything—and still I could sense Isla's disappointment.

"Fun? Are you serious? The crisis folks are coming tonight. They're going to give us a media strategy and we're going to follow it word for word. I guarantee you it doesn't include dancing the floss for the paps," my father says.

"Sorry, Dad," Hudson says, and even though I've been hearing Hudson call my father "Dad" all my life—and it too is accurate—it always chafes. In my mind, my dad belongs to us, not to him. Which is unfair. And selfish. I don't know what it is about my brain that divides us into teams. "Just so you know, you don't say 'dancing the floss.' You just say flossing."

"To what do we owe the pleasure, Hudson?" my mother asks, and her tone is hard and angry, a slice. Usually, she's warm to my half brother, even when he doesn't deserve her kindness. Once he showed up so loaded to our big Easter brunch that he passed out in the backyard. Instead of getting angry, my mom put him to bed upstairs so he wouldn't disturb the guests. She didn't even yell at him later after everyone had left.

I got yelled at that day, though, for taking off my tights, the ones with cute bunnies on the knees, in the bouncy castle. She said my behavior was "unladylike" and "unbecoming" and that I hadn't been "raised in a barn."

I was eight, only beginning to learn the contours of my mother's professional life, how even hosting a brunch and a bouncy castle in the backyard required a certain level of performance.

"Oh, hello, stepmonster," Hudson says, which is what he calls my mom. She pretends not to mind, but I did once hear her complain about it to Dad: *If he has to be offensive, at least he could try to be a bit clever.* "I was worried about you guys. Wanted to make sure everything was under control. As you know, I have a wee bit of experience getting into trouble with the law meself."

If for a moment, even after his front-lawn performance, any of us has been clueless enough to hope that Hudson was clean, our hopes are shattered when he starts to sway to the right and has to reach for the console table to steady himself.

"For Christ's sake," my dad yells, voice cracking. "We are not dealing with this right now."

"I see a lot of suits here. Last time I was arrested you refused to pay for my lawyer," Hudson says.

Although my dad likes for everyone to think he's low-key and relaxed, Hudson's problems weigh on him in a way

I'm sure the rest of us don't fully appreciate. Sometimes, out of nowhere, my dad will say, "I hope Hudson's okay," when what he really means is, "I hope today is not the day that Hudson dies." Sometimes I wonder if it's not the fact that I don't like Hudson that keep us from being close, but the subconscious understanding that if I were to let him into my life, I'm likely to one day get my heart eviscerated.

Indifference seems a safer strategy. I don't want to be Isla staring sadly at an empty chair, like she did when he didn't show up for her award ceremony or even the dinner afterward. I don't want to let him leach joy from moments of glory.

"Hey, Hud, did I tell you about my science fair project?" Isla asks out of nowhere. "It's actually pretty cool. I looked at what happens when you feed male fish estrogen. Come on, let me show you."

Isla grabs Hudson's arm, and at first I think, *I'm sorry, Isla, but he doesn't care about your science project unless it's made out of heroin,* and then I catch her eye. Again, I'm the dense one. She's trying to get him out of our mom's way. I take my cue.

"It is pretty amazing, and I, like, hate science," I say. Isla leads Hudson upstairs and I follow behind, partially to be a human buffer in case he falls and takes Isla down with him.

Once we're safely ensconced in Isla's room, she closes the door behind her—to minimize his potential for damage, I assume—and when he again lists to the side, she points to her bed. Hudson obeys, curls up on top of the covers, and rests his head on her pink satin pillowcase.

"Some major shit happening here," he says.

"Yup," Isla says, making no move to show him her project. She doesn't seem angry, though that's always how I feel when I see Hudson high. She seems only sad and frustrated, like he's an equation that she should know how to solve. "Some major shit."

"Your mom might go to jail for, like, *twenty years*. The most I've ever faced is like five. I find the whole thing very ironic."

"That's not really what *ironic* means," Isla says. I want to scream at them both: *Mom is not going to jail for twenty years, you idiots. It was only a college application!*

"I can't believe you cheated on the SATs, Chlo. I can't decide if that's the nerdiest thing I've ever heard or totally badass," Hudson says.

"I didn't cheat," I say, for what might be the hundredth time, though I wonder why I feel the need to make this excuse to him. It wouldn't matter to him one way or the other. I bet he's not even curious. One added cruelty of addiction—it turns you into a narcissist. "I didn't know."

"Yeah right," Hudson says, and then, "Wait, are you eighteen yet?"

"No." I know what he's driving at. If I were, and the feds decided I knew about everything, I could be charged as an adult. That was one of the very first questions Kenny asked me when we sat down to talk: *Are you eighteen?*

"Lucky bitch," he says, and closes his eyes. His words cut, but I shake them off. Hudson can't hurt me. Not when he's too busy hurting himself.

We wait a minute. Wait some more. Isla pokes him to confirm that he's passed out. She puts her hand on his chest to make sure he's still breathing. You never know with Hudson.

She reaches into his pocket and takes his phone.

I stare at her, shocked.

"What? This way he can't sell a story to the tabloids," Isla says. "Or at least this will make it harder."

"Did you really do a science project on fish?" I ask.

"Of course not. The fair isn't until the spring. And anyhow, you can't experiment with hormones like that. It would be animal cruelty."

"I love you," I say, feeling suddenly thankful for my sister. If things had been the other way around, if she had ruined my life, I wouldn't be nearly as generous about trying to help sort it all out. I throw my arms around her and kiss her cheek.

"Stop being weird," she says.

CHAPTER SIXTEEN

Then

The SAT results are posted Friday morning, two weeks after I take the test. I want to check them alone, but of course, as with everything college admissions related, this has ballooned into a family affair. Thankfully, Isla had jazz band practice before school, so she's not here to witness my final mortification.

"Let's do this," my mom says, all pumped up, clapping to release her nervous energy. She's wearing her workout clothes—Lululemon yoga pants and a sports bra, the same outfit from her "Celebrities: They're Just Like Us" photo in *Us Weekly*. Even though she's almost fifty, she doesn't require a shirt.

"Please calm down. I already told you I bombed it," I say. I'm not nervous about my score—it will be, no doubt, embarrassingly low. That's what happens when you eeny-meeny-miny-moe half the questions. I'm only nervous about how my parents will take the news. After all the money spent, the countless hours of private tutoring, and a testing accommodation, these results will confirm for them their deepest, quietest suspicion: that their eldest daughter is, in fact, a moron.

I don't want to watch that disappointment play out on their faces in real time. I don't want to see the inevitable sag and the exhale, and worst of all, their attempts to hide it all so they can protect my feelings. There will be hugs and tears and a reflexive need to comfort me; all the while I'll know they're making eye contact over my head and having their own terrible conversation.

"Stop being so negative, sweetheart. I bet you did great," my dad says in a voice I recognize from childhood, the one he'd use after I fell, when he'd scoop me up so fast that I wouldn't have time to notice the hurt. I'm sitting in front of what we call the "home computer," which is the desktop in the playroom, although we each have our own laptops and iPads and iPhones. Between us, there are at least twelve other gadgets I could have used that would not have required me to sit here, with my parents standing behind me, so close I can not only smell but also feel their hot coffee breath. Their bodies tent over mine, as if to shield me.

I should have done this in the bathroom, before they woke up, behind a locked door. I could have stepped straight into a steaming hot shower to scream afterward.

I want to remind them that the SAT isn't a group sport. Neither is college admissions. But that will only make things worse. I know my parents. They will take this score like a punch.

I want to ask them to please not scoop me back up this time—no conciliatory hugs—that we should each retreat to our corners after to lick our own wounds. I don't know how to say this without hurting them.

I sign in to my College Board account and take a deep breath.

"Right there, honey. Click there," my mom says, pointing with a long, blue-polished fingernail to the results link. She's the only person in the world over the age of twenty-five who can get away with blue nail polish. "I'm so nervous and excited. I'm nervited!"

"Mom," I say.

"I'm excervous," my dad says.

"Stop, guys," I say.

"Relax. This is going to be so great. Click it already!" my mom says.

"Give me a second." I close my eyes. I think: *I am lucky. I am lucky. I am lucky.*

I list all my good things: Levi and me on the beach, him saying *I like you.* I think of Shola, how even if we end up at colleges on opposite ends of the country, she'll still be my invisible safety net. I think of my health, and my parents' health, and Isla's. I think how I've never known food scarcity. How I could have been born in Syria or South Central, instead of Beverly Hills.

I think about the word *privilege,* the good edges of it, the reassuring ones, and how it applies to me on every front in every way.

I think: *This doesn't matter. This doesn't matter. This doesn't matter.*

"It *does* matter," my mom says, which makes me realize I must have said this last bit out loud.

"I know," I say, defensive. "I'm trying to keep things in perspective."

"A little late for that," my dad says, and laughs, though I have no idea what he means. I think I've kept my panic hidden pretty well, all things considered.

"I swear, if you don't press that button, I'm going to do it for you," my mom says, and so I click.

My scores appear on the screen.

Reading, 720. Math, 720.

Wait, what? I double-check again that it's my name on the top and that this isn't someone else's file.

There has to be some sort of glitch.

A total score of 1440—720 reading, 720 math. That's two hundred forty points higher than the last time I took the test.

Two hundred forty points.

"Holy crap! Yes! Yes! Yes!" my mom cheers, and kisses my cheek, and then does a happy dance, which in her case, apparently, takes the form of some sort of cha-cha.

"Well done," my dad says, and hugs me tight from the back. I don't turn. I'm still staring at the screen, bewildered and frozen. I check the question breakdowns, and I must be remembering incorrectly, because it seems like there are way fewer marked wrong than I guessed on. How could that be? Could I have had some bizarre, magical sixth sense when randomly picking? I click over to my percentiles: 97 percent across the board.

"These are wrong," I say, without thinking. I don't understand. "They must have mixed up my scores. I have to talk to Mrs. Oh."

"Chloe," my dad says. "Look, it's right there. You did it, honey. All those practice tests. All that early morning studying. You did it!"

"We're so proud of you," my mom says, grinning, a sheen of sweat on her forehead. She was more nervous than I was. "See? Hard work pays off."

"It doesn't make sense." My parents exchange a worried glance, and I get a whiff of that familiar disappointment: *Why does Chloe have to make everything so hard?*

"Of course it does, sweetheart. It makes perfect sense," my dad says.

"There's no way," I say.

"Don't look a gift horse in the mouth," my dad says, and taps the screen again. His voice is sharper, with a tightness I only ever hear when he's on the phone with work people, what I think of as his *cut the crap* tone. I don't understand the undercurrent of anger, and so I shake my head, smile, feel the slightest bit of relief.

1440.

"This is great. This is best-case scenario. Be happy," my mom says, looking from my dad to me and then back again. "All I ever want is for you to be happy, Chlo."

I make a conscious attempt to suck up her joy. She's right. This is best-case scenario, actually better than best case, because I never allowed myself to consider the possibility of scoring this high.

I let my mom pull me out of my chair so we can cha-cha together, though mine is worse than hers. I allow myself a minute to revel.

Maybe I'm not as stupid as I thought.

Maybe I do not need to create my own, new category of smart, after all.

I text Shola.

> **Me:** 1440
>
> **Shola:** !!!!!!!!!!!!!
>
> **Me:** I know, right?
>
> **Shola:** AMAZING! I'm so proud of you!
>
> **Me:** There has to be a mix-up
>
> **Shola:** Come on. Stop that. You EARNED THIS
>
> **Me:** I mean, I did work my ass off, but . . .
>
> **Shola:** But nothing!
>
> **Me:** 1440 shouldn't be a big deal to you Ms. 1560
>
> **Shola:** Don't do that. It's a HUGE DEAL!!!!!!!
>
> **Me:** I raised my score 240 points. That doesn't sound like too much? Like there's a glitch in the matrix?
>
> **Shola:** No glitch, bitch. That should be your senior quote
>
> **Me:** 1440!!!!

Shola: Well, I always said you were a genius

Me: You've never once said I'm a genius

Shola: You're right. I didn't. But I love you, you beautiful smart human whose value comes not from how you fill out a Scantron on a standardized test even when it gets you a score as kickass as this, but whose value comes from the beauty within. Nothing standardized about you

Me: Love you too you big nerd

CHAPTER SEVENTEEN

Now

Five days after my mom is arrested, the first encrypted group text arrives via Signal, an app Isla downloaded to our new cells. She says it's a less dangerous, more private way to communicate, and so this is how she and I talk when not face to face. Through software used by spies and terrorists.

Kenny agreed that this was a smart precaution. We don't want to risk hacking or wiretaps.

I still don't quite understand how it has come to this: that I have my own lawyer, that he didn't think it paranoid or ridiculous to imagine that my phone could be compromised, that criminal charges against me are still entirely possible. That I receive encrypted messages from other kids targeted by the FBI.

The first one arrives with a mellow *bloop*, and there it is: my first introduction to my co-scandalees.

> **PhinnyB:** Welcome to this fully encrypted group
> text chain for those of us I could locate who are

also caught up in this thing. RULES: Do not show your parents. Or lawyers. Delete each message after reading. Leaks will not be tolerated. No discussion of legal strategy. OK? I figured we could all use a friend to vent to

ALC: Did you guys know?

Slyse: No idea. I feel so stupid

ALC: Me too. My twin sister knew I think, but I didn't. How screwed up is that? We're 17 by the way. In the clear, probs. Delete this

Slyse: I heard they sent target letters to some of the kids. Is that true? Can anyone confirm?

PhinnyB: Yup. Got one. I'm 20

ALC: I'm not allowed to talk to my mom. Like it's currently court ordered that we can't talk about the case

Slyse: I never want to talk to my parents again

PrettyPen: This is a nightmare. I keep waiting to wake up. I can't go back to school. It's humiliating

Thelgster: I think they're going to kick me out. I guess it doesn't matter. My grades are dogshit anyway

PhinnyB: Ig, you in college too, bro?

Thelgster: Sophomore. Yale

PhinnyB: SCC junior. We're so screwed

After the first text breaks the seal, the messages come in fast, one after the other, so quickly, I can barely keep up. Is this legal?

I scan the handles in the group and it's not hard to trace each of them to the complaint, which I finally read yesterday, peeping through the fingers I held over my eyes. Reading it gave me one specific sort of rare victory—it felt exactly as bad as I had anticipated.

PhinnyB is Phinneas Black III, the heir to the KetoBagel fortune; ALC is Apple Lennon Chesterford, whose dad is the head litigator at a large New York Law firm and whose mom is a well-known health influencer; Slyse is Sly Sanderson, whose mother runs a hedge fund in Connecticut (dad unmentioned); TheIgster is Igancious Smith Wollingham IV, who is the son of two real estate developers in the Bay Area; and PrettyPen is Penelope Grace Giffords, whose mom is a famous supermodel married to an ibanker. Usually Penelope goes by Penny Grace. She posts makeup tutorials on YouTube that Isla and her friends like to watch.

> **ALC:** I can't imagine my mom going to jail. She's vegan and only wears organic fabrics and has, like, a zillion allergies. Do they accommodate that stuff in jail? I mean she needs a special pillow at hotels or her eyes get puffy

I decide to jump in. I'll stay away from the topics Kenny warned me not to talk about. No confessions. No details about what happened last fall. But maybe this can help me, a support group of sorts, the opportunity to find safety in numbers. They are the only people in the world who under-stand what I'm going through, how it feels.

Yesterday, I sent Shola a text from my new phone.

Only five words: *I'm scared. I miss you. Chlo*

She hasn't written back.

I try to shake off that sickening hum of terror, the un-folding of my dirty crevices of guilt, the words that play on repeat in my brain: *Well, you got what you deserved.*

Me: NO ONE is going to jail

PhinnyB: Welcome Missy's kid! I feel like you might have this worst of all

Me: Umm, thanks?

PhinnyB: I meant the paparazzi. Every five minutes I get a news alert about your mom. By the way, it took mega-balls to wear that SCC shirt when she was arrested. Nice one

Me: An accident

ALC: Your parents didn't sit you down the night before?

Me: ?

ALC: Apparently the feds gave advanced warning or something to everyone. I swear when my parents told me, it was like learning there was no Santa Claus. They were like—it's about to get real, buckle up. And I was like, Mom, stop talking like your Twitter feed

Well, at least one thing is explained. Why my mother seemed to be expecting eight FBI agents at our door that morning, though clearly she assumed they'd be fashionably late. My fear, a sticky thing, a constant sheen on my skin, turns rancid and transforms into a burgeoning rage. I feel the prickle of sweat at all my pressure points.

How come my parents didn't warn me? Is it that they didn't trust me? Or they assumed I was too brainless to understand?

PrettyPen: I didn't even want to go to college. My parents made me apply

TheIgster: You really think no one is going to jail?

PhinnyB: I think they're all going. Every last one of them. But only the adults

ALC: Me too

TheIgster: YOU are an adult, Phin

PhinnyB: Nah man, like a real adult. We were kids following along with our parents. We had no choice. No one wants to see us go to jail

TheIgster: Hope you're right

PhinnyB: I hate to say it but I think people want to see Missy in stripes tho

Me: I'm out

PhinnyB: Wait, come back. Just being honest. Sorry

Me: I get enough crap already. I don't need it here

ALC: I don't think he was trying to give you crap. I think he was saying this is all a pr disaster and people are like, super obsessed and mad. So much madder than I would have guessed they'd be. Like people pay to get into college all the time. They build buildings and endow departments. Why is this any different?

Slyse: And your mom is famous, so . . .

Thelgster: I don't even understand how this is illegal. How could this be mail fraud if no one sent anything through the mail? I don't even know HOW to send a letter

PhinnyB: Seriously, I'm sorry, Chloe

PrettyPen: Hey will you guys hit up my Insta page? I'm losing followers by the minute

CHAPTER EIGHTEEN

Then

Levi holds my hand as he walks me to my locker. It's casual, a loose link, like we're not trying to make a big fuss.

"We need to celebrate your new score," Levi says, and bumps my hip with his. Every time he touches me, I can hear the tiniest click in my mind: it's me taking a picture to capture the moment so I can savor it later like I'm my own paparazzo. "I have a student council meeting after school and then tennis and an AP physics quiz tomorrow. So crap, we won't be able to do it today."

"Remember when they promised us that senior year we'd get to coast?" I say.

"I don't know who *they* are, but *they* definitely lied."

"The patriarchy. A bunch of lying liars who lie," I say, which doesn't even make sense, but Levi laughs anyway.

"I can't even think about coasting until I have an acceptance letter in hand, and even then, did you know they can rescind it if you don't keep up your grades?" Levi asks.

"The patriarchy can rescind your college admissions?"

"You just like saying the word *patriarchy*."

"I also like the words *onomatopoeia* and *solipsistic*. Those are my top three, I think. Ooh, and *rabble-rouser*," I say, but he doesn't take the banter-bait.

"Can you imagine you finally get into your dream school, and they're like, 'Nope, sorry, we changed our minds because you blew that math test'?" Levi's getting into Harvard, just like Shola. He's never blown an exam in his entire life. The more time we spend together, the more I realize that that which he has always made seem effortless is not effortless at all. This boy *likes* to work.

When he rubs his eyes, that habit that unravels my insides every time, it's because he's exhausted. I actually feel a weird relief in seeing all of the effort behind his success. It gives me an easier, albeit still uncomfortable explanation for my being toward the bottom of my class.

Watching Levi, I consider for the first time that maybe I'm not not-smart, I'm lazy.

I think about his *Nope, sorry, we changed our minds*, and I wonder if that will happen here, between us. He'll rescind this hand-holding and the kissing, and for me, he'll turn out to be another overreach. My heart will be destroyed in all its onomatopoeic glory: *blam, splat, kapow*.

"When you send in your acceptance, just say *no backsies*. It works for the cooties." I throw my books into my locker, and Levi laughs again and brushes his lips against my cheek. If kisses could talk, this one would say: *I enjoy you*. And if it wasn't weird, I'd say: *Please don't stop*.

"No backsies," he says.

"Chloe Berringer, report to Mrs. Oh. Chloe Berringer, report to Mrs. Oh," the office receptionist announces over the loudspeaker, interrupting our moment.

My stomach clenches. Of course, I already know what's to come. Mrs. Oh will sit me down in her office and will make official what I already suspect: the College Board screwed up my results. I did not get a 1440. Moron status reconfirmed.

I think about my parents' inevitable disappointment. *Crap*. This morning, my mom ran around the house chanting *SCC! SCC! SCC!* despite the fact that even with these new scores, it's still a big long shot.

"Uh-oh," I say.

"I'm sure it's nothing." Levi kisses my cheek a second time, like he can't resist, and I melt, despite the anxiety surging through my veins. "Okay, got to get to class. But: Saturday. You, me, celebratory tacos."

"No backsies," I call after him, and then for no reason at all, maybe because it's my default factory setting, as soon as the words are out, I feel like an idiot.

I sprint to Mrs. Oh's office. If my entire future is about to unravel, let's rip this Band-Aid off fast.

"Chloe," Mrs. Oh says, and I can't read her face. She's in her thirties, and wears tortoise-shell glasses and wide-legged linen pants. Something bulges from her chest, and it takes me a minute to understand: she's holding a sleeping infant in a sling. She sways side to side. "Come sit down. I'm going to stand and rock and pat. It's a whole routine and we don't want to wake the little monster."

"I don't know how this happened," I say, fumbling, because how do you say, *Well, it was fun while it lasted. Back to Planet Mediocre?* Mrs. Oh smiles at me, puts a comforting hand on my shoulder, and then goes back to her rocking.

"I wanted to congratulate you," she says.

I'm unable stop my right leg from bouncing up and down, a nervous habit that drives my mother bananas when we go to restaurants. "Stop that jackhammering," she'll say in a whisper under her breath, because of course she can't yell at me in public. And I'll stop, until ten minutes later, when she puts her hand on my knee and I realize I'm doing it all over again.

Maybe my shaking leg is how I got an accommodation. Maybe not everyone has so much constant, nervous, unfocused energy. Maybe I'm not lazy, I'm wired.

I wonder if I will accidentally wake the baby. I can't see its face, but a puff of black hair sprouts out from Mrs. Oh's elbow, like she's sporting a Troll doll.

"Fourteen forty. A two-hundred-forty-point increase is practically unheard of. I love seeing hard work pay off," Mrs. Oh says. She opens my file with her free hand. It's all spread out on the desk—my grades, my extracurriculars (even a photo of Cesar), my scant AP classes (I took world history because it has the highest pass rate), and these scores. All my measurements taken and then used to determine whether or not I am worthy of a particular brand of future.

"Do you think? I mean, could there be some mistake?" I ask.

Mrs. Oh peers at me for a moment with a bizarre intensity, and then as if coming to some sort of decision, she throws her head back and laughs.

"I wasn't kidding," I say.

"Chloe, you did it. You worked your ass off—pardon my French, little monster," she mutters to the baby. "And you did it. The College Board has never once, at least since I've been doing this job, had a mix-up."

"I guessed on a few questions." I don't confess to how many. I don't make clear the reason that this score report *feels* like an impossibility is because I'm pretty sure it is one. Or if not impossible, then magical. I've never been good at probability, but I'd put me guessing my way into a 1440 at similar odds to my winning the Powerball.

Then again, people do win the lottery sometimes. And when they do, they don't call it a mistake; they call it luck.

"Well, either you guessed correctly or got enough of the other questions right. I wouldn't look a gift horse in the mouth, sweetheart," Mrs. Oh says. Hearing that expression for the second time this morning makes it no less annoying.

"Right."

"I've been looking over that original list of schools we discussed last month. Now listen, I'm not going to lie to you. I think most are still a reach, but before I thought you'd be wasting the application fee even trying. Now I think it's worth going for them."

The baby starts to stir, so Mrs. Oh increases her rocking. It had never occurred to me that Mrs. Oh could be a mom. Then again, I never think of my teachers' outside-of-school lives. It's like they cease to exist as soon as I leave the Wood Valley front doors.

"So you think I could get into a place like SCC?"

"Who knows? At a certain point, it's all a crapshoot. You're not a legacy, right?"

"No."

"Well, that would have helped."

"You can say I won't get in. It won't hurt my feelings. I think my parents are being unrealistic," I admit.

"Listen, are you the strongest candidate from Wood Valley who has SCC on their list? Of course not. It's a super-popular school among our student body, and your grades aren't stellar. But do I think you should still apply and cross your fingers? Yeah, why not? Maybe they'll take more of us this year. Maybe they're fans of *My Dad, My Pops, and Me*, or they'll think your parents could one day be generous donors. There are all sorts of calculations here that we're not privy to."

I feel the ickiness I always feel when anyone suggests I might be treated differently because of my parents, like there's no such thing as my earning something on my own. And then I tell myself I don't care. If my mom starring on a sitcom in the early aughts is what pushes some admissions person over the edge, so be it.

I *am* Joy Fields's daughter.

It's not like it's a lie.

CHAPTER NINETEEN

Now

"Why are you keeping *me* locked up?" Isla asks. "If you hadn't noticed, I wasn't the one who got arrested around here." We're in the kitchen at seven a.m., the only chance to talk to our parents before the army of suited professionals arrive. They come hungry and mean, like a zombie apocalypse.

We've been home from school for an entire week, and Isla's itching to get back to Wood Valley. When she's not reading legal blogs, she catches up on homework and reads the day's class notes, which she gets emailed daily by her friends. I, on the other hand, haven't cracked open a book. I don't see the point.

I've sent Shola more texts, and Levi, too, and each time I hit send, I feel an irrational surge of hope that never gets rewarded.

After this, the day will turn its attention to the grinding bureaucracy of our lives falling apart: meetings and phone calls and referrals and PowerPoint presentations. The PR and crisis folks and the lawyers will jockey for my mother's attention, a constant tug-of-war from the living room to the dining room. PR almost always wins. My mom feels way more comfortable debating the merits of a *People* magazine cover interview vs. a tell-all exclusive with *20/20* than facing her legal situation.

She doesn't want to learn about mandatory federal prison guidelines.

When the lawyers insist she sit down and listen, she cries weird silent tears that fall down her face in perfect straight lines.

"I can't deal with this," my mom says, which has become a frequent refrain in this house, and one I understand. She reaches for the bottle of Xanax, which now lives on the kitchen counter for easy access. Before, it lived in my mother's medicine cabinet, the pills only making a sly appearance in her silver engraved pill case for long-haul flights.

Every day, the trouble grows with a terrifying momentum. My mom has been fired. My dad has a meeting with his board of directors next week, when he too is likely to lose his position. There's talk of a $800 billion class-action lawsuit, a sum so outrageous, my father actually laughed when the lawyers mentioned the possibility. Hudson has been MIA doing God knows what, and we pretend not to be worried about him. We pretend not to think that he might be the other shoe that's about to drop. We've canceled our trip to Mexico to celebrate my mom's fiftieth birthday, since she had to surrender her passport as a condition of her bail.

I don't care about the vacation, but I do think about her passport. I heard my parents murmuring about an account in the Cayman Islands, how maybe they could come up with a plan to leave the country if it became absolutely necessary. *I've always liked Zurich*, my mom said.

They stopped talking when they saw me. No one defined *necessary*.

I made the mistake of setting up a Google alert, and op-eds across the country celebrate the idea of my mom going to jail, declare her (and by extension me) a symbol of everything that is wrong with our country. Even debates that have nothing to do with us—immigration? health care?—somehow pivot back to the scandal, how the 1 percent take more than our fair share, how we hoard our privilege. How we've corrupted every system, that we are emblematic of a perversion of capitalism.

Off with our heads.

Under all this lies the terrible quicksand of fear. What if they are right? What if it's true that we are terrible, horrible, no-good, very bad people? If I allow myself to dip my toes into that idea, that I am not actually the hero of my own story but a villain, I quickly find myself neck deep.

And, of course, there's the heartbreak that slithers in late at night, when I'm alone in bed, the darkness so heavy I can't breathe. Sure, I can handle the humiliation of Levi temporarily blocking me. I can understand that he needs time. Time I can give. Time I have in spades. What hurts the most, what sends me into the fetal position, is thinking about Shola. I've sent her increasingly desperate text messages:

I'm sorry

I need you

I can't do this alone

Please

I'm begging

Of course, no response.

"If I don't go to school, I'm not going to get into college, no matter how much you pay the next Dr. Wilson. You want to ruin my future too?" Isla says, and this shuts my mom right up. My sister has always known how to angle the knife, especially with my mother. Sometimes I wonder why they don't get along with the same seamlessness that my mom and I do. I think it's because they are eerily similar people—stubborn, competitive, compulsively diligent—who can't help but be as hard on each other as they are on themselves. Isla's 4.4 GPA, it turns out, is not unlike my mother's abs.

"I'll drive you, Isl," I say, because my sister is still a few months away from getting her license. "I can drop you off a block away so you don't have to be seen with me."

"Thanks," she says.

"Carrie will get you a driver," my dad says, and it comes out like a command. He too reaches for the Xanax bottle, shakes one into his palm, pauses, shakes another. His hair is wet and neatly combed, and he's wearing a stiff, white shirt, fresh from the dry cleaner. A small way, I think, of signaling to the rest of us that he still has this all under control. "Chloe is not leaving this house."

I don't know if this is a punishment—am I *grounded?*—or if this is for my own protection. It doesn't matter. Even though my mom has been negotiating our first public outing since the scandal broke with the crisis people, I have no interest in going anywhere. That's what we've been calling it around here—"the scandal"—which I think is a cop-out. The word *scandal* divorces us from our own culpability, makes it sound like something that happened to us instead of something we've done.

Paloma says we need the photographic evidence to show that things are business as usual in the Fields-Bellinger family, that we are close-knit, happy. *Celebrities: they're just like us.*

The only place I'd like to go is the Reading and Resource Center to see Cesar. We are well into *Harry Potter and the Chamber of Secrets,* and I miss hearing about his day—who he played with at recess, whether he got his name written on the board for talking without raising his hand. But I realize going there would be selfish for a variety of reasons, not least of which I'd be using my friend for reputation rehabilitation. More importantly, the last thing Cesar or his mom needs is media sniffing around them. I did text Rita, though, to let her know I wouldn't be back for a while, and to pass along my new number in case Cesar needs anything in the meantime.

I wrote *Tell him I miss and love him and I'm so sorry and I'll be back soon.*

I haven't heard back from her, and I wonder if Rita has decided, without telling me, that I'm no longer welcome there. I decide that's another rejection I would not survive. I am Cesar's backup, no matter what. Rita cannot—will not—banish me.

I imagine walking out the front door of my house into the bright sunlight. I imagine facing the paparazzi who are still, a whole week later, camped outside, cameras aimed liked the FBI's guns.

I don't think I can stomach it.

My new phone buzzes, but it provides no escape.

There's a text from my lawyer: *I'll be there by nine. It's important. Prepare yourself for news.*

The coffee that mere minutes ago felt like a lifeline does a quick crawl up the back of my throat.

I reach for the Xanax.

"Don't even think about it," my dad says, and slips the bottle into his pocket.

CHAPTER TWENTY

Then

Levi and I lie on the picnic blanket he keeps in his trunk. Of all the details I've gathered about him over the years, that may be the one that's most surprising to me: He's ever-ready for a pop-up picnic.

"What did you write your college essay about?" I ask. My head rests on his stomach, and my laptop sits on my knees. He's reading *Crime and Punishment* and has a pink highlighter tucked behind his ear. I scroll through the common application essay prompts: *Discuss something that inspires you. . . . Tell us about a challenge you've overcome. . . . Elaborate on some of your interests outside of school.*

Levi inspires me. It's challenging to negotiate with Levi out of the friend zone. My biggest interest outside of school is kissing Levi, because kissing Levi is, to borrow an SAT word, transcendent.

Of course, I know that I can't actually write my application essay about Levi, that not only is the idea pathetic, but it will also be shot down by both Dr. Wilson and Mrs. Oh.

Even my small brain should stretch beyond the confines of a boy. It should be singing more complicated, fulfilling songs than simply a ditty that repeats: *Levi, Levi, Levi.*

And yet: *Levi, Levi, Levi.*

Dr. Wilson said to write about whatever I wanted, that he has a professional writer on staff who will help clean up my essay later. Mrs. Oh said to *dig deep and tell the story of Chloe Wynn Berringer.* The problem is there really is no story of Chloe Wynn Berringer. At least, not yet.

"I wrote about having cancer as a kid and that's why one day I want to become a pediatric oncologist," Levi says, his body stiffening below me.

"Wait, you had cancer?" I put down my computer and roll over so I can see his eyes. Though our MO generally is to keep things light between us, this seems too important to gloss over. "How did I not already know this?"

"It was before you knew me. I'm fine now." He does a flipping-a-pancake motion, so I turn around, back to the way we were lying, head to chest, the universal couple-in-the-park position.

We are a couple in the park, I tell myself with a secret thrill.

"That must have been rough," I say. Here's what I want to know but don't ask: *What kind of cancer?* and *Could it come back?* and *How are you so amazing?* Also *That's not fair and I'm so sorry* and *Thank you for sharing with me.*

"Yeah, it sucked. Though I think it was harder on my parents and my sister. I was too little to really understand."

"How old were you?" I can feel his hand in my hair, a slow combing.

"Seven." I squeeze his ankle, the only body part I can reach. My reading buddy Cesar's age. Cesar, who is both impossibly young and also impossibly old, someone who has lost too much already and still is made joyful by a Pokémon card. I think about a smaller version of Levi, rendered bald by an IV drip.

The sadness sets deep.

"That kind of explains your fears list. Why you worry so much about disappointing your parents, maybe?" I ask Levi. I'm seeing Cesar tomorrow. I make a mental note to bring him something special for moving up a reading level at school. Maybe I'll stop at that gaming store on Melrose, find a powerful Pokémon card that no one else in his class will have.

"You'd think it would be the opposite. Honestly, it's not them. They'll be happy no matter what I do, so long as I'm healthy. But you're probably right. Maybe I'm desperate not to disappoint them because I feel like I already have. No one wants a sick kid." He stops, letting the thought sink in. "Wow. That's the first time I've ever articulated that."

"What happened to you . . . it's not your fault." I wonder if Levi would have told me this if we were face to face, or if this is information I'm only learning because the two of us are talking to the sky and not to each other. "You don't need to make up for it."

"I know."

"Isn't it so weird how we can know things but not know them at the exact same time?"

"You should be a therapist," he says, and I laugh. "Seriously, you're really good with people. That's why I always ask for your advice."

I smile and soak up Levi's compliment. For a second I try to picture myself as a therapist. I can see the slick couch (a velvet cobalt) and even the notebook (cloth, hardback, pink Shinola), but the rest—college, graduate school, training—I can't even fathom. Me capable of setting a goal like that—*becoming a therapist*—and managing to follow through.

When I think about growing up, I mostly imagine a meandering crawl through my bucket list—kayaking the dunes of Namibia, seeing gorillas in Rwanda, hiking the entire Na Pali Coast, celebrating New Year's in Times Square, visiting a hedgehog cafe in Tokyo, dancing costumed at Burning Man. Nailing the perfect Coachella look. Taking Cesar to Disneyland and getting him his own Mickey ears cap with his name embroidered on the back.

That last one I'll check off before I leave for college.

Last year, my mom said, apropos of nothing, "I bet you go into PR," and when I asked why, she shrugged and said, "I don't know but it's full of girls like you." I didn't ask what she meant by *girls like you*.

What kind of girls? Stupid girls? Rich girls? Empty girls? Boring girls? Not-so-pretty girls?

I like to think she meant it as a compliment. If Paloma is anything to go by, you can be a boss in PR. But I've noticed she's never suggested this to Isla.

"So what's your essay about or"—he gestures to my blank screen—"going to be about?"

"No idea. I have absolutely nothing to say."

"That's not true. Tell them about you."

"Nothing bad has ever happened to me."

"Getting into college isn't the pity Olympics."

"I know. But they ask about a challenge you've overcome. My life has been, like, mostly challenge free," I say. I feel Levi laughing, his belly jiggling my head, though this time, I think, he's laughing at me.

"We should all be so lucky, Chlo."

CHAPTER TWENTY-ONE

Now

Kenny arrives wearing an olive cashmere sweater and khaki pants, which I appreciate because it makes it easier for me to pick him out of the lawyer lineup. The bloated and under-slept faces of the many middle-aged white men and women who crowd our house have become indistinguishable in their shades of gray. They sit hunched over laptops, fueled by the empty adrenaline of the billable hour.

The PR people are, at least, easier to tell apart. They're better, more casually dressed. High-waisted pants and fash-ion sneakers and the tips of tattoos peeking out at the collar-bone. Painted nails and fake smiles.

I follow Kenny into my dad's office. He shuts the door and motions for me to take a seat. My body feels electric with nerves, and I wonder if people can short-circuit. I pic-ture this all ending with me in an institution, catatonic from stress overload, a far cry from the SCC student my parents had so desperately hoped I'd become.

"Okay, so I have bad news and I have slightly less bad news," Kenny says.

I don't say anything but I feel myself shrinking, as if I can collect my atoms and tighten them into a ball, out of his reach. Smaller and smaller I go. I want to disappear, become a puff of air to be walked through. Not the same as wanting to die, but not far off either.

How could there be more bad news?

"You got a target letter," he says, and again I don't say anything. I'm afraid if I open my mouth, screams will erupt, loud and long and deranged. I don't cry like my mother does, dainty and clean. I'm all snot and red eyes and I spread my sad around, like germs or loneliness. "Let me explain what this means. It means that you are the target of a criminal probe. It does not, I repeat, it does not mean they will necessarily bring charges against you."

"But they could," I say, and it's not a question. "This is them saying *we might*."

"Yes."

"But I thought they were only targeting people over eighteen? Only legal adults." I wonder why I thought this. Did I have an official source for this information? From the Signal text group? From Kenny? As usual, I wish I was more like Isla. She'd have taken notes in every meeting with her lawyer, and then typed and color coded them for later reference. Then again, Isla would never have gotten into this mess in the first place.

"We thought they'd draw the line there. It seems they've chosen not to."

"Why?" I ask, which is not what I really want to know. What I really want to know is what will happen to me? Am I going to jail? A juvenile detention center?

I wouldn't last five seconds in either place. In my whole life, I've never once thrown a punch. I get queasy at the sight of other people's cracked heels. I can't poo in public restrooms.

"Can't say for sure, but I think it's because people are pissed as hell about this, even angrier than anyone anticipated. They don't like being reminded that the system is rigged," Kenny says in a neutral, way-too-casual tone. I no longer appreciate his sweater and khakis. This is serious business. He should be wearing a tie.

"What about the kids whose parents buy buildings to get them in? Doesn't that happen all the time? Why aren't they getting target letters?"

"That's not illegal," he says.

"If what my parents did was illegal, then that should be too," I say, and then realize I'm not helping myself. The whole thing feels unfair. Like I'm being held to account for how this complicated world works. For its arcane laws and unclear lines.

How should this have played out? I remember that list Mrs. Oh had handed me after our first meeting in the fall, all the places she said would be a "more natural fit" for a student like me.

What was so wrong with those schools?

I think about Levi and me on the picnic blanket: *We should all be so lucky, Chlo.*

Shame finger-crawls up my spine.

We were so greedy.

I consider the word *unfair,* how it has never once applied to me. Not even now. Maybe especially not now.

"What's the slightly less bad news?" I ask.

"My friend at the US attorney's office seems to think that they aren't really that interested in hauling a bunch of kids into court. Won't look good. They have the public's support. They want to keep it."

"Okay."

"He says this—you, specifically—is all part of their scare tactics. They want to pressure your mom into a plea bargain," he says. "They think she'll be more likely to accept a plea with prison time if it means keeping you from being charged."

"How is this slightly less bad news? This feels like worse news. Like it's either me or my mom, or maybe both of us going to jail."

He doesn't answer, cocks his head to the side, in a way that reminds me of Fluffernutter. I feel like walking out of this room, begging one of the million more serious lawyers in the living room to represent me.

"The cops think I was in on it?" I ask.

"Well, it's the US attorney's office for Massachusetts, not the cops. But yes. They think you knew," he says, pausing to let this sink in. "They must have at least some evidence to back this up."

"I want to tell you what happened." I mentally replay the last eight months, as if fast-forwarding the video, and my mind catches. I hover above myself, think about the word *evidence*. What could make them think I knew? What *did* I know?

"Nope." He holds up his hands, like I'm about to assault him with my words. "I know it seems helpful to unburden yourself to me, but it isn't. There are restrictions once I know things, and I don't want to know things. Capisce?"

"No."

"*Capisce* means *understand* in Italian. Or maybe it's in the Mafia? I actually don't know." Kenny takes out his phone, presses a button. "Siri, what does *capisce* mean?" He looks at the screen, turns it toward me. "She did a Google search for cat piss."

"Kenny," I say.

"Right, sorry. I love that you can immediately ask any question you have in the whole world to a device that fits in the palm of your hand. And then you know the answer. Just like that." He snaps his fingers, like the world is so easy and simple, black and white.

"Really? Then ask Siri: Is Chloe Berringer going to jail?" I'm only half joking. I feel borderline hysterical. My brain sloshes around in my skull, useless, shriveling. "Seriously, though. Am I going to jail?"

I want to tell Kenny my story, not as a confession or even as a means to absolution. I want to better understand, to turn this into something that makes sense. I want someone to write me a field guide so I can understand the extent of my own culpability.

What evidence?

No, a story is for bedtimes and sitcoms and Hallmark

movies. Not for potential felons. A story won't protect me. I need to grow up.

"You're going to be okay, Chloe," Kenny says, and I take him at his word, as if his words mean something. I will be okay.

Only hours later, when I'm wide awake at three a.m., do I realize he never answered my question.

And so, alone in the dark, I ask Siri: *Is Chloe Berringer going to jail?* but she doesn't answer. Apparently I need to unlock my iPhone for that.

CHAPTER TWENTY-TWO

Then

"Please tell me you did not just say you are jealous of Levi because he had cancer and gets to write an essay about it," Shola says before school the following Monday while she reapplies her red lipstick in her locker mirror. I wonder what it would be like to move through the world in her body. To be tall and striking and beautiful, to make people stop on the street and ask *Who is that?* But even while I think those thoughts, I know that this description is missing a huge part of the story. That by virtue of her skin color, Shola gets none of the perks of my invisibility, or of my presumption of harmlessness. Since she's had her license, she's been pulled over twice driving her parents' car for no reason at all. And at Wood Valley, where she sticks out—not only because she is in the minority at our mostly white school, but because she refuses to play the high school conformity game—she's met with less admiration and more mystification.

"Of course I didn't say that. I'm not a monster." I knew

that applying to colleges would be stressful but I didn't realize it would feel like this—a constant tightening. Last term, the principal ran a required seminar for both parents and students discussing ways to ease anxiety during this process. The hour-long PowerPoint presentation included tips like "Establish a daily meditation practice" and "Put a Post-it on your bathroom mirror that says: 'Where you go to college does not define you.'"

I assumed I'd be mostly immune to the pressure, though, like I've been throughout my time at Wood Valley. I've never been terribly concerned when I bombed a test. To be honest, I've never put myself at risk for any real rejection, at least not in the way Shola and Levi have. I'm not a good enough actress to expect a part in the school play or popular enough to run for student council or ambitious enough to want the EIC position on the school newspaper, not that I'm interested in any of those things anyway. This will be the first time, with the exception of middle school (and in that case my parents did all the hard work), that I've ever applied for anything.

"Chloe, you know I love you, but you really need to check yourself," Shola says.

"What? Why?"

"You literally said, out loud, to my face, 'it's so unfair that you get to write about being a scholarship kid and Levi gets to write about cancer,'" Shola says, in what's supposed to be an imitation of my voice, but is really a generic, obnoxious whine. For the record, I did not say that.

"That's not what I said and you know it. I was simply

making the objective observation that I'm the least interesting person I know. And I have no idea how to spin that for an essay."

"Define *interesting*," Shola says, because she never lets me get away with anything.

"I'm an average student with average grades and I haven't, you know, written a book on molecular biology or played with the New York Philharmonic. All of a sudden, it feels like you need to be special to get into college," I say.

"Or rich," she says.

"Why do you have to make everything about money?" I feel bad as soon as the words are out of my mouth. Shola doesn't make everything about money. The world does. And Shola is the only person at Wood Valley brave enough to point that out. Which is yet another reason why the rest of the student body remains mystified by her. It's uncomfortable to hear the truth. "Anyway, that's not what I'm talking about."

"Chlo, when you say 'least interesting' what you really mean is 'most privileged'—like nothing bad has ever happened to you, wah, wah, too bad, so sad—and the idea that you'd complain about that is like the height of entitlement."

"Stop being smarter than me. I can't keep up," I say with a smile, trying to lighten the atmosphere.

"Bullshit," Shola says, then slams her locker door and walks away.

Later, we sit together at lunch, but it's obvious Shola's still annoyed. She spends the whole time jabbing at her phone, probably complaining about me to her other, non–Wood Valley friends. We're under a tree in the quad, our favorite spot, and I wish Levi were here to smooth things over.

If Shola wasn't mad, I'd say *I miss Levi*, and she'd snort and say *You are so ridiculous.*

Levi's at a student council meeting, and since he's busy every day after school this week, I won't be able to spend any real time with him again until Saturday night. I'd like to ask Shola what she thinks will happen when he comes over this weekend.

"I'm sorry," I say, and she looks at me, and then back at her phone. "I really am, Shola."

"You're not the only person in the world applying to college, you know."

"I know that."

"This is super stressful for me too." Shola puts down her phone and plays with the grass. Pulls up individual blades, one by one, and then lines them up in her hands.

"You're going to get in everywhere, though."

"See. That's what I mean. You say that, but you have no idea—"

"Shola, you're brilliant. You work hard. You have practically perfect grades, you do a ton of extracurriculars, you're—" I start ticking off her attributes on my hands.

"Black?" she interrupts.

"Give me some credit. I was going to say you're amazing at everything you do." I block out the memory of my dad talking to Dr. Wilson, his unfair jab at Shola. I think about all the times other kids at Wood Valley have made snide comments about her being a shoo-in, and how Shola clenches in response. Maybe she has more reasons than I realized for being ready to graduate and move on.

"I'm totally overwhelmed, Chloe." Her eyes fill with tears, even though she's not usually a crier. She's more the type to go cold and quiet. "I've been tutoring the Littles and it's not going well. And then the FAFSA is a nightmare."

"What's a FAFSA?" I ask, gripped with the sudden terror that I've missed some essential application step.

"Exactly." She wipes at her face with the backs of her hands and stands to leave.

"Shola, please, wait." She sighs the sigh of the eternally weary.

"It's the financial aid form."

"Oh. Right. Sorry."

"It's why I'm not applying early decision anywhere, even though that would up my chances of getting in. I can't commit to any school, even Harvard, until I know exactly how much aid I'm being offered. And did you know some colleges aren't need blind? They actually take into account whether you can pay full tuition when considering your application. I'm not the one making it about money. They are."

I didn't know any of that.

"I still bet you get a full scholarship to Harvard," I say.

"Harvard doesn't offer merit scholarships."

"Oh. Well, Harvard's a dick, then."

"Yeah," she says, and smiles the tiniest bit.

"And you're the best. Like if you look in the dictionary, it would say, 'Shola: proper noun, meaning the opposite of a dick.' That should be *your* yearbook quote."

"Tell me more."

"And any school that doesn't give you full financial aid plus a full scholarship so you *make* money on this whole college deal is a loser school not worthy of the presence of you," I say.

"Amen," Shola says.

"Sometimes I'm an insensitive, overprivileged white-girl idiot."

"We do know this," she says, and her tone changes. "Maybe it's time you worked on that." I reach out my insensitive, overprivileged white-girl idiot hands, a small gesture, and she takes them.

CHAPTER TWENTY-THREE

Now

I find my mom in flannel pajamas eating cookie dough ice cream at the kitchen table at four-thirty in the morning. Her hair is pulled into a loopy bun, and her face gives off the metallic smell and sheen of her expensive serums. My pristine mother has gone slack with sadness. I think, *And this is just the beginning.*

We have only been living in this new hell for ten days. What will she look like by summer? I can't imagine her beauty unraveling like the hem of a sweater. Then again, I never could have imagined any of this either.

"Hey," she says, waving her spoon. She doesn't meet my eyes. She keeps them trained on the container. I assume since she's denied herself this simple pleasure for so long, the Ben & Jerry's cookie dough ice cream holds extra magic. This is the kind of self-care I can get behind.

I sit down next to her and take the spoon from her hand. Help myself to a hefty bite. She doesn't ask what I'm doing up this early. She doesn't have to. No one sleeps in this house anymore.

"Get your own," she says, and we both smile as I go for more. "No, seriously, there are six cartons in the freezer."

"Six?" I ask.

"Moment of weakness. I wanted to try lots of flavors. There's also a stash of M&M's—did you know they make caramel ones now?—and Mallomars. Also, vodka and a fresh baguette, because apparently I eat bread now. Thank God for Carrie. She even brought me a Costco-sized Nutella. Think they have Ben & Jerry's in the big house?"

"We need to talk," I say. She closes her eyes and opens them again, as if her lids are heavy and they need a millisecond's rest before facing me. I can't tell if this is because she's medicated or because she's upset.

"Isn't it my job to force you to have the big talks?"

"Mom."

"I thought we'd already covered this. It's pretty simple. A man puts his peni—"

"Mom!"

"I'm kidding. Relax."

"How many Xanax have you had?" I ask.

"This is my second pint. Works better than the Xanax."

"What's Raj going to say?" Raj is my mom's trainer. Thinking of him makes me think of all the hundreds of people we know, maybe even thousands, who have heard the news. When they think of us, they'll only think about this: that I'm such a dumbass that my parents had to pay someone off to up my SAT score, and then bribe my way into

153

college. Even worse: How many of them are celebrating our fall from grace? I would bet almost all of them.

I wonder if Rita explained to Cesar the real reason why I haven't been able to see him. I wonder if his mother saw my mother being led away in handcuffs on television, and if she now regrets all those cookies she made for me at Christmas. Maybe she'll ask Rita to reassign Cesar to a different buddy.

"Eh, Raj'll understand. You know he's pretty much the only person who reached out to check on me. With everyone else, it's been like total radio silence. I've barely even spoken to Aunt Candy, since she acted all shocked and insisted, 'We did things the legit way for Philo.' Which, no way. You'd think felony charges are contagious or something."

I don't float my alternative theory. That people are too disgusted to talk to us. That we carry the stench of the rotting and rotten.

"I'm so mad at you."

"I know. You should be."

"I'm so mad at you." I shout it this time, loud enough that I wonder if there are paparazzi still outside, even at this hour, and if they can hear me.

"I know." She reaches for my hand, and I pull away. She can't touch me. I'm not ready for that. I worry her fingers will singe my skin. "The problem is we aren't allowed to talk. Not about the big stuff. The judge said we aren't supposed to discuss, you know, the thing."

My mom says this calmly, rationally, like she has accepted the concept of not being legally allowed to talk to her own daughter. I remember us sitting right here in the fall, celebrating my first kiss with Levi.

"The thing? Is that what you're calling it?"

"My alleged crimes," she says, finally looking up at me. She takes in my disheveled hair, the toothpaste on the boob of my T-shirt. My eyes are swollen from crying. My nail beds are crusty with blood, since I've taken to chewing on my cuticles. There's a burn in my gut: the churn of fear and guilt. "Because you could be called as a witness or, you know, be charged—"

She stops here, and as if in slow motion, she crumbles. Her forehead rests on the table. Her arms wrap around her knees. A sound like a horse's whinny escapes through her lips or maybe her nose. I want to rub her back like she used to rub mine when I was home with a fever.

I also want to punch her in the face.

I didn't know you could feel blistering love and hate at the exact same time, but here we are.

"So now you want to follow the rules," I say, remembering Kenny's warning. How I'm not supposed to talk to my mother. Funny that it's the only thing I can think of to do. A few years ago, we learned in school that you should never throw water on a grease fire even though that's our natural instinct when we see flames. That's how it feels to turn to my mom—like she is both the water and the fire.

I think of Isla up in her room, probably googling away. A better use of my time, and yet.

"The lawyers say that—"

"I don't care what the lawyers say, Mom." I feel hot all over and icy at my back, like thinking about a fever has brought one on. "I *need* to talk."

"I . . . I . . . Chloe, I don't even know what to say. I messed up. Real bad. I have never been so scared. I didn't know," she says. And the echo of my own words, *I didn't know*, the shallowness of them, makes me realize anger can be cumulative. I feel layered in rage, like coats of paint.

"You didn't know what? That this could all blow up in our faces? That you could go to jail? Which part didn't you know?"

"I didn't know it could . . . I'm scared of saying too much—"

"Are you serious?"

"You could be subpoenaed. I don't want you to have to lie. Listen, I don't want to make any more mistakes." She licks an errant drop of ice cream off her fingertip, and I notice her nails are chipped. Of course, she didn't make her weekly mani-pedi appointment. I examine her more closely. Look for signs of other maintenance slipping. I grab the spoon again, more aggressively than necessary, and take another bite.

"Let me put it this way: Everything I've ever done, I've done for you. Because I thought it was what was best. For you." Her chin wobbles, and her face is wet.

"No," I say.

"It's true. I love you, Chlo. Nothing matters except for you and Isla." She pauses. Lining up her delivery, trying a different tack. "And, of course, Ben and Jerry."

"This isn't funny. This is not a late-night show where you have to be charming. This is our lives!"

"I know. I'm trying to explain—"

"Don't you dare pretend any of this was for me." It takes me a beat to realize I'm yelling. I don't care. I point the

156

spoon right in my mother's beautiful, perfect, sagging face. "This was for bragging rights. So you wouldn't be embarrassed by me. Don't you dare lie."

She shakes her head, and she looks like her Missy bobblehead doll. Big-eyed, unhinged.

"That's not . . . It wasn't—"

"Everything was a lie."

"I love you," she says. "I love you, I love you, I love you."

"This isn't about whether you love me, Mom."

"But it is. That's exactly what it's about. I love you. That's my job. And you are almost all grown. While I can, I need to do what I can, anything I can to—"

I pick up the ice cream container and throw it hard against the wall. It falls to the floor, bounces once, and lands near my mother's feet. Nothing spills. She picks it up and hands it back to me.

"You need to put your back into it," my mom says, suddenly calm and sober. A cold devastation coming off her in waves. "Plant your feet."

I don't throw it again. The carton is, like me, frustratingly useless. I should have thrown my water glass instead. Just another bad decision.

I should have let it shatter all over the floor.

We deserve to step on glass.

CHAPTER TWENTY-FOUR

Then

"I'm not going to sugarcoat. This essay reads like a parody of an LA rich kid," Mrs. Oh says. She hands me back my paper, which after a quick glance, looks free of edits. I'm confused. I'm used to Mrs. Pollack returning my English assignments covered in red pen.

Mrs. Oh is sans baby today. In our last meeting, she found a Cheerio in her pixie cut and casually popped it in her mouth.

"You didn't write any comments."

"Because you should throw it in the trash and start over. Actually, burn it."

"You said that the admissions committee would find my mom's career interesting. I figured I should write about that." I attempt to say this as matter-of-factly as possible. To keep the wobble out of my voice.

"This reads like if your mom's Wikipedia page and an Instagram influencer's diary mated and had a college application essay baby."

"That's mean."

"You're right. I'm sorry. I'm a little punch-drunk from lack of sleep." Mrs. Oh doesn't look sorry, though. She looks like she wants to laugh. "But did you have to mention that you once got a free Chanel bag?"

"It was an example of how the stylist system works."

"Really? Because it sounded like you thought acquiring that bag was an accomplishment that should get you into college."

Mrs. Oh is right. My essay is a joke.

"Listen, Chloe. It's my job to be real with you. Do you want me to be real with you?"

"Not really?" I say, but I nod anyway. This hurts, though not too badly. It would have hurt more if I had worked harder on the essay.

"You're a senior in high school. If you want to be treated like a serious person, you need to act like a serious person," Mrs. Oh says, and readjusts herself on her chair, stretches her back, and groans.

"What if I'm not a serious person?" I ask.

"Listen, you can't all be academic superstars. I get that. But then don't bother applying to SCC if you're going to phone it in."

"You're right," I say, because she 100 percent is. I don't want to be a parody. "I'm sorry I wasted your time. I'll do better with the next draft. I promise."

"Good."

"Want to hear something weird? My private college counselor said my essay was great." This is true. He sent me and my mom an email that said: *Great job, Chloe! We are full steam ahead on all our big plans!* And then he inserted the winking face emoji, which seemed a poor choice, in my opinion. Like it discredited the compliment that preceded it. Then again, in my experience, old people don't know how to use emojis. My mom always sends the hugging hands when she means to wave hello.

"Then she should be fired immediately." Interesting that Mrs. Oh assumes Dr. Wilson is a woman. I don't bother correcting her. "Honestly, this essay could even jeopardize your chances of getting into your safeties."

I glance out the window. Levi's standing on the green, gesticulating widely in front of a crowd of seated students. He's running a student council meeting and from this side angle, I can see Sophie's—his ex—face. She's watching him the way I sometimes catch myself watching YouTuber makeup unboxing videos, openmouthed and with longing.

"Are you listening?"

"Yeah. Sorry. Just Levi." I gesture out the window, and Mrs. Oh looks at me like she understands. "Anyhow, I promise I'm unpacking your feedback." I'm parroting Mrs. Pollack, but I like the way it sounds. Perhaps I should use the word *unpack* more outside the suitcase context. It makes me think of Russian dolls and accordions and unfolding that manual that Isla was born with and I wasn't.

Mrs. Oh pulls at her shoulder, sniffs, grimaces. "Goddamn little monster. I was wondering what that smell was and it turned out to be me. Spit-up. Great."

"Babies," I say inanely.

"Chloe, sorry if this feedback feels harsh. I'm Team Tough Love here at Wood Valley."

"Mission accomplished, but no worries." I live in a world of protected feelings and of cushioned blows; there's a strange relief in Mrs. Oh's brutal honesty. "So what should I write about then?"

"Isn't it obvious?" She points at me with a pen, and I see her hands are stained with ink. She must have marked up everyone else's papers, and I feel embarrassed all over again. "You should write about you."

"I did write about me."

"No, you wrote about how fun it is to live with a B-list celebrity," she says.

"Did you just call my mom B-list?"

"The sleep deprivation makes me loose lipped. Please don't tell her I said that. I really need this job." Mrs. Oh looks at me with desperation, and then wipes at her shoulder with a McDonald's napkin. After a few attempts she gives up.

I mime zipping my lips.

"Thank you. Okay, to sum up this meeting, your mom is the best, A-list all the way. You are also the best. You worked so hard to get your SATs up. This essay, however, is not the best. Now get the hell out of my office. I need to pump."

When I check my email later in the day, I see Dr. Wilson's assistant's name pop up in my inbox.

To: Joy Fields, Richard Berringer
Cc: Chloe Berringer
From: drwilsonassist@drwilson.com
Subject: North Hollywood Testing Center

Dr. W says got your message but seriously do not stress about essay

My mother must have immediately called Dr. Wilson in a panic when I texted her after my meeting with Mrs. Oh: *Mrs. O says essay sucks. Need to rewrite even for safeties.*

As usual, my mom is incapable of digesting anything calmly. This is not an emergency. I spent two hours working on this draft. It won't kill me to push a little harder.

I reply to the message—*I'm not stressed, happy to revise*—and before I hit send, I notice that there's a trail of emails below between my parents and Dr. Wilson and his assistant. Apparently, this crew likes to communicate without cc'ing me.

To: Joy Fields, Richard Berringer
From: Dr. Wilson
Cc: drwilsonassist@drwilson.com
Subject: North Hollywood Testing Center

Woot woot

Woot woot? Seriously? I guess I'm not missing much. The email is dated the day after I took the SAT. I scroll down farther, to the previous email from my mother, same date.

From: Joy Fields
To: Dr. Wilson
Cc: Richard Berringer, Wilson-assist
Subject: North Hollywood Testing Center

So happy! All went smoothly. Thanks for everything.

I can't imagine what my mom had to be so thrilled about the day after the SAT? It wasn't like I left the test feeling optimistic. Maybe she was convinced the accommodation had worked its magic? Or maybe they worried that someone would question whether I was actually ADHD at the exam? That doesn't make sense. Dr. Wilson took care of the paperwork, but I got the clearance from the SAT board directly. I saw the letter with my own eyes. It was 100 percent official, 100 percent legit.

From: Dr. Wilson
To: Joy Fields
Cc: Richard Berringer, Wilson-assist
Subject: North Hollywood Testing Center

It's a go

This last one was dated three days before the exam. I read through the emails again, this time from bottom to top. I feel a little queasy but can't put my finger on why. Like when you walk into the gym locker room and sense, by the sudden awkward quiet, that the girls were talking about you but then the moment shifts and you tell yourself you're being paranoid.

What's "a go"?

My phone buzzes and I click away from email and over to my text messages.

Mom: Don't worry darling. Spoke to Dr. W. He'll get someone on staff to rewrite

Me: No! I want to do it

Mom: You did do it, sweetie. Rewrite was wrong word. They'll clean it up, add a little sparkle

Me: Mom!

Mom: What? You're so stubborn. Like your father. I know you have a lot on your plate lately

Me: It's my essay!

Mom: Of course. Still, nothing wrong with a little help

Me: Let me try again first

Mom: You sure?

Me: YES

Mom: Okay. By the way, it wasn't a Chanel bag. It was a Birkin.

CHAPTER TWENTY-FIVE

Now

Isla pokes me awake with her Converse-clad foot, square in my ribs.

"Just checking to make sure you aren't dead," she says.

"Aren't you supposed to be at school?"

"It's four in the afternoon." I would have guessed it was still morning, and yet I take that as my cue to pull my bright white comforter over my head and burrow back into the mattress. I've always been a little shy about my undercurated bedroom, which, if I'm being honest, was modeled directly from a page in the Restoration Hardware Teen catalogue.

Isla's room, on the other hand, has a shelf crowded with all her various academic awards, a Malala poster, and an overflowing bookcase. Her bulletin board, which hangs above her desk, is crammed with her favorite quotes and Polaroid pictures of her friends smiling and holding up stick mustaches.

You walk into Isla's room and you think, *I know who lives here.*

You walk into mine and you think a designer decorated the place for a vapid, generic teenager.

Today, I take refuge in its blandness. Maybe, if I'm forgettable, this entire scandal will be too.

"Chloe!"

I can't think of a single reason to get up. I realize my not going to school is a situation that will eventually have to be addressed, but not today, not when any moment the feds could arrive to arrest me. When everyone at Wood Valley hates me. When it feels like I no longer have anything resembling a future.

If I leave the house, I'll be accosted by the paparazzi. Not that I have anywhere to go.

This might be what jail is like, I think optimistically, and then remember that jail will not have Netflix, two-ply toilet paper, or Intelligentsia coffee on demand. It will not have my delicious pillow-top mattress or hot showers or Fluffernutter.

I cannot go to jail. Neither can my mother. My mom can take or leave the dog, but when we were on vacation in Saint Martin, she freaked out when Carrie forgot to pack her La Mer.

I need to come up with a better strategy than simply repeating "I didn't know" over and over, like those words are a magic spell. How do you prove a negative? Ironic that my best defense is exactly what got me into this mess in the first place: *Your Honor, I was too oblivious to realize what was happening. Exhibit A, the SAT. Even my own parents think I'm a moron.*

I saw Proctor Dan on the news yesterday and wouldn't

have recognized him if it weren't for the caption under his picture: BREAKING NEWS: ACCUSED TEST TAKER TO ENTER GUILTY PLEA IN COLLEGE ADMISSIONS SCANDAL. Gone were his tie-dyed T-shirt and flip-flops and chill vibes. Instead, he was grim-faced and clean-shaven and wearing a blue suit. According to the reporter, who looked eerily like a younger version of my mother, all smooth hair, giant lips, and tiny hips, Dan has been proctoring as a side hustle since he graduated from Yale five years ago. Apparently, he's presided over hundreds of SATs and ACTs at three test centers around the country "controlled" by Dr. Wilson.

The scam was simple; after the student left, Proctor Dan would fill out and submit a completely different Scantron. He guaranteed a score within a twenty-point range.

I'm impressed despite myself.

Then I wonder: Did my mom specifically request a 1440? If I were paying $15,000, the amount she is alleged to have paid for this part of Dr. Wilson's services, I would have gone for the full 1600. Or maybe not. No one would have believed I could score that high on my own.

When the breaking news alert came on CNN last night, which has been on silent in the background downstairs all day every day, my mom let out a string of expletives that would have made even my father and Paloma blush. Kenny later explained why this was more bad news: Proctor Dan's plea means that if my mom's case goes to trial, he will likely testify against her. If I get charged, he could testify against me too.

I never should have eaten his chips. I should have suggested he trim his toe hairs.

"You need to get up," Isla says. "Mom is bombed out of her mind on Xanax. I think yesterday put her over the edge. Dad is locked up in his office with the lawyers. He's hired his own separate team too. I need at least you to be okay."

"I'm not okay."

"Yes, you are. We're going to get through this," she says in the steely, determined tone she usually reserves for her academic life, student council meetings, or class presentations. The *we* is mighty generous of her, considering.

I wonder if she's still getting death threats on her old phone. I check mine regularly to see if Shola or Levi has reached out, which, no surprise, they haven't. Instead, I'm still assaulted by hate texts: *die cheating bitch.* The number of messages has decreased; their nastiness has not. I read every last one of them. Sometimes I read them twice. In the shower, I repeat the words out loud under the rush of the faucet: *lying scum of the earth, lying scum of the earth, lying scum of the earth.*

"You should pack a bag and get as far away from this family as you can. You deserve better than us," I say.

"Aww, did you just say something nice to me? That's a first," Isla says.

"Don't get too excited. We set a low bar. I assume you haven't committed a felony lately." I sit up and examine my sister, who is wearing ripped jeans and an old T-shirt, and looks as underslept as I feel. I mentally bump her higher on my worry list, which is long and overcrowded, and bleats like rolling credits in my brain.

"How's school?" I hold her gaze so she has to tell me the truth. Unlike my mother, who is after all, a professional, Isla is a terrible liar. She looks away, pretends to be fascinated by the window. My curtains are drawn, and in a burst of paranoia last week, I duct-taped their edges to the wall. No way am I going to fall victim to a telephoto lens.

"Tell me," I demand.

"Better than being here, I guess. Some jerk vandalized my locker, though." Isla pretends this is no big deal.

"Who? I'll kill him."

"That's what you need. A murder charge on top of everything else." She says this with a half-smile, and I surprise myself by smiling back. I hold up the sheet and pat the bed, which is not something I'd normally do, not now that we are grown, and Isla hesitates for a minute. I think she's going to say she has to do her homework or study or research legal precedent. Instead, she surprises me by crawling in beside me. She feels warm and small and I'm gripped with a sudden fear that this will be the last time we ever get to do this. We used to snuggle all the time when were kids, and chat late into the night in our matching footie pajamas. But somewhere along the way, like how we stopped playing with dolls or baking together or racing to avoid being a rotten egg, we stopped this too. Without fanfare or a decision.

I imagine it was my fault. I met Shola and banished my precocious little sister to her room across the hall.

"I saw Shola." She says this quietly, tentatively, as if reading my mind. I haven't told her Shola has gone radio silent, but she knows. Otherwise, Shola would be here.

"You did?" I swat at the renegade tear snaking down my cheek. Sometimes it astounds me to think about how much I've messed up my life. I remember how once, when we all had to go visit Hudson in rehab, he stood in front of us in this room that smelled of nicotine and stale coffee and read a letter detailing all the ways he'd wronged us with his addiction. Apparently, he stole money from my backpack. He missed pretty much every one of Isla's birthday parties. He once fed Fluffernutter a laced cookie. The list was long. As he talked, his hands shook, and when he said the word *sorry*, his voice cracked. That I think was the hardest part for him— that single word—and I remember thinking that he, and his therapist, had it all wrong. We were family. We weren't tallying his sins. I didn't care that he stole my money. I was waiting for him to promise to never use again.

"She stopped me in the hall. Asked how you were," Isla says.

"What did you say?"

"I told her that she should call you if you she really wanted to know."

"You're a good sister."

"Duh," Isla says.

"Seriously. I don't say it enough."

"Dude, you don't say it ever."

"Sorry," I say, thinking of how maybe Hudson didn't want to make promises he didn't know if he could keep.

"You know that picture of Mom with her dummy?" When my mom was sixteen, she competed in a Junior Ms. New Jersey pageant and her talent was, I kid you not, ventriloquism. There's this great picture of her, with '80s bangs, in a taffeta pink ball gown, smiling at the brown-haired dummy in her lap. My dad had it framed for her fortieth birthday.

"Yeah."

"I wonder what she was like back then."

"I bet pretty much the same—well, before this all happened—though with more hair spray."

"Yeah," Isla says, and I can feel it. We are both thinking about that young, naive version of our mother, whose greatest hope was to be Junior Ms. New Jersey. Who even learned to talk out of the side of her mouth because she was so desperate to win. "So can I borrow your clothes when you're in jail?"

I stick my pointer fingers in Isla's armpits in that way she's hated since she was tiny. For a moment, it feels like before, when I hadn't yet ruined everything. When poking at each other was only a game.

"Okay, too soon for prison jokes," she says, tucking her elbows close to her sides. "Got it."

Later, I check my Signal, and there they all are, my fellow college scammies, swapping messages, like a Greek chorus.

> **ALC:** My sister got a target letter
>
> **Slyse:** I got one too
>
> **Thelgster:** Yeah, turns out they are OUT FOR BLOOD. No one is off limits
>
> **PhinnyB:** We're all so fucked. My parents are taking a second mortgage on the house to pay legal fees
>
> **PrettyPen:** My little sister was like, "Are we going to be poor now?" And my parents laughed. First time I heard them laugh since this all happened, so at least I think we're good on that front

PhinnyB: Shut up Penny. You and your Instagram and YouTube are the reason why the whole world hates us

PrettyPen: WTF did I do? What's your problem?

PhinnyB: All those ridiculous lipstick tutorials and whining into the camera. "College is a state of mind." You have no idea what the real world is like

PrettyPen: Give me a break. People need to chill

PhinnyB: Do you even get it?

TheIgster: People hate us. HATE

As usual, I can't decide if I want to weigh in. Isla would tell me to listen to my lawyer. To shut the hell up. But I don't feel like shutting up. I haven't spoken to anyone who was not my family or being paid for their legal services in two weeks.

Me: They should hate us. If I wasn't me, I'd hate me

PrettyPen: That's ridiculous

Me: You know what? I do hate me. We are disgusting

PrettyPen: Speak for yourself bitch

Me: No seriously. I'm not saying I knew anything, but it doesn't matter does it? What we knew? We were all playing our parts in this game. We thought we deserved everything and it didn't matter who we hurt to get it

PrettyPen: I didn't hurt anyone!

TheIgster: TBH, I didn't deserve Yale. I knew I wasn't smart enough to go there

PhinnyB: I wanted SCC more than anything else in the whole world. And I loved every second until they kicked my ass out

TheIgster: Did you hear about that black lady from Connecticut who went to jail for five years because she pretended to live in a better school district?

PhinnyB: That's messed up

PrettyPen: We have better lawyers. Also, I hate to say it, but it helps that we're all white

Me: That's exactly my point. Why should she go to jail while we don't?

PrettyPen: Oh now you're arguing we should all go to jail? Nice Chloe. You're garbage

TheIgster: Maybe no one should go to jail for trying to help their kids

ALC: We definitely over-incarcerate in this country, especially people of color

Slyse: My parents weren't trying to help me. I wanted to go to art school. They wanted me to go to Princeton. They did this for their bragging rights

PhinnyB: I'm so scared. I can't go to jail

Me: I'm scared too

Thelgster: Me too

ALC: Me too

PrettyPen: You guys are pussies. There are six production companies who want my film rights. Just you watch, this will be the best thing that's ever happened to us

Slyse: Can we drop Penny from this group text?

Thelgster: Done

CHAPTER TWENTY-SIX

Then

On Saturday night, my parents head out to some charity auction, Isla sleeps over at a friend's house, and so for the first time since our shift in status, Levi and I will be alone, indoors, possibly in a room with a bed. When I swing open the front door, he's leaning against the wall, fresh from the shower, so handsome it makes my soul ache and my insides quiver.

We have plans to "watch a movie," and so I lead him downstairs to the screening room. I figure this is the way to go, not directly up to my bedroom, which seems too forward, especially because I don't know what I want to happen tonight. With his hand in mine, me leading him like I know where we're going, this seems naive and I feel overwhelmed, which is how I feel all the time lately. Like I'm constantly living that recurring dream I have where it's finals week and I've forgotten to go to math class all year.

"Don't worry. Levi's totally a virgin," Shola said yesterday when we were eating Friday tacos, which is what we do every week and is exactly what it sounds like. Eating tacos on a Friday, not tacos made out of Fridays, which Shola has posited would be totally better: *Imagine if we could package the feeling of Friday last bell into a taste? We'd be gazillionaires.* "Based on national statistics and popular belief, teenagers have way less sex than pop culture suggests. Also, Levi has no time to get it on. He's too busy trying to take my spot at Harvard."

"You're both getting into Harvard."

"He's a legacy, he's president of our class, he's on the tennis team, *and* he fences, which my parents wouldn't even let me try because the gear is like crazy expensive, and he obviously doesn't need financial aid, so he can apply early. You know what's messed up? Levi probably thinks *I'm* trying to take *his* spot."

"You're both getting in," I said.

"This is a zero-sum game. There are only so many spaces, and most of them are reserved for full-paying kids like Levi, again contrary to popular belief."

"Popular belief seems to be very unreliable."

"And yet, it is, by definition, quite popular. Anyhow, if you start to freak out at any point, you can stop or you can slow down, and you can even say 'Hey, Levi, this is all new for me.'" Shola says this like we're in health class and she's the teacher. Which to be fair, is our usual dynamic. I always joke that Shola seems to be perpetually twenty-five—still young enough to be fun and spontaneous, and yet mature enough to have seen some stuff.

"Honestly, I'm more worried about the opposite. What if I, like, attack him?" I asked.

"Different strokes for different folks, I guess," she said.

"No pun intended."

"Your dad is way hotter," she said.

Levi and I are sitting on the oversized leather couch in the screening room scrolling through our movie choices. He lands on the new romantic comedy about a workaholic woman who doesn't have time for love. I don't mention that I've already read the script since my mom was up for the role of the mean boss, and it's terrible. She lost out to the blond lady from *Desperate Housewives*, the cool, harried-looking one married to the shaggy guy from *Shameless*.

Doesn't matter. I assume we won't do much watching anyway.

Two hours later, we're horizontal on the couch, the popcorn long since kicked over and likely hoovered up by Fluffernutter. We've been kissing, long, tender kisses, and short, brutal ones, and Levi's hands are everywhere. My lips feel puffy and sore and I think, *So this is what our mouths are for.* I wonder if he's left a mark on my neck and decide I kind of hope so; this is a night I'd like to remember. My fingers explore his chest. I think maybe growing up has its perks.

"Movie's over," Levi mumbles into my ear as his hand spans my stomach, and it sears my skin like a brand. "Fine film."

"The best ever. Should win all the Oscars." My head arches back as I feel his breath on my neck. This is the feeling we should bottle into a taste and turn into a taco.

"Oh, I know this movie," a voice says. The lights come

on. Too bright and too sudden and Levi and I scramble up-right. I'm grateful, suddenly, in a way I wasn't mere moments ago, that we are both still fully dressed. "Director said they wanted to go 'in a different direction.' I mean, I don't get the appeal, personally."

"Mom!" I say, and feel my face flush a deep red.

"Hi, Mrs. Berringer. I mean, Ms. Fields," Levi corrects, and I have to fight a giggle. His eyes are round, and it looks like he thinks my mom might chase him off the premises. They've met before, obviously, but always under more neutral conditions—back-to-school barbecues, dropping me off at the Grove with Shola, middle school graduation.

"Call me Joy, Levi. We're practically family, after all," she says with a devilish grin, and I want to kill her.

"Funny," I say.

"Listen, you can't spend hours fooling around in the screening room and expect me not to tease you a little."

"We . . . we were watching—" Levi says, and gestures inanely toward the television. "It was about . . ." But he loses all words as my dad comes down the stairs and stands behind my mom. My father, if you only get to see him like this—immaculate suit, face puffy from what I would guess are a couple of cocktails, his body enormous next to my petite mother—can be intimidating. He looks like a movie star from the '40s. He's slick and rough featured, and seems tougher than the life he currently lives. The crooked nose on his face, broken by a punch and unfixed, remains like a badge of honor from his hardscrabble childhood in Detroit. So does the small scar on his left cheek.

"Hello, Levi." I swear my dad drops his voice an octave to

mess with Levi. "I see you've been having a pleasant evening with my daughter."

I roll my eyes.

"Sir," Levi says, and nervously rubs the back of his head. Levi has no way of knowing that I'd already planned to give my mom a detailed account of my night. Earlier, on her way out the door, my mother blew me a kiss, winked, and said, "Enjoy yourself, sweet pea."

"Please call me Richard. Sir makes me feel ancient." Levi will never call my dad Richard, of course, and so what has happened here is that Levi will call my dad nothing at all. Which is fine by me.

"Well, this was a fun chat. You guys can go upstairs." I do a shooing motion. "We'll be up in a sec."

My mom ignores me.

"How's the college search going?" she asks Levi. She's wearing a black cocktail dress and her hair is pulled up Audrey Hepburn style. An oversized teardrop diamond necklace rests delicately in her cleavage. She's stunning. What does Levi think when he looks at her? That it's a shame the apple fell so far from the tree?

"We'll see soon. I applied early to Harvard. Fingers crossed," Levi says.

"A Harvard man. Impressive," my dad says. My father went to a small community college back in Michigan, and despite his own obvious success, he's obsessed with fancy credentials. About five years ago, my dad went to a Wharton Business School executive conference, and even now, he'll say, "When I was at Wharton . . ." and not correct other people when they assume he actually graduated from there.

"Well, not yet," Levi says.

"Chloe is going to SCC," my mom declares, and I don't only want to kill her, I also want to die.

"Mom!"

My dad elbows my mother in the ribs, and she looks at him, confused, then looks back at me.

"What? You totally are," she says.

"She has to get in first," my dad says.

"I like to be optimistic. I have it on my vision board," my mom says, and I wonder if she might have broken Raj's rule and had more than one glass of sauvignon blanc. Maybe it turns out a woman can't live on celery and endive alone.

"I didn't know you wanted to go to SCC," Levi says, and I look away. There's a reason I don't talk about college with him. My distant reaches are his safeties.

"It's a long shot for me, so . . ."

"The good news is that Harvard and SCC are on opposite sides of the country. I don't think your arms are that long," my dad says, and laughs, like this is funny. It is not funny.

"Oh my God," I say.

"Joking!" he says. "I'm so sorry you got stuck with the worst parents in the world who let you have full run of the house, with a boy no less, while we were busy doing the hard work of raising money for kids with cleft palates. The wine was terrible, by the way."

My dad winks, and my mom links arms with him to lead him up the stairs.

"Don't worry. We're going before you disown us," my mom says.

"Too late," I call out after them.

"Are they always like this?" Levi whisper-asks, once my parents are out of earshot.

"Unfortunately, yes."

"Explains a lot," Levi says, and I can't tell if that's an insult or a compliment.

CHAPTER TWENTY-SEVEN

Now

My mother sits hunched at the head of the table, looking strung out. She's dressed at least, after having spent most of the past month, like me, in old pajamas. Today she's wearing an ivory silk blouse tucked into a high-waisted skirt and sensible navy flats. I imagine this ensemble was labeled "serious business" in her closet by her stylist. We've been summoned for a family meeting, which in this new bizarro version of our lives, means my parents, Isla and me, and ten lawyers plus Paloma.

"Let's get started, shall we?" asks the lawyer who seems most in charge, Mr. Spence, though of course it's not a question but a demand. He's old and white and his watch costs more than four years' worth of college tuition. "We wanted to convene to have a final discussion of Joy's options before her court appearance. Chloe, as I've told your counsel, the judge has dropped the gag order, so you and your mom can talk freely, though beyond this conversation, I'd still advise against it."

I turn to Kenny, who sits next to me, here to represent my legal interests vis-à-vis my parents, which feels bananas and like overkill, but he insisted. He nods.

"Okay," I squeak.

"Because of the totality of the evidence, as well as the possibility of Chloe and/or Richard being charged, we strongly advise that Joy take a plea deal. We can push the prosecutors to commit to a recommendation on the low end of the sentencing range, and also have them promise not to go after anyone else in the family. We can end this nightmare."

"Don't worry about me," my dad says, with a manufactured jauntiness that doesn't match the rest of him. He's all stiff horizontal lines today—forehead, lips, the crease of his shirt. "Stuart thinks they would have charged me already if they could have. If they had the leverage, they would have used it."

The guy my dad hired to represent him, Stuart, grunts in agreement and reaches forward to place a hand on my dad's shoulder, as if to tell him to be quiet.

"Any plea would include jail time?" my mom asks. She takes a sip of water, and her hands are shaking so badly, a few drops land on the table. She wipes them with her sleeve, and this gesture, so unlike my mother—reflexive and uncouth—unnerves me.

"In all likelihood. Sentencing discretion varies dramatically by judge, so it's somewhat the luck of the draw. As we've discussed, public opinion is not with us. You very well might get a judge who wants to make an example of you," Mr. Spence says. "We can push for ankle monitoring, but it's a long shot."

"So if I plead guilty, I will go to jail," my mom repeats. The lawyers at the table exchange uneasy glances. It's obvious this is not the first time they've had this conversation with my mother and this is not the first time she has refused to understand. Last term when I took a psychology elective, we learned about the Kübler-Ross stages of grief: denial, anger, bargaining, depression, and acceptance. I want to call up Mrs. Santiago and ask her if the model can be applied to all the other unforeseen terrible things that can happen to a person, like being arrested by the FBI.

My mom seems stuck at denial.

"To a minimum-security federal prison, not a jail, but most likely yes. For a much shorter period of time than if, say, we go to trial and you lose, which is a real possibility. Minimum guidelines then say twenty years."

My mother starts to laugh, unhinged and hysterical, and then once she hears herself, she stops. She takes another sip of water, again spilling, and it takes all of my willpower not to take her glass away.

"Twenty years. Two decades," my mother says. "I mean, that's . . . that's a long time for trying to help your kid a little."

"Joy," my dad says, and puts a steadying hand on hers. "We're going to figure this out."

"How? How are we going to figure this out? By me going to jail? Not you, me. Even though you were just as involved—"

"Joy," Mr. Spence says, stopping her. Apparently, he went to the same law school as Kenny. The one where they teach you not to let your clients say too much.

"This is ridiculous," she says, changing direction, since it's in no one's interest, not even my mother's, to implicate my dad. "I've already lost my job and my reputation. I accept that. Haven't I been punished enough? Explain to me how this is any different from buying a building to get your kid in."

"What you did and buying a building are both unethical, Mom. The difference is what you did was also illegal," Isla says, her voice steely, uncompromising, not softened by even a drop of sympathy, though perhaps with more than a drop of condescension. I feel a surge of admiration and love for my sister, but then fear too. What does she think of me? What does she think I deserve?

I know I will never get rid of the stink of this, but I have to believe that Isla will.

We were greedy, so disgustingly greedy, and yet, my mother has a point. How big a price must we pay? *Twenty years? Isla's future too?*

Here's the truth: If my parents had openly offered to endow a building at SCC, I wouldn't have said no. I would have been psyched. My parents didn't not buy a building because it was *unethical*. They didn't because they couldn't afford to. We are not Aunt Candy rich.

"This is why we thought it vital that the rest of your family chimes in," Mr. Spence says, and another lawyer hands him a file. He opens it, closes it, opens it again, as if he's wafting legal wisdom into the air.

"When you say *chimes in*, you mean *pressures me to plead guilty*," my mom says, and the way she cocks her head to the side, stubborn and determined, looks so much like Isla, that

I feel shaken. Usually, I think of it the other way around: Isla reminds me of our mom. "I'm not ready to do that yet."

"Time is not on your side," Mr. Spence says. "Other defendants are going to start to plead out, and each time they do, you'll be in a worse bargaining position. Dr. Wilson is already cooperating with prosecutors, as is the proctor, who will one hundred percent make the government's case stronger by testifying against you. I'm talking about the other parents caught up in this case. Our plan requires you, as the public face of this scandal, to be the *very first* to take full responsibility with an emotional heartfelt public apology, in the hope that sincere remorse will lead to the greatest amount of leniency."

"From a PR perspective," Paloma jumps in. "You put out an apology press release about all the mistakes you made, blah, blah, blah, you love your children too much, blah, blah, and then we'll start your reputation rehabilitation tour. We'll leak that you and Richard are in counseling and meeting with spiritual advisors. You'll talk about how you lost sight of your wholesome Midwestern roots because of this scam artist. You fell victim to the pressures of modern parenting in a cutthroat place like LA," Paloma says, nodding. She's smiling, like this—my mother's confessional media lap—could be fun.

"She's from New Jersey, not the Midwest," Isla says, and Paloma shoots her a death glare.

"We'll find a photogenic priest looking to build his social. We'll book you to tell your side of the story on *20/20*. Or maybe *The View*. That's more your demo. Women thirty to sixty," Paloma continues, jotting a note, with what I notice is a pink glitter pen. "Maybe you write a book. That might be a win-win. Could be a cathartic way to spend your time while you're . . . in . . ." She pauses here. I think she's going to say *incarcerated*. Instead, she reaches for and finds: "Indisposed."

"How nice of you to think of hobbies to occupy me in *jail*," my mother says, like everyone else in the room is an idiot and keeps forgetting the only relevant point here.

"Prison," Mr. Spence corrects.

"Prison. The clink. Behind bars. Where. I. Will. Be. Locked. Up."

"They have a strong case, Joy," Mr. Spence says. "It's not a slam dunk, but it's pretty close. There are arguments we can make in court, of course. There are always arguments. But you have to understand these are very serious charges against you, and you're in much deeper legal jeopardy than many of your codefendants. Some of them were caught up in the SAT scam, but not the bribing of coaches at the universities themselves, or vice versa. You are charged with both," Mr. Spence says.

"I didn't bribe anyone. I made a donation to a charity," my mom insists, and this time, it is me who laughs, though it comes out as a desperate puff of air. I reread the complaint again last night, all two hundred pages, and I'm still blown away by how simple the scam was. Parents paid money to a nonprofit, and Dr. Wilson then used that money to pay off coaches at various schools across the country to add students to their team rosters as recruited athletes. Once deemed a recruit, voilà, the student was pretty much an automatic admit, despite, you know, *not playing the sport*.

According to the application to SCC that Dr. Wilson

submitted on my behalf, I'm a renowned pole vaulter. This is hilarious for a number of reasons, not least of which, I still have a scar under my chin from when I tripped with a pair of scissors in kindergarten. Had to get seven stitches.

In other words, I learned my lesson early about not running with pointy objects.

This scheme, falsely identifying me as an athlete, was what Dr. Wilson called the side door to admissions. The front door is the way Levi got into Harvard: blood, sweat, and tears. The back door is the way Xander got into Princeton: His parents donated a library wing. The side door was the only way in for people like me: not smart enough to get in on their own, not quite gilded enough to buy their way in legally.

"I'm also worried that if you don't plead guilty, the prosecutor will pile on more charges—tax fraud, conspiracy— that can add additional significant time," Mr. Spence says. I notice his cuff links are tiny gold handprints, a surprising choice. Mr. Spence must have his own family. Perhaps the four-figure hourly rate he's currently accruing camping out at our house is being spent on private school for his own precious children so they too can one day go to law school at Stanford and defend actresses from criminal charges.

"I am not going to prison," my mother says.

"I think you should plead guilty, Mom," Isla says.

"Me too," I say, my voice froggy, like it hasn't been used enough lately. "But not because of my target letter. Because otherwise it's too big a risk for you."

"No way," my mother says.

"He said you could get a sentence of twenty years," I say. "That's longer than I've been alive."

"Actually more if you throw in a money-laundering conspiracy charge," Mr. Spence says, and I can tell, for whatever reason, my mother refuses to acknowledge this possibility. Maybe she thinks he's trying to scare us. If he is, it's working on me. "Also tax fraud. If you wrote the donation off."

"No one is going to put me in jail for twenty years for doing what I thought was best for my kid," she says, not answering. "It's not like I'm one of those antivaxxers who doesn't care that they are putting children with cancer at risk for getting the measles. Come on. Find me a judge who's a parent. Put me on the stand and I'll have them weeping in minutes and convinced they'd have done the same exact thing for their kid."

"It doesn't work that way," Mr. Spence says. "We don't get to choose our judge and we can rehearse, but we can't urge you to lie."

"Don't be ridiculous. Put me in, Coach. I'm an actress. I can make them understand."

"Mom," Isla says. "You know what a judge is going to think? They'll think how unfair it is that their kid had to play by the rules when yours didn't. Or maybe they'll have a kid who needs a legitimate accommodation, who has a real disability, not a made-up case of ADHD, and because of *you* those will be harder to get now."

Isla is unintimidated by this room full of lawyers or my mother. She's riding that same wave of righteous indignation that has fueled angry op-eds across the country, all calling for us to get the book thrown at us, or maybe it's more personal than that: She's pissed because my greedy mother took her down too. I understand the rage, the desire to yell in my mother's face, to ask her to get this part over with so we can move on to the next. I think this not-knowing has to be worse than whatever is to come. It's the waiting that kills you.

Or maybe Isla is being Isla. Practical to the core. My mom *should* plead.

"And then what happens? We have to visit you in federal prison every weekend for twenty years. Take a plea and do a few months, Mom. Grow up. Take some responsibility," Isla says.

"I didn't know," my mother says.

"Didn't know? That's all you and Dad and Chloe can say. *I didn't know.* What does that mean? Tell me!" Isla is yelling, and the lawyers shuffle through files and stare at their phones to pretend they're not watching this shitshow unfold. Or perhaps one of them is live tweeting our disaster in real time.

"I didn't know it could land us here. I mean, jail."

"Prison, Mom," Isla says snottily, in a voice unlike her own. Like she's borrowing a persona to get through this.

"Screw you," my mother says, slamming the glass of water down on the table. This time she leaves the splashed droplets. "Screw all of you."

My mother storms out of the room and slams a door behind her.

"Well, that went well," Isla says, eerily calm. She remains dry eyed, while tears streak my face. I feel messy and unhinged. I've been so worried about my mom, I haven't really considered what this all means for me, especially if she doesn't take a plea. What if the US attorney isn't bluffing and they're serious about charging me too? "We should have Aunt Candy tell her that she'd plead guilty. That will get her on board."

"You didn't have to push so hard, Isl. She's scared. She'll come around," my dad says. I can't see if he's wearing cuff links, because his sleeves are buried underneath his suit jacket. If he is, they're likely diamond inflected. He'd never wear tiny handprints.

It's weird to imagine him deciding to put on his suit upstairs knowing the only place he was headed was our dining room.

"She doesn't have time to come around," Mr. Spence says. "The longer she waits—" But he doesn't get to finish his sentence because phones all around the table blink, buzz, and beep at the exact same. A *New York Times* alert: *Silicon Valley mom Penelope Wallingham is first parent in the college admissions scandal to plead guilty.*

"Time for a new plan," Mr. Spence says, and throws up his hands. Apparently my mother's phone is also signed up for news alerts, because not two seconds later, we hear the sound of something shattering upstairs.

CHAPTER TWENTY-EIGHT

Then

"Things are blowing up. Did you hear about that letter Mrs. Oh sent out to the parents of all seniors?" Shola asks. We're in English 4, and we've broken into small groups to discuss whether we agree with literary scholars that the epilogue of *Crime and Punishment*, which neatly ties up the novel, cheapens the rest of the book. I still have not read it, though I did read the SparkNotes. The dude gets sent to prison in Siberia for murder and falls in love. I decide I'm a believer in tidy endings, of bad guys getting their due.

Epilogue for the win, I write in my notes.

"What letter?" I ask.

"Mrs. Oh is pissed. She's been getting anonymous phone calls from parents trying to sabotage other kids' college applications," Shola says, whispering, because Mrs. Pollack is making the rounds. I read notes over Shola's shoulder: *Thematic tie in to consciousness of guilt and whether R. actually "owns" his actions. Does he truly atone? What about S.?* I have no idea what any of that means. She might as well be speaking Yoruba, which, incidentally, she can understand. Reason #495059 why Shola should and will get into every college she applies to.

"Seriously? This is a thing that people do?"

"Yup. Happens a lot. Rumor has it that Axl's mom anonymously reported that Simon was arrested for underage drinking last year but his parents got the charges dropped. She called from a blocked number, but Mrs. Oh totally recognized her voice. It's super nasal, like if a pug could talk."

"Why would Axl's mom do that?"

"I guess the hope was that Mrs. Oh would be required to notify the colleges Simon applied to." Shola raises an eyebrow, like she's not at all surprised, cynicism being on brand.

"But Simon and Axl are best friends. They do everything together." I try to imagine my parents, who have clearly lost their minds about the admissions process, resorting to that kind of direct sabotage, especially targeted against someone I care about, like Shola. They would never. Not in a million years.

"Apparently they're applying to the same schools, have pretty much identical applications, because they do all their extracurriculars together. Except Axl is number fifteen in the class and Simon is fourteen, and his parents are like super-entitled bazillionaires, so . . ." Shola shrugs, as if this is all to be expected when rich people play a zero-sum game. It occurs to me that maybe she's not a cynic but a realist.

I still don't understand why they make the stakes feel so high. Maybe it's because where we end up going to college is on the final parental report card. Maybe our parents have grown accustomed to the adult equivalent of A pluses in the rest of their lives. Or maybe they truly buy into the foolish belief that where you end up going to school defines who you are and who you will one day grow up to be.

"Everyone has gone bananas," I say. I look over to Axl and Simon. They are mid-debate with Levi, who apparently has strong views on epilogues. Levi catches my eye, smiles, and then goes back to his argument. I think back to Saturday night, and my hand reflexively touches my neck.

Even if I somehow manage to avoid being dumped before summer, Levi and I have a built-in end date. No one who looks like Levi—and who also happens to be cool and smart and kind—goes off to Harvard with a long-distance girlfriend.

"No kidding. I had a stress dream last night that the Littles tanked the ISEE and didn't get into Wood Valley and I didn't get in anywhere, not even my safeties," Shola says. "Then my parents made us form a family singing troupe to make money, like the von Trapps."

"You could work the Santa Monica pier," I suggest.

"I could spray myself gold and stand on Hollywood Boulevard. Be a human statue," Shola says. "I'm tall enough."

"It's all going to be okay, you know," I say. "Everyone ends up where they're supposed to go."

"How very Zen of you, Chlo." Shola jots down more notes about the book, somehow managing to have a full conversation with me while simultaneously processing the thematic underpinnings of *Crime and Punishment*.

"Just so you know, I'd never call the school and tell them about the time you pocketed that nail polish from CVS," I say.

"That was an accident!" she says, eyes wide. "And I returned it."

"I know. You went up to the cashier and offered to pay double," I say, and laugh.

"Whatever. I'm a Goody Two-shoes. This is not new information."

"It's annoying. You don't even let me copy off you," I say, trying to grab her notebook, which she blocks with an elbow. "What's the good in having a genius for a best friend if you don't let me cheat?"

"Somebody's got to keep you honest," Shola says.

CHAPTER TWENTY-NINE

Now

On the forty-second day of what I've come to think of as my house arrest, Mrs. Oh calls on my new cell. I have no idea how she got the number, though I'm guessing through Isla. For a minute, I wonder if I should hang up and call Kenny. Could I incriminate myself with Mrs. Oh? Could she be subpoenaed to testify against me or my mother or both of us? Could she already be working with the authorities to entrap me?

"Chloe. First of all, are you okay? How are you holding up?" Mrs. Oh asks, and the concern in her voice, the fact that she might actually care how I am, instead of hating my guts like the rest of the world, makes me want to weep with gratitude. I'd assumed she was furious with me. Wood Valley, which used to be known for their academic rigor and astronomically high percentage of Ivy admits, is now synonymous with the college cheating scandal. Since the news broke, Mrs. Oh's letter last fall, the one in which she complained about parents behaving badly in the admissions process, has gone viral, prompting an op-ed in the *New York Times* about the death of empathy and how unethical parenting is creating a generation of entitled monsters.

It was strange and disorienting to realize they meant me. I'm the monster.

And just as strange and disorienting to realize they weren't wrong.

"Hanging in," I say.

"You're a tough kid. You're going to be fine."

"What do you mean by 'I'll be fine'?" I ask, and hope she realized that I'm not trying to be a smart-ass. "I'm sorry. I'm honestly asking."

I lie on my bed and stare at my chandelier, which has become my new favorite pastime since I've given up social media. There are no answers for me up there, though. Only a lonely light fixture, currently overused because I'm still too scared to open my curtains.

"You'll put this behind you and maybe even be a stronger, better person for the experience. You'll go on to live a long and authentically good life. You'll end up more empathetic and ultimately have a fuller understanding of your own privilege not in spite of this mess, but because of it. That's what I mean by *fine*."

"Huh. Thank you." I savor her words for a minute. I wonder if there's any chance for me to emerge from this as someone who feels anything but pure self-loathing. I've spent much of my life feeling stupid, and now I feel stupid and dirty and ashamed. I'm not sure I'll ever feel worthy of Mrs. Oh's definition of *fine*. "Hope you're right."

"I keep remembering when we talked in the fall about

your SATs. I should have done something. I should have listened better. I think you were trying to tell me what was happening, in your own way, and I might have saved you from this going so far—"

"Let's not. I mean, I'm not supposed to talk about it." It occurs to me that if called to testify, Mrs. Oh could mention that meeting in her office, and my obvious suspicions that something was off with my test. Can she incriminate me? What did I say exactly? Or did I make it clear that I knew?

No, that's not possible. Because I didn't. Not really.

Did I?

"Fair enough. So we have some orders of business."

"Okay," I say, when I really want to say is *Mrs. Oh, I'm sorry I let you down. Mrs. Oh, I'm so bone tired of bad news. Mrs. Oh, please don't testify against us.*

And also, this: *Mrs. Oh, your baby is very lucky to have you as a mom.*

"We need to set out a plan for you to graduate. I understand why you haven't been in school, but you can't just stop coming and still expect to get your degree." I hear the bell in the background, and then the jumbled noises of five hundred kids finding their way to class. I'm hit with a sudden longing for my normal life and for the old, clueless me. I want to throw books into my locker and eat frozen yogurt with Shola and be bored senseless by calculus. I want to gossip about prom and eat Friday tacos and float on an oversized flamingo raft in the pool without thinking about telephoto lenses. I want to go to Wood Valley Giving Day, even though I complain about it every single year because you have to wear a hard hat and use tools and the dusty construction site ruins your sneakers. I want to visit Cesar after school and hear all about how he's been doing on his weekly spelling quizzes.

"I've reached out to your mom and dad to discuss these arrangements, but they haven't returned my calls," Mrs. Oh says.

"Yeah, they're a little distracted." The irony isn't lost on me that my parents, who have micromanaged every moment of my life at Wood Valley, who have literally become the poster children for the term *snowplow parenting*, are now not legally allowed to talk to my school advisor, or at least my mother isn't. "So how do I graduate? Obviously I can't go back."

"The year is winding down anyway. It's already May. We can offer you independent study, assign final projects and special exams for you to do from home. Everyone understands there are extenuating circumstances." Right. Again, this is not what I expected. I thought Mrs. Oh would have tried to convince me to return to school. Clearly, they don't want me spreading my cheating cooties all over campus.

I wonder if the headmaster, Mr. Hochman, considered expulsion. I wonder if Mrs. Oh talked him out of it.

No backsies, I think.

I remember Mrs. Pollack's class, and how she went on and on about the idea of culpability—the various ways we end up paying for our sins. I think of all the people across the country who would like to see my mom and me sent to a Siberian labor camp. And then I think about how my mother hasn't left her room in the forty-eight hours since our disastrous family meeting. She's been eating Xanax like candy and telling Dad over and over that she's still confused about why what she did is considered a crime at all. Occasionally, I hear her mumble the word *Zurich*.

I get it, though. Why what she did—what we did?—was a crime.

"Thank you. That sounds super fair," I say, thinking that my parents or Carrie can hire me a tutor to help. A beat later I realize that I don't want them to. I need to manage this on my own with a little hard work. "I'll do whatever you need me to do."

"Good. Glad that's sorted. So then about prom."

"I'm not going." Last week, I finally received a text from Levi. It was only six lines. My very first breakup haiku.

> I'm sorry about prom
>
> But what happened was messed up
>
> Not ready to talk
>
> I'm not sure when/if
>
> Obvi hope it works out for you
>
> But this is goodbye

I, apparently, am not even worthy of full sentences, or the writing out of the word *obviously*. Which, come on, it probably would have been the faster choice with autofill.

"Right, okay. Good. We were worried about paparazzi, so—" Mrs. Oh clears her throat. The bell rings again, and all that background shuffling comes to a stop. I picture Shola in class finding someone else to talk to when Mrs. Pollack makes everyone break into small discussion groups. I picture Levi taking Sophie to prom instead, and kissing her on the dance floor, and not giving a second thought to the fact that it was supposed to be me there with him. *Obvi.* "One more thing, and I'm sorry about this, truly I am, but SCC is rescinding your acceptance. You'll be getting a letter soon."

My friends on Signal had warned me this was coming. The future that had so recently seemed inevitable—me in my dorm room at SCC becoming whomever I'm meant to become—disappears. I remind myself that I don't want to go someplace where I don't belong, that everyone hates me there anyway, and most importantly, that I never earned my spot in the first place. None of that lessens the sting.

For a week, I'd had the pleasure of basking in my parents' evident pride, of walking through the Wood Valley hallway flaunting my brand-new SCC sweatshirt, of scrolling my SCC class hashtag on Instagram. I'd felt important and special and chosen. Now I wonder if what my parents were experiencing was nothing like pride at all. Only a perverse relief. Or if there was pride, it was because *they* had found the side door, the secret handshake to get me in.

In the complaint, there's an email my mom wrote to Dr. Wilson after I got my SCC acceptance. She sent him a high-five emoji. That's it. No words. Only the high-five emoji. Out of everything I've read and for reasons I'm not sure I can explain, that one hurts the most.

"Yeah. Okay," I say, my voice thick. "No SCC. I figured."

"I know it sucks."

"No. I mean, yeah, it sucks. But they're right to rescind. I don't. I wouldn't. I can't anyway." I stop talking, give up. She knows what I mean. SCC belongs to fictional alterna-Chloe. Liar Chloe. I stare again at the chandelier, willing it to give me answers, or a plan, or a road map. Something to get from here to whatever comes next so I can hop over this terrible part. I feel myself sinking into my mattress and I imagine the pillow top suffocating me slowly. "I don't know what I'll do now, though."

"That's okay," Mrs. Oh said. "You'll figure it out."

"I'm not sure I believe you," I say.

"That's okay too," Mrs. Oh says.

CHAPTER THIRTY

Then

The first morning of Thanksgiving break, I sleep till one in the afternoon. Despite the fact that our teachers know we're all in the middle of college admissions, they haven't let up on the homework. I've been up late every night this week trying not to fall further behind.

I've scrapped the essay Mrs. Oh hated, and I've rewritten it from scratch. What I end up with won't win any awards, or be excerpted in the *New York Times*, like Maverick Stone's— last year's valedictorian—essay was. That was about a kid who convinced his parents to defect from Scientology while in middle school. I still think mine's good enough to send off.

Even Mrs. Oh agrees. When she handed it back, it was covered with red pen, but she also said, *Well done, Chloe*, which felt better than I would have thought. The closest thing I've gotten to a gold sticker at school.

Now it's in the hands of Dr. Wilson and his on-staff writer, for what he called a "quick copyedit." I imagine there might be some tinkering, but at least I wrote the gist of it myself. I wrote about the real me, which is to say, unlike my classmates who all seem to already know who and what they want to be when they grow up, I admitted to not yet finding my passion or myself. That I'm hoping college will be the venue that helps me to do so.

Okay, so nothing mind-blowingly original, but at least it's honest.

"Get up, lazybones. Dr. Wilson needs a photo of you," my dad says, and barrels into my room and opens the blinds. The sun streams in through the window. I can hear the buzz of a lawn mower and Isla conjugating Spanish verbs. The number of these sorts of mornings are running out, and I want to hold on to them. My bed, the sounds, the promise of a familiar, unchallenging day.

"Seriously, get up," my dad says, and sits down on my duvet. He's in golf clothes and smells like fresh laundry. He whacks me on the head with a pillow.

"Stop!" I sit up, laughing, and block my face with my arms.

"I don't know your phone code or I'd find a picture myself. Is yours face or finger ID?"

"I'm not giving you my phone. What do you need a picture for?" I ask.

"For your college applications," he says, like this is perfectly reasonable.

"You don't need to send a picture with a college application."

"Dr. Wilson said we did. Joy, didn't Dr. Wilson say we needed a photo?" he calls to my mother, who comes running.

"We need a photo. Yes," my mom says. She's wearing her usual weekend uniform: leopard-print running tights and a matching sports bra and no shirt. I stare at her midriff. To be clear, I don't begrudge my mother her figure. I happily choose food. And free time. And my mental health.

"What is that?" my dad asks, pointing to my mother's face, which is covered in a terrifying Korean sheet mask.

"It does good things to your skin. Dr. Roth said to use one every third week, so Carrie set a reminder on my calendar."

"Huh."

"Mom, your abs look insane," I say.

"I know, right? Paloma has me doing a fitness cover shoot later. If you look closely, you can see some of them are painted on with tanner." I squint, and sure enough, the lines appear hand drawn. Still, if you painted a six-pack onto my abs, they'd look like Hawaiian dinner rolls.

"Photo. For Dr. Wilson. Now." My dad pulls up an email on his phone and squints at the small type. "Only requirements are you facing forward where we can see your face and neck."

"Can someone please tell me why Dr. Wilson needs my photo, particularly one showing my neck?" I ask for a second time.

"I think it's for some sort of profile," my dad says, and my mom shakes her head in exasperation. Isla does this killer impression of mom yelling at dad: *Richard, get that phone out of your face and listen to me for once.* In all fairness, my dad *is* an epically bad listener, which is one of the many reasons we have Carrie. My parents have found a way to outsource all of the things married people usually nag each other about. That might be the secret to their mostly blissful union, come to think of it, enough money so that neither of them has to cook or clean or negotiate who picks up the dry cleaning or the kids.

"It's for his website," my mom says, elbowing him.

"I don't want to be on his website," I say.

"Stop being difficult," my parents say in unison.

"It would be good if you can find one where you look a little tan," my dad says.

"Why?"

"You need to look a tad Latino," my dad says, again as if he's making sense.

"But . . . I don't know if you've noticed, I'm not Latina," I say.

"There's a little Argentinian on my side," my dad says, and holds up his forearms, which are perfectly tanned. From weekly golf under the California sun. Not genetics.

"Ignore Dad. It's not a thing," my mom says. She grabs my phone, flashes it in my face so she can bypass the passcode, and then pulls up my photos. "Ooh, this one is cute of Levi."

"Hands off, Joy. He's too young for you." My dad pinches her butt and she squeals.

"Here. One from the beach in Maui. You look stunning," my mom says, and messages the image to herself. "Done."

"The one with me in a bikini? Oh my God, do not send that to Dr. Wilson."

"Relax. He just needs your face and neck," my dad repeats.

"What are you even talking about?" I ask.

"Shush," my mom says, though I don't know if she's talking to my dad or to me. She glances at my phone again. "Ooh, time's up. Need to take off this mask. It's all tingly."

"I know how to make you tingly," my dad says, and I groan, because boundaries.

"Can I go back to sleep?" I ask, though I have no plans to go back to sleep at all. I plan to lie here and listen to Isla through the wall, and memorize the sound of that lawn mower. I plan to luxuriate in my waning life.

"Fourteen-forty on your SATs. Got your essay in. I think you earned it, love," my mom says, handing me a silk eye mask from the side dresser.

"Sweet dreams, princess," my dad says. And then they both blow kisses from the door.

CHAPTER THIRTY-ONE

Now

This time, the meeting is held in the playroom, my family sitting on the wraparound couch, while a man I've never met before and who despite his suit and tie doesn't seem like a lawyer, stands in front of us, fiddling with the television. A tattoo peeks out from his sleeve, and it occurs to me you can tell a lot about a man from how he decorates his wrists.

"Do I need to call Kenny?" I ask, because this is how we live now. Before spending time with my parents, I need to consult my lawyer.

"Not for this," my dad says. "This is Mr. Forster."

"Call me Michael."

"Michael, who are you?" Isla asks, and somehow manages to adopt a tone that is authoritative without being rude. She immediately gives the impression that she, not my parents, is the one in charge here. Instead of going to college, I should take life lessons from my sister.

Michael looks bemused. I guess he's not used to being

addressed directly by sixteen-year-old girls, particularly ones dressed in pajamas decorated with tiny llamas crossed with unicorns, that have the commandment *Be a Llamacorn!* written in script across the chest.

"I'm here as part advisor, part therapist, part—"

"Oh crap. Are you the priest that Paloma wanted to hire?" Isla asks. "You should know, she's only using you for reputation rehabilitation and social media exposure. We're all atheists in this family, though Chloe leans agnostic."

"Isla, listen to the man," my dad says. Usually my father puffs up when Isla shows off her smarts, and it would be my mother who'd get annoyed by the interruption, but today my mom sits next to me on the couch, quiet and subdued. She smells of that potent cocktail of Xanax and defeat.

My dad, on the other hand, looks like he's had twenty gallons of coffee and needs to pee. He wipes his sweaty forehead with a paper towel. He has opted out of his suit jacket for this one, instead wearing a deep blue linen shirt, the sleeves rolled up to the elbows. Instead of using the app on his phone, he gets up to lower the temperature on the Nest and then sits back down.

"I'm not a priest. Far from it, I'm afraid. I'm actually a prison consultant."

Isla laughs out loud when he says this, long and hard, and I glare at her to stop.

"Sorry, I didn't realize that was a thing. You and your love of consultants. Did Aunt Candy recommend him too?" Isla's voice is thick with scorn and sarcasm. She looks at my parents, and they both look at the ground, unwilling to meet her eyes. She's no longer trying to control her anger, or even keep it on a tight simmer. Somehow we knuckleheads have managed to outsmart her and bring her right down with us.

Michael clears his throat and gets started.

"So to more fully answer your question: Who am I? Ten years ago, I went to a minimum-security federal penitentiary for embezzlement and tax evasion. At the time, I thought my life as I knew it was over, and in some ways I was right. It was. But, and I realize how this is going to sound, prison was also the best thing that ever happened to me," Michael says.

"Are you going to try to get my mom to plead guilty? If so, I'm here for it," Isla says.

"Nope. That's your mom's choice. I'm here to help make it an informed one," Michael says, and claps his hands together, like he's the coach and we're Little Leaguers and the time for messing around is over. I can't get a good look at his tattoo. It seems serpentine. "The prospect of prison can be really scary, especially to people like you and to people like who I used to be—"

"You mean rich," Isla fills in.

"Don't be crass," my dad says, but Michael looks at Isla and laughs.

"Being wealthy is part of it, sure. Though I meant people who are used to having complete control over their lives. Prison is by definition a loss of control."

"Can we stop using that word?" my mom asks, her voice small and tight. Fluffernutter, sensing the tension, jumps into her lap to soothe her, and my mom runs her fingers through his fur.

"What word?" Michael asks.

"Prison," my dad says.

"Yes," my mom says. "That one."

"Sorry, no. I can't do that," Michael says. "From everything I've read, you're going to have to get used to both that word and the idea. And with all due respect, Ms. Fields, the sooner you realize that, the better off you'll be. So how about we start immediately," he says, clicking on his Power-Point presentation, and I realize this may be the very first time I've ever heard someone talk to my mother this way, striking right through her artifice to the truth. *Tough love,* Mrs. Oh would call it. I may have snowplow parents, but they too live their own kind of snowplowed existence.

The opening slide reads *On the inside: the ups and downs of prison life.*

Next, a picture of Michael looking about fifteen years younger—thirtysomething, thinning hair, long-limbed but with a paunch, wearing a flashy suit and sitting on the edge of a wide wooden desk. A finance cliché. Exactly who I imagine both Axl and Simon will grow up to be.

Click. Michael again, this time in his orange prison garb, thicker, stronger, his paunch ironed out into muscle. He has a shaved head, a whisper of a scar at his temple, and he looks straight into the camera. He's smiling in this one. With teeth. I can see his full tattoo: a snake up his arm, curling around the neck of a lamb at the elbow.

A little too obvious.

The pictures present two versions of the same man. I disturb myself by finding the second significantly more attractive.

"One bonus of prison. Lots of time to exercise," he says with a wry grin.

His lecture is long and detailed, teaching all of us way more than we ever wanted to know about minimum-security federal penitentiaries. The ways to structure your life as an inmate, like waking up early while there's still fresh toilet paper, and avoiding team sports so you won't find yourself in front of the prison doctor. To ration your commissary funds, because they tend to go fast. How you need to make allies instead of friends.

I watch my mother's face as he talks. She looks both riveted and nauseated. Maybe reality is finally sinking in.

"I hate to admit when I'm wrong," Isla says, once Michael has finished and asks if we have any questions. "But Aunt Candy did good this time, for once. Thank you for that. Super informative. I give it five stars on Rotten Tomatoes."

"Ignore Isla. She's just angry," my dad says dismissively, and as soon as the words are out of his mouth, I can tell that my father, in his usual blunt carelessness, has without noticing lit a match. I feel Isla tense next to me—her teammate has veered to the other side—and so I put my hand on hers, in what I hope she'll understand is a *calm down, I got your back* gesture. She shakes me off. She stands up so quickly that so does Fluffernutter, barking.

"Of course I'm angry," Isla says. She's been dancing on the edge all morning, all week, and we're going to see her jump. "I'm freaking livid."

"Isla, please sit down," my dad says, and I can tell by the way his words come out that he's too tired, too broken to put out this fire, even though normally he relishes his role as the family mediator. He likes to play the levelheaded dad smoothing out the hotheaded women around him, just like dads do on sitcoms.

"When you did this, when you lied and cheated and scammed, did you for one single second think about what was going to happen to me when this all came crashing down? How this would ruin my life too? I've done every single thing right. Gave you a million silly awards for you to brag about. I'm fluent in Mandarin, for God's sake, even though I really wanted to focus on Spanish. I was on track to run for president of the school next year, but nope, not going to happen. Now I'm lucky when I can get through the afternoon without getting bodychecked by some idiot who got rejected from SCC." Isla, my robot sister, who's always so self-contained and practical, who puts her head down and follows the bread crumbs her teachers leave for her until the early hours of every morning, shouts while tears stream down her cheeks. "I know what you're going to say. This isn't about you, Isla. You're not the one who might go to prison. Why do you have to make everything about you, Isla? But you know what? I'm part of this family too, even if no one else seems to notice."

My mom looks at Isla and her mouth hangs open. Isla looks back at her, waiting for something—an apology, a hug, an explanation. Anything. They've had blowups before, obviously. No mother and daughter, especially ones as stubborn as these two, make it through the teen years without their fair share of screaming matches. But usually they fight over silly things—a tone of voice, Isla's rejection of all things vegetable, Isla not getting enough sleep—and they recover quickly.

My mom picks up Fluffernutter, places him back in her lap. She leans her head back against the couch and says nothing. But instead of grabbing her end of the argument so they can shake it out in all its epic glory, she stays there, too still. I think about Isla and me as kids, how we'd squeeze our eyes shut and put our fingers in our ears and say "lalalalala" when we didn't want to hear what the other was saying.

"Isl," I say, and then she turns to me, eyes ablaze. A feral animal stuck in a trap. As if she's realizing that no matter how much a stink she raises, she's never getting out of this family.

Isla is strong and smart and will be fine, by every definition of the word, and this, it turns out, might be the thing that unravels her. Because I know we'll continue to take her competence for granted, we'll continue to take comfort in the fact that she doesn't need us, we'll continue to allow her to never be satisfied with something as small as *fine*.

She's not me or Hudson. We're the ones who have continually proven to need special tending.

"What, Chlo? What?" she asks.

Still it's not fair for us to see how far we can bend her till she breaks.

"I'm sorry," I say, and reach out to touch her, but she steps backward. "I'm so, so sorry."

"I know you are," she says, and walks away.

CHAPTER THIRTY-TWO

Then

Shola: The Littles rocked the ISEE!

Me: YAYYYY!!!!!!!! All test practice with them paid off! You're Teacher of the Year!

Shola: I'm so relieved. You don't even know. I haven't slept in like a week

Me: Watch out Wood Valley! Here come the Littles!

Shola: Don't jinx it! They still have to get in with scholarships

Me: THEY WILL!

Shola: We need so much admissions mojo right now. I honestly think I'm more worried about them than me

Me: You're such a better big sister than I am

Shola: Yeah you're right. I rock

Me: You coming over today?

Shola: I wish. Still have to help my parents. They had so much food leftover they invited everyone over again today for Thanksgiving 2.0

Me: Come on. I'll pull out the unicorn float

Shola: Don't tempt me with the unicorn. You know how much I love that thing

Me: You love it more than you love me

Shola: You come in a close second tho. Your dad comes in third

Me: SHOLA

Me: Please come over. Levi's boarding in Vail. Argh, I'm so mad we didn't go away this year. I'm soooo bored. I don't want to have to swim alone

Shola: Tough life you have C 💁

"Read a book for once," Isla says when she comes into the playroom and sees that I'm still playing Xbox. My essay is in, the SAT nightmare is over, my boyfriend (I really, really like that word) is away—I'm allowed to kick back, guilt free.

She flops down on the couch with a giant bag of potato chips—contraband in this house—and opens up a fat novel. "Nerd," I say.

"Do you think the *My Dad, My Pops, and Me* reboot is going to get picked up?" Isla asks. She puts her book down, and I see the title, *Crime and Punishment*. She's reading my homework for funsies.

"Probably. Why?" I ask. I can't remember the last time I voluntarily spent a night at home with Isla, but I do that constant math that seems to follow me everywhere these days: only six months left of the two of us living under the same roof, and then probably never again for the rest of our lives, so I pause my game to sit with her.

"Is it wrong that I kind of don't want it to?"

"It's what Mom wants, so yeah, I guess," I say, surprised. The reboot is definitely a good thing—it could kick my mother up a notch, move her from B list to, well, B+. I'm proud of my mom's success, even if other people denigrate her work as fluff just because it's targeted to girls. (I've noticed that no one seems to crap all over the men who star in action movies.) Also it's not easy to sustain a career in Hollywood like she has, especially when you're an aging woman.

"I feel like, I dunno, and you probably won't understand this, because you two are besties so it's different for you, but I mean, she hasn't even asked how junior year has been going." We never talk about the fact that I am closer to our mom and she's closer to our dad. I will not insult her by pretending I don't know what she means. I nod. "Still, this is it. The most important year of high school and she's totally checked out."

"Come on. You're Isla. You're acing all of your classes and kicking Wood Valley ass." I wonder if my mom and Isla aren't as close because my mom has decided that Isla is like one of those low-maintenance plants. The more you tinker, the more you mess her up.

217

"Still," she says, and so I pat my little sister's head, like she's Fluffernutter.

"Sorry, dude. Your success gets tedious. But fine, I'll bite. How's junior year been going for you?" I wonder if maybe for the first time my sister could be struggling. Did school suddenly get hard for her like it did for me? I was fine in seventh grade and even mostly in eighth, and then in ninth I started to sink under the weight of all that homework and expectation. I became resentful that every choice I made—classes, sports, extracurriculars, even summer break—was tied not to what I enjoyed the most, but to what everyone thought would look best on a résumé. And I can't even blame my parents. It was everyone. Activities turned professional and hardcore. Dabbling was no longer allowed. No more being bad at stuff and doing it anyway just for fun.

"Kicking Wood Valley ass, of course," she says, smiling. "Like you have no idea. My advisor wants me to consider adding an extra AP to my schedule."

"I hate you," I say, and she shrugs, like *It's all in a day's work*.

"Seriously, though, you really don't think things have gotten a bit out of control here lately? Like a little gross?" Isla asks.

She waves a hand, and so I look around to see what she could be talking about. The pool guy outside skims leaves. My dad practices his golf swing in the backyard. My mom is at Dr. Roth's, her second home, getting a laser peel.

"I'm not following," I say.

"Your sneakers came predirtied and cost like eight hundred dollars."

"Your point?" I ask. Dad calls Isla "our good little liberal" because she's always making us recycle and bought us water bottles made of cork with aluminum straws, and last year, when we flew on Aunt Candy's private jet that one time, she tried to convince my parents to offset the environmental damage with carbon credits. She gets into arguments with my dad all the time about the need for affordable housing in Los Angeles and calls him a NIMBY-ist, which was a term I had to look up. Apparently, it stands for *Not In My Backyard* and means that you are pro-liberal ideas, except when they directly impact you or your house or your wallet. To be fair, she nailed him.

"That's a lot of money. A lot of families in the United States don't even have eight hundred dollars in their bank account. I bet Cesar's family doesn't."

I groan, because this is a low blow, bringing up Cesar. I examine my sneakers.

"They aren't predirtied. They're strategically dirtied, which is a whole different thing."

"Also, you don't have ADHD, Chloe."

Here's what this is all about. Not my Golden Goose sneakers. That was only the appetizer, her opening segue. My stomach knots up, and I feel my face redden. Of course, even though I never specifically told her about my accommodation, Isla lives in this house and so has overheard me and my parents endlessly discussing the SAT. I guess there was no way to keep it a secret at home.

I tell myself I have nothing to be ashamed of. *A doctor diagnosed me.*

"A doctor diagnosed me," I say, but it comes out too practiced, too defensive, like I said it in my head first.

"Right," she says. "Listen, I'm glad you did great. Seriously, I am. But—"

"But what? It's really none of your business anyway." Isla took the PSAT last year and she scored so high that had it counted, she'd be a National Merit Scholar. Still, she'll be putting her hours in with Linda soon, learning the tricks to aim for a straight 1600.

Isla picks up her book again, as if she's done talking about this. And then she looks at me, square in the eyes, like she's lining up a shot: "Did you tell Shola about your accommodation?"

Another low blow. My sister has terrific aim.

"Why would I?"

"I don't know. Why wouldn't you?"

"Because," I say.

"Well, I think it's generally a good policy never to do anything that you're too ashamed to tell your best friend," she says, and I take a deep breath while I let the urge to punch her in her smug face pass. "Or, you know, your sister."

CHAPTER THIRTY-THREE

Now

Paloma decides it's time for me and my mom to leave the house. She's not worried about our mental health, even though sometimes at night, my mother and I pass each other wandering around upstairs, restless and hollow-eyed, eye masks tented on our foreheads. The Beverly Hills version of the undead. During the day, we do much the same, except our route stretches between the kitchen and the playroom and our eye masks are discreetly packed back in our nightstands.

Eight other parents have pled guilty to their charges, and each made the sort of impassioned apologies Mr. Spence recommended. Every time another person folds, my mom's bargaining position weakens. Paloma and the PR team have concluded that we need to switch the media narrative.

Even my Signal group has gone quiet now that we find ourselves in different boats, or maybe I've been dropped the way they dropped Penny. My mom is not the sole holdout, but she's by far the most visible.

"What do you think? You guys could shop at Erewhon

for salads? Go to a yoga class? Get juice? How do you want to play this?" Paloma asks. We are in the kitchen, which is the room I spend the least amount of time in these days, because there's always a man in a suit loitering around the giant coffee urn and pastries, talking too loudly on his cell.

I don't like to be near the lawyers. I always get the sense they're sizing me up, wondering how I could be so dim as to need to cheat to get into college. *It's not like SCC is an Ivy*, I heard one mumble once into his phone. *I mean, then I might get it. But SCC, man, really?* That guy was wearing crimson socks decorated with tiny Harvard emblems, and I realized you could tell a lot about a man from his ankles too.

"What do you think, sweet pea?" my mom asks. She's leaning on her elbows on the kitchen island, as if she can't hold herself up on her own.

"You okay, Mom?" I ask.

"What? Yeah. Just tired," she says. "Don't worry. I surrendered the Xanax to Dad to dose out more reasonably. I know I was getting a little *Valley of the Dolls*."

"Maybe we should go to a yoga class to relax? But then everyone will look at us," I say.

"That's the point. We *want* people to look at you. We're going to tip off the paparazzi," Paloma says, getting that grin she always gets whenever she says the word *paparazzi*. Like it turns her on.

"I still don't understand the point of this," I say. I asked Kenny whether it was okay if I left the house with my mother and he said, "Sure, spend time together while you can." After we hung up, my dad said, "Twenty bucks he bills you for that phone call."

My dad talks a lot about billable hours now—it's his fallback conversation; he uses it the same way he used to babble about his last golf game. Both are equally uninteresting. From what I can gather, his annoyance about the cost of all this is not based on real concerns about our finances. Even with both of my parents out of work and mounting legal bills, we have a long way to go before we need to start worrying about money. My dad sat Isla and me down to reassure us about all of this when he agreed to step down from his firm, as if our concern about our depleted trust funds was the thing keeping us up at night. Truth be told, I hadn't really thought about it, being much more concerned with the whole "my mom and I potentially going to prison thing."

"The point is that for six weeks the headlines have been saying"—Paloma points at me with one of her pink fingernails and puts on a monotonous, newscaster voice—"Pimpleton Von Wildenstern the Eighth has pleaded guilty to charges in the college admissions scandal that has rocked the nation. Meanwhile, Joy Fields, known for her longtime stint on *My Dad, My Pops, and Me,* continues to roll the legal dice despite mounting evidence against—"

"Enough," my mom says. "We get it. Yoga. We'll do yoga."

Paloma puts a finger to her ear, like she's Secret Service, voice dropped low and serious. "Scheduling it."

Twenty-four hours later, after my mom has had her makeup and hair done—all so it looks like she's wearing no makeup and that her hair was casually thrown back into that perfect ponytail—we find ourselves doing the downward dog at eleven-thirty in the morning. Paloma wants my mom to seem easy, breezy, all calm, cool, and collected. Like she's confident she'll beat the charge. I turned down my mom's offer of a blowout and instead am going au naturel. I'm tired of the world thinking I'm a spoiled, entitled brat, though come to think of it, not sure the image of me looking sweaty in front of 9021-OM will help matters much.

When I come downstairs, though, Paloma sends me right up to change.

"Stripes are *not* a good idea," she says.

Her plan, once I've changed into something that can't be used for a *Daily Mail* pun, is pretty straightforward. We take the class, and then when the paparazzi surround us upon exit, my mother will repeat these exact words, which she practiced more than her People's Choice Awards acceptance speech: *Unfortunately, I'm unable to discuss the details of the case at this time, but I'm so grateful for the outpouring of support for me and my family that has come from not only all over the country but all over the world. Thank you from the bottom of my heart.*

Then she's supposed to follow with a wink and her trademarked Missy line: *You're the bestest!*

My job is to stand next to her in a solid color and not throw up.

There has been no outpouring of support. As far as I can tell, very few people have reached out, with the notable exception of Raj, my mother's personal trainer, who kindly passed along exercises to relieve her overworked adrenals. Even Aunt Candy has gone radio silent after her big claim that she had no idea about Dr. Wilson's scheme, and instead used him for only legitimate consulting services. Right.

Occasionally, during our middle-of-the-night crossings, my mom'll murmur: "You'd think she'd at least check in on me. When she discovered that Charles had that mistress in Tokyo, I was on the first flight out."

I understand how my mom feels. I may not have coached Shola through an extramarital affair, but we have been through whatever the high school equivalent might be. This is the longest I've gone not speaking to her since we met, and often, still, I catch myself talking to her in my mind.

"Please don't hate me," I find myself saying, on repeat, as if Shola can hear me. If I believed in vision boards, I'd put a selfie of us smack in the middle and write the word BFF in bubble letters.

The only person I've heard from is Cesar's mom, who a week ago, out of the blue, texted me a picture of Cesar hanging upside down in the park, knees looped over a tree branch. Her message was brief: *Sorry about your troubles. Cesar says to send this. Hope you come back soon.* I have re-read that text a hundred times, run my fingers along the words like they're rosary beads.

So much unearned empathy in those three lines; they make me swim in painful gratitude.

At first Paloma's plan goes off without a hitch. When we walk in, a few people titter, but mostly they do that LA thing of recognizing my mom and then intentionally looking away.

I imagine later they will call their friends and be like, *Oh my God, you will never guess who I just saw.*

The class kicks my butt; yoga for these women is apparently not about finding inner peace, but about finding inner abs. My mom's perfect makeup-non-makeup beads up on her forehead. Since I've done no exercise over the last few weeks other than lifting croissants into my mouth and walking my quiet dopey laps around the house, my body burns. Still, I tell myself this isn't so bad, even with the covert glances. Maybe my self-imposed solitary confinement is unnecessary. Next time, though, instead of sweating, I'm going to sneak out to see Cesar, and we'll sit in that double rocking chair my parents donated to the center for my sixteenth birthday and pretend to wear our invisibility cloaks.

When we finally reach the end of class, the instructor, a bendy brunette, looks straight at my mother when she says, "Namaste." It turns a beautiful word into a rebuke. We pretend not to notice.

"Ready?" my mom says, before we step outside to face the planted paparazzi.

"No."

"We can do this," my mom says, which is the first time since the scandal broke that I see echoes of the mother I recognize. Cameras have the opposite effect on her than they do on normal people—when they're around, she turns calm and composed and charming.

We step outside into madness. I hold my mother's hand to stay steady and reflexively look down to avoid the assault of flashes and shouted questions, the press of bodies moving in closer. My mom's wedding ring, which Paloma insisted she wear despite the fact that her fingers swell in downward dog, digs into my hands.

My mom delivers her speech and it seems to go off without a hitch. I echo it in my head, and make a mental note not to mouth the words along with her. This is supposed to seem impromptu, and ever the actress, my mom throws in a few casual *umms* and thoughtful looks into the distance so as to appear she's coming up with the words on the spot. Just as she's about to deliver her trademark line at the end, she stops, because she notices Paloma pushing her way through the crowd and signaling to cut it short.

The reporters shout questions into the void—*Will you serve time? Why did you do it? Chloe, are you mad at your mom?*—as we move toward Paloma's outstretched arms, her nails spiking at the ends. For the first time in my life I'm relieved to see her; she will use her Jedi superpowers to get us out of here.

"What do you have to say about the additional charges against you that came down in the last hour?" My head jerks up. I can't see who is asking, if it's a real journalist or a tabloid. I'd expected only TMZ here or E!, but there are news trucks lined up the street with legitimate letters along their sides: ABC News, CNN, MSNBC.

My mother's phone is currently buried deep in her bag and powered down. 9021-OM has a strict no-cell policy, so I didn't even bother to bring mine. What have we missed?

"Conspiracy to commit fraud and money laundering are pretty serious allegations. Each count alone is twenty years.

Do you now wish you had pled guilty?" the reporter continues.

My mother looks up and for a split second I see the fear on her face, a blast of tightness so quick I doubt the camera caught it, and then the actress Joy Fields clicks back into place.

"Thanks, y'all. You're the bestest," she says, with the trademark wink, and then Paloma ushers us into the back of a waiting SUV with tinted windows. Once inside, my mother crumbles.

"I'm so sorry. I tried to get to you in time but there was traffic, goddamn LA, and I called the studio and they wouldn't put me through, even when I told the twelve-year-old at the front desk it was an emergency. I tried everything." Paloma, whose job it is to remain unruffled, looks distraught. She grabs my mother's hands, and for a minute, Paloma seems like a human who cares about what is happening to my mother. Not like a PR cyborg.

"More charges?" my mom asks, eyes watery, pupils gigantic. "So if I'm found guilty, that means even more time in prison. More than twenty years?"

"I'm not a lawyer, but yeah, I think so. We can get Mr. Spence on the phone," Paloma offers. She's texting as she talks, probably some sort of SOS to her team. "Or Richard. We can call Richard."

"But he didn't say anything about Chloe, right? They didn't charge her?" my mom asks, and my stomach bottoms out. Until recently, I hadn't realized terror was something solid, a physical weight to be borne, a desperate paddling to keep your head above water despite the persistence of gravity. I feel pressure in my chest and a dull humming in my ears. It's a logical conclusion. If their goal is to break my mother, I'm the best and easiest route.

"No, I don't think so," Paloma says, and I try to still my shaking bottom lip. My mom grabs my hand and kisses it.

"It's okay. We're going to be okay, Chlo," she says, and uses her inner elbow to swat hard at the tears coursing down her cheeks. I think about the power of telephoto lenses and the mechanics of tinted windows. Whether this scene will play out on television screens across the country tonight. If the world will see what I see: two broken people, a loving mother tending to her daughter, or if they will see something altogether different. Us getting what we deserve.

I've turned so paranoid, for a second I wonder if this was Paloma's plan after all—to reveal this moment, us at our most vulnerable and not the sturdier version in front of the yoga studio that preceded this. Nah. Even Paloma is not that diabolical. She's recovered, though, and looks away from our emotion. Her AirPods are back in her ears, her eyes on her phone.

"Can someone please text Carrie and let her know we need more ice cream?" my mom asks.

CHAPTER THIRTY-FOUR

Then

Levi, Shola, and I lounge on oversized floats in the pool—a swan, a unicorn, and a flamingo, respectively—trailing our fingertips lazily in the water. It's eighty degrees in early December, and though we're supposed to be long past wildfire season, the hills up and down the coast are ablaze. The hint of smoke hangs in the air, like a distant barbecue, or a warning.

"No one is talking to each other. Like Axl is super pissed at Simon, because he told his mom about the drinking thing, which he only did because he thought it was a funny story. He never thought his mom would call the freakin' school and report it. And Simon is pissed at Axl, because I don't even know why, and he's like, 'Even if we both get into Penn, we're totally not rooming together now,'" Levi says. His face has that fresh-from-Vail chap, and he's mussed his wet hair into spikes. I wonder when I'm next going to get him alone. Since Thanksgiving break, he's been either away snowboarding or with the fencing team on weekends, and his schedule is too packed for him to see me after school. I guess that's the price you pay for a fighting chance of getting into a school like Harvard—you sacrifice innumerable opportunities to hook up with your ready and willing girlfriend.

"Boring," Shola says, sipping from the LaCroix she tucked into her float's cupholder.

"Weird question: Did you guys have to submit a photo with your college applications?" I ask. I'm wearing a two-piece black tankini that shows only a sliver of skin between top and bottom, though my mom suggested I borrow one of her sexy white suits that has full side cutouts and connects in the middle with a gold O. Even in this one, I feel naked and exposed, and I hold myself low in the bucket curve of the raft.

"Of course not," Shola says.

"Not like a head shot or anything. Though I think we might have to put one in my athletic profile, of me in my fencing gear," Levi says, and then without even being discreet about it, he checks out my mother, who strides over in a tiny, hot-pink bikini, cell phone pressed to her ear.

At least she didn't wear her thong.

"Right," I say.

"Hold on, Candy," my mom says into the phone, and then she stops in front of me. Her toes are also painted a hot pink, and she wears a thin ankle bracelet and the sort of leather sandal you'd imagine came from a beach vendor in Mallorca, though they really came from Barneys. Her face is swallowed by enormous sunglasses and a giant straw hat—my mother takes no chances with sun damage. My guess is that the swimsuit and accessories and shoes and even the nail polish were all bundled together in her closet and labeled *pool day* by her stylist. "Sweetheart, don't forget we have a conference call with Dr. Wilson in half an hour."

"I couldn't forget if I wanted to. Carrie put five different alarm reminders on my calendar," I say, and blow out a puff of air. Most of the time, I'm happy to be the daughter of Joy Fields, and for all the privileges that come along with it. Today, I'd prefer she took herself elsewhere.

"Thank God for Carrie," she says, and then into the phone: "Thanks again for the Dr. Wilson reco. That man's a miracle worker."

"Who's Dr. Wilson?" Shola asks after my mother has finally walked away. My mom lounges on the opposite end of the pool, far enough away that we can't hear her chatting away to Aunt Candy, but close enough that we can see the long expanse of her tanned legs. "You okay?" Shola asks, redirecting my attention. She drops her voice to a whisper so Levi can't hear. "Is this about your ladyparts?"

"My ladyparts are fine, thank you very much," I whisper back. Then in my normal voice: "He's my college admissions counselor."

"Isn't Mrs. Oh everyone's college admissions counselor?" Shola asks.

"Yeah, but my parents hired him privately. To help 'package' me." I do gross air quotes and roll my eyes, to signal to her that I realize the whole thing is ridiculous.

"Do you have one too?" Shola asks Levi, her voice turning up in panic. "I thought Wood Valley recommends against them."

"I'm using the lady my sister used when she applied to

Harvard," Levi says. "She's the one who suggested I take up fencing a few years ago, because it's one of those sports that's not available everywhere."

"Your sister goes to Harvard?" Shola repeats. Although she likes Levi the person, because everyone likes Levi the person, she hates Levi the applicant. She calls him "an admission officer's wet dream."

"Went. She graduated last year," Levi says.

"So is this another one of those things everyone does and no one talks about? *Everyone* pays for a private college counselor even though we are not supposed to?" Shola asks.

"Not everyone," I say.

"This feels like the time I found out all those summer community service programs you guys do cost thousands of dollars, when you could, like, drive fifteen minutes to Skid Row for free," Shola says.

"Hey, I don't pay to work at the RRC," I say defensively.

"Didn't your parents give a giant donation last year?" Shola asks, and I regret telling her this fact, which, for the record, wasn't some quid pro quo to let me volunteer, but something I was genuinely proud of. Because of my parents, the Reading and Resource Center was able to hire another full-time coordinator and triple the number of new books in their library. "Sorry, that came out wrong," Shola says.

"My guy has that sleazy-car-salesman vibe. I kind of hate him." I paddle over to her so that our rafts are side by side. "You would definitely hate him. But, Shols, don't worry. You don't need some idiot holding your hand. You're going to get in everywhere."

"I really wish you'd stop saying that," Shola says, and

when she gently pushes my flamingo away from her uni-corn, I pretend not to notice.

"Great job on that essay, Chloe! Really unique perspective on your mom's career," Dr. Wilson says over the phone half an hour later. I'm in my bedroom, wrapped in a towel, while both of my parents are also on the line downstairs in my dad's office. I bet my mother is still in her bikini. Thank God we aren't on FaceTime.

"I appreciate that but I switched essays, remember? I wrote instead about discovering who I am in college?"

"Right, right, forgive me, of course. Yes, loved the new one. Even better than the one before. More honest," he says. "The real you."

Dr. Wilson is presumably somewhere on the East Coast, though for the life of me I can't remember where. Connecti-cut, maybe. I picture him outside, perhaps on the veranda of a country club, a gin and tonic in hand, a sweater tied dain-tily around his shoulders. Then I remember it's December and likely cold. I revise the image in my mind's eye. He's by a fire in a fancy lodge sipping bourbon. He's the kind of jerk who would wear loafers, without socks, and I bet when he goes on vacation, he shoots large animals and calls it a sport.

"Thanks," I mumble.

"We're all systems go at this point. I just need your com-mon app log on," he says.

"Why?"

"Because it's my job to make sure this all goes off with-out a hitch. That all the proper paperwork is in, all the boxes checked. I've learned from experience that it's best if I do it myself," he says. I hate his condescending tone, the insinuation that I can't manage to get my own applications in without somehow screwing it up.

"But it's done," I say. "All I really need to do is press submit. I was waiting for the final go-ahead from you."

"Chloe," my mom says in her warning tone, the one that means *stop being a pain in the ass.*

"This is how everyone does it. I do the final send-off. That way I can sleep at night knowing we made every deadline. Senior year at Wood Valley is no joke. Let me take this small thing off your plate," Dr. Wilson says. I don't bother arguing, because I see no harm in it. Maybe he'll have better mojo somehow.

"Okay, just please make sure you have the right essay," I say, and then give him my password.

"Of course," he says.

"So, wait, does that mean I'm done? Like done-done? I've officially applied to college?"

"Yup. I'll email you confirmation tomorrow morning when everything has been sent in, but yeah. You wait for the acceptances to roll in," he says, and I snort. Despite all the professional help and the SAT bump, none of us believe I'll have a large number of schools to choose from. My list, as Mrs. Oh has pointed out innumerable times, is full of mostly reaches. "You worked hard, Chloe. You should be proud of yourself."

"Thanks," I say, accepting a compliment I'm not sure I deserve. I sometimes think about what would have happened had I put in the hours over the last few years on my schoolwork, like Levi and Shola obviously do. I decide not to dwell on that. As our meditation teacher taught me, no need to stress about that which we cannot change.

"You can hang up and get back to your Saturday afternoon. I have some bookkeeping stuff to handle with your mom and dad," Dr. Wilson says.

"All right, thanks again." I tap the phone, as if to hang up, and then on impulse decide instead to continue listening. I'm not sure why. Maybe residual anger at my mother for flaunting her bikini in front of Levi? (Is it flaunting when that's how you look? Isn't my mother allowed to wear a bathing suit?) Or perhaps Dr. Wilson's casual dismissal chafed? Like I'm not central to this process.

"So yeah," Dr. Wilson says. "It's two hundred fifty k now, and two fifty on acceptance."

I assume I've misheard him. *Two hundred and fifty thousand dollars?* That can't be right. That's what *k* means, though, right? Thousands?

Are they talking about payments?

I'm not great at math, but that's more than double four years' tuition at a place like SCC. Dr. Wilson hasn't really been much of what my dad calls a "value add." It's not that hard to push the submit button on the common application. Even if he wrote the entire thing himself, which of course he didn't, *five hundred thousand dollars?* I feel sick.

"We make the checks out to that Horizons Unite and Cares International, right?" my dad asks.

"Yes. The underprivileged children thank you," Dr. Wilson says, and barks a laugh, which my parents awkwardly echo. "Plus, it's totally tax deductible."

That makes a whole lot more sense—my parents making a charitable donation—though it is far larger than what they normally give, and I don't understand why any of it's funny. Or why it would be conditional on my acceptance.

Just two weeks ago, my parents had a fight about buying a table at yet another fund-raiser Aunt Candy was throwing in San Francisco. The buy-in then was twenty grand. I know this because my dad kept repeating it over and over again: *Twenty grand, Joy, twenty grand. That ain't peanuts, especially for something to blow smoke up Candy's ass. We just gave to Chloe's reading thing. We're not like Charles. I've done the math. His money is so busy making money that, literally, when he pees he makes twenty grand.*

I know my parents are, relatively speaking, well-off. Most people might see us as rich. But we aren't rich-rich. We aren't Aunt Candy rich. Or even Xander's family rich. We don't have homes scattered around the globe or a private jet or a yacht. Why would they write a five-hundred-thousand-dollar check to Dr. Wilson's charity?

That's *half a million dollars.*

It makes no sense. I decide I must have misheard them. My head swims as I tune back in to the conversation.

"Nothing warms the cockles of my heart like the words *tax deductible*," my dad says, and this time my mom delivers her on-camera version of a laugh, which sounds like a box opened, an explosion of confetti. I can picture how she must look too—her eyes wide, white teeth gleaming, her neck pale and exposed, the delight of a mom seeing her toddler after a long day of work. A magazine once remarked that my mother had a Katharine Hepburn laugh, and I know back in New Jersey, when she was a waitress-slash-actress, she'd watch old movies and re-recite the lines because she couldn't afford acting classes. I bet she sat in front of a mirror and perfected that laugh, just as she perfected crying on cue, and the one-two punch line on sitcoms.

I think: *What the hell is going on?*

I think: *Maybe there are some things I don't need to know.*

CHAPTER THIRTY-FIVE

Now

Isla watches cable news on the television in the playroom, vacuuming up the new information. The headline JOY FIELDS FACING UP TO FORTY YEARS BEHIND BARS scrolls endlessly across the bottom of the screen.

"What would putting Joy Fields in jail actually accomplish? She's not dangerous. Wouldn't it be better for society if she were severely fined or forced to endow a scholarship for underprivileged kids? That seems more commensurate with the crime, surely," a talking head, a bald white guy with square tortoiseshell glasses argues. "Force her to turn that so-called charitable donation into an actual charity."

"First of all, in this country, it's supposed to be a fact that if you break the law, you suffer the consequences. But because Joy Fields is a white actress with a pretty smile, she doesn't have to serve time? No. Literally hundreds of thousands of people of color have been put away for so much longer for so much less. There's a mom of four kids in Oklahoma who is currently serving twelve years for marijuana possession," a white woman, with a Drybar blowout, argues back.

"But then isn't the argument that we should have less incarceration generally, not that we should put Joy Fields in prison?" the man argues.

"Maybe, but my point is that not until we see equal administration of the law, not until I see the mass release of African Americans from our nation's prison, will I start losing sleep over whether this overly entitled, overly privileged, cheating—"

Isla clicks the TV off.

"What were you watching?" I ask.

"You guys have lawyers to explain stuff to you. I have MSNBC," she says, matter-of-factly.

"How bad do you think—"

"Bad," she says, fast, unblinking.

"Do you agree with that woman? That Mom deserves to go to prison?" I don't add what we both are thinking. That if she thinks Mom does, then she probably thinks I do too.

"No. I mean, if she were some stranger, maybe? But she's Mom. So of course not."

"I get that, I think." Lately, when I lie on my bed and watch the chandelier sparkle, I dip my toe in that quicksand and let myself understand why everyone is so angry at us, how we became the focus of so much seething resentment. I try to let go and see this from the outside. How Shola might look at our case, or even some rando in Nebraska. I think it boils down to this: I already have too much I did nothing to earn, and then I went ahead and stole from someone who was running all the bases.

"I'm scared, though. I'm scared she's blowing her shot of this not ruining the rest of her life and ours. If she has to go away for, like, a year but that's it, she could do that. She could. We could handle that too," Isla says. Neither of us even bothers grappling with my mother's hypothetical innocence. We know she did it. Of course she did.

Or more accurately, they did. The only reason we don't have to contend with my dad's guilt is because he's likely to get away with it.

The question is, what's the most palatable punishment? Our circumstances don't allow us to tackle morality so much as practicality.

"But twenty? Or forty? That's insane," Isla says.

"I can't imagine it. Mom in an orange jumpsuit. Mom, not here."

"What she did, what we all did, was wrong," she says, and I can see her swallowing back tears. Strong, impenetrable Isla. "We shouldn't just get away with it."

"*You* didn't do anything," I say.

"I keep thinking about what it means to know something. Like whether the concept of knowing is something active or passive. When does something graduate from being a suspicion?" Isla brings her arms around her knees, turns herself into a girl ball. Leave it to my sister to boil down everything I've been thinking into a simple question. Even now, I haven't quite come out the other side. Kenny could lay out an argument on paper and prove to a court that there's little evidence I was in on my parents' plan. And yet, that's nowhere near as reassuring as it should be.

"Yeah, I've been thinking about that too. Though probably in a less smartypants way."

"I knew, I think. I mean, I didn't know-know. I couldn't explain it all like they do in the complaint. But I knew enough," Isla says, looking straight at me, deliberately holding eye contact.

"You didn't know. You couldn't have," I say.

"There was stuff on the printer." She nods, as if convincing herself this is the right thing to do, unburdening herself. Saying this out loud. Her confession. "I saw the pole vaulting picture. And I knew about the SATs. I heard them talking to Dr. Wilson."

"Stop. Let me call Kenny. We need to make sure you're protected." The prospect of my mom and me facing legal consequences is terrifying, but the idea of Isla being brought into this is unimaginable. I used to think that scene in the *Hunger Games*, when Katniss steps up and volunteers as tribute, was ridiculous. That she would risk almost certain death for her annoying little sister? Now I get it.

I'd go to prison for life to keep Isla out of this mess. I really would.

"I'm fine. Safe. Whatever. I can't be . . . you know, I'm too far removed. I did my research. I can't be held responsible for having dishonorable parents," she says with a shaky laugh.

"Why didn't you say something to me, then?" I think about how that conversation could have gone, if we could have avoided this mess in the first place.

"I tried."

My brain short-circuits for a minute, and then I remember. Thanksgiving break. Isla asked about my supposed ADHD and I thought she was being judgmental. How if she wasn't so good at test taking, she too would understand the pressure of the SAT. I had it all wrong. She knew we'd gone over the edge and was looking for me to help pull us back.

Did I know then about Proctor Dan?

Isla is talking about passively knowing, and I wonder if there is such a thing as aggressively, actively choosing *not* to know.

A 1440 was magic, a vision board made manifest, what felt like the work of God, not man.

But I've never believed in magic. Or vision boards. I'm still fifty-fifty on God.

I was, *am*, such an asshole.

"Did you like *Crime and Punishment*? The book, I mean." This is my way of telling her I know exactly the conversation she's talking about.

"Oh, I never got past page twenty."

"What? I saw you."

"I knew my reading it for fun would piss you off," Isla says, and I laugh and hit her with a throw pillow. "I should have stopped you guys. Or spoken up more. Then this never would have happened."

"Isl, you're the smartest person in this house and maybe the best, but it's not your job to keep us from . . ."

I stop, trying to think of the best way to put it.

"Cheating?" she asks. "Breaking the law?"

"Among other things, but yeah, that," I say. "You've done

nothing wrong. Do you hear me? Nothing. I'm not going to lie to you and say the same about Mom and Dad and me. But *you* did nothing wrong, no matter what you did or didn't know or whatever the word *know* even means."

I take a firm grip on her shoulders, force her to make eye contact. I don't want her to carry guilt on top of everything else. We screwed up enough of her life already.

I volunteer as tribute, I want to shout.

She's again in her llamacorn pajamas, and she looks delicate and small, the less-tough, more adorable version of my mother. I think about the rage I felt when I saw her reading Dostoyevsky. I feel shaken by my predictable pettiness.

"We never should have put you in this position in the first place. Okay?"

"Okay," she says.

"You deserve better than us," I say.

"Nah," she says.

"You do."

"Can I borrow your clothes when you go to prison?" she asks again.

"Isla!"

"Still not funny yet. Got it," she says, and then tackle-hugs me.

CHAPTER THIRTY-SIX

Then

"So tell me, how do you feel about Boston?" Levi asks. He bounds up to me in the hall, throws one arm around my shoulder. As usual, he's glowing. His cheeks are pink and recently warmed, and I want to rest the backs of my hands against them. I want to kiss his ears at their jaunty jagged tips. I wish we could find a cozy corner somewhere to make out—the back of the library, a janitor's closet—but this is real life, not a teen movie. We have exactly two minutes to get to English 4.

"Well, for one, I hate the Patriots. All that winning is boring. And then they had to go and cheat also? They suck," I say. "Boo."

"Okay, not team Brady. Got it."

"But they have the Liberty Bell, which is cool, even with the crack. I'm a sucker for a perfect imperfection," I say.

"That's Philly, not Boston."

"Duck tours. I love duck tours," I say triumphantly, looking up into Levi's perfect face. If it wasn't weird, I'd take out my phone and snap a selfie with him. Capture the two of us in this moment—him aglow, me basking vicariously—so I can have it to relish later, when this is inevitably over. I want to hold on to our casual flow, remember it beat by beat. "I took one in Boston once, and it was awesome, because they are both a car and a boat. Like a real-life Transformer."

"Okay, this got so off track. Let me start over: I got into Harvard!" he announces.

"What? Really? You got in? It's official?"

"I got in! It's done." I turn around to face him and he picks me up and swings me in a circle.

"Congratulations!" I bury my face in his neck. I plant ten tiny kisses and then I wish kisses were like seeds and that they'd grow so I could keep him. He'd normally be opposed to this sort of public display of affection—we hold hands at school and that's it—but today, *Harvard day*, he makes an exception. No wonder he's glowing.

"I can't believe it. I mean, I knew I had a shot, but I don't know. For the rest of my life, I'm going to get to say I went to Harvard." I don't remind him that he's getting a little ahead of himself and that he still needs to get through four years. Then again, unlike me and my SAT scores, I doubt he's worried that his acceptance is some sort of glitch. He belongs at Harvard. He'll do great there.

"I knew it. Never had a single doubt," I say. "And for what it's worth, I'd love any city you were in. I could even become a Patriots fan."

As soon as the words are out, I cringe. Both cheesy and presumptuous. Great. Levi and I haven't talked at all about what next year means for us. I'm assuming the worst-case scenario—sometime in the next six months, I'll get my heart smashed into a thousand pieces. Then I'll go off to college—probably somewhere far away from Boston, despite the fact that I wasn't joking and I do dig a good duck tour—and I'll be distracted by all the shiny newness of freshman year. Eventually, I'll get over Levi and he'll transform from a person into an indelible memory. He'll become the story I tell new friends when we stay up late into the night talking about our first loves.

Levi doesn't seem fazed by my uncharacteristic gushing.

"Harvard!" he says, like he still doesn't quite believe it. I spot Shola farther down the hall, and when she sees Levi, she comes running over.

"You got in?" she asks, eyes wide.

"I got in," he says, his grin so big it eats his whole beautiful face.

"Congrats. I'm really happy for you," Shola says, giving him a big hug. I'm sure on the inside she's jealous and rightly pissed off that she didn't get the benefit of applying early decision even though it's her first choice too.

There's still room for her at Harvard, of course, assuming they cough up enough financial aid. Last year, they took eight kids from Wood Valley, which means there should be about seven more spots.

"I heard Bodhi and Palmer got in too," Levi says. Okay, five more. Still, I have faith. One of those has to have Shola's name on it.

"That's great," she says. I look over at my best friend in awe. She's either an amazing actress, or she's legitimately happy for him. I'm floored by her generosity. I almost say, *It will be you next,* but instead I grab Shola's hand and squeeze, and she squeezes back, and we have a tiny conversation that way.

Me saying, *It will be you soon,* and her saying, *Fingers crossed.*

"Fingers and toes," I whisper out loud. And she nods and closes her eyes, like I've said a prayer.

CHAPTER THIRTY-SEVEN

Now

My mother turns fifty with little fanfare. We don't celebrate in Mexico as originally planned. Instead, she spends the day in a federal court in Boston, where she officially pleads not guilty. I still don't quite understand why the case is happening in Boston and not here, but since my dad's fear of the billable hour has finally sunk in, I decide it's unnecessarily expensive to ask Kenny. Instead, I make a mental note to ask Isla to explain it to me later.

I watch my mom walk into the courthouse on CNN and then again on MSNBC. She wears a boring black suit, loose-fitting, purchased specifically for this event and never to be worn again, and fake chunky glasses. She left her supersized diamond engagement ring at home, and so she wears only her simple gold wedding band and no other jewelry. Her nails are painted a pale pink, her hair is blown out straight with the ends tucked under—no sexy beach waves—and again she dons the makeup-no-makeup look. The lawyers told her to dress conservative and harmless, "like a mother, not a Hollywood actress," whatever that means.

What is a mother supposed to look like? I wonder. I remember last fall when my mom pretended to make pancakes for *Marie Claire*, how she rocked an apron and red heels. I remember Paloma later complaining that she wasn't Gwyneth enough—another version of motherhood altogether, all-natural, organic, condescending. I think about my real mom in a fluorescent bikini, nagging me about our call to Dr. Wilson, reading scripts on the couch, tucking me into bed every night with an *I love you.*

Even when she's facing felony charges, my mother's forced to play a role. If Shola were here, she'd lecture about the dangers of performative femininity, how my mom is stuck playing a game she can never win. How we all are, in our own way.

I wish my mother could go to court in Wood Valley sweatpants and her hair tied back in a silk scarf, the look that most seems like home to me.

I wish my mother had taken the plea bargain and then this court appearance would be an ending, not a beginning.

I wish this didn't feel like one more terrible mistake at the end of a long line of them.

My father is in Boston with my mom for moral support, though all of the lawyers collectively agreed that it was better if he stayed back in the hotel room. Safer for him to remain under the radar, rather than remind the prosecutor of his existence. Mr. Spence accompanies my mother into the courthouse, arms linked at the elbow, guiding her past the bevy of cameras. My mom follows Paloma's instructions, which have changed course since the yoga studio incident—this time my mother is supposed to keep her eye-line down, remain serious and demure. Play it "accidentally in-over-your-head and scared," Paloma said, and for maybe the first time, Paloma's instructions 100 percent match reality. I imagine this is exactly how my mother feels.

There will be no tossing off catchphrases this time. None of us is at our "bestest."

The house feels empty with my mom and dad and Mr. Spence away and the rest of the lawyers returned to their own offices for the time being. Even Cristof and Carrie were given a few days off. The paparazzi are no longer camped out in front of our house, and since I still refuse to venture out into the world, Isla and I are left with a credit card for Postmates. Our only instructions are to keep the alarm set around the clock and to occasionally feed ourselves, preferably with a vegetable or two. My mom, in a moment of Gwynethness, also left me her essential oils kit on my nightstand—she has her travel set—to rub on my wrists for stress relief.

Use as needed, sweet pea, she'd written in a note.

While Isla's at school, I wander from room to room, lonely. I let my fingers drag along the spines on the bookcase but can't bring myself to read anything. I switch on Netflix and then turn it off again. Too many choices. I click over to Instagram and create a fake account—I find a black-and-white picture of Dostoyevsky to use as my profile picture, and I set my location as Siberia. I feel ever-so-slightly clever, until I remember I still haven't read the book. Maybe the reference makes no sense at all.

I click over to Levi's feed and learn that today is Wood Valley Giving Day. He posts a picture of him and Simon and Axl. In it, all three of them look sweaty and hold nail guns in the air like Charlie's Angels. It's supposed to be a day of community service—building houses for low-income families—but looking at Instagram, I can see my classmates are filled with that restless, excited end-of-school year energy and that they're doing more chatting and selfie-taking than working. I wonder if people are still talking about me, or if they've moved on to more important matters. Picking college roommates. Dress-shopping for prom.

It's a weird feeling—this desire to be forgotten. I've spent my whole life wondering about the opposite. If I could find a way to leave behind a mark, to move beyond my own mediocrity. If I could one day be more than simply my famous mother's daughter.

The doorbell rings, and I freeze. My brain scrolls through worst-case scenarios: A reporter. No, the FBI here to arrest me for real. I pull up Kenny's number on my cell. I decide if it's the cops, they'll at least give me a chance to call my lawyer.

I curse my parents for not having a peephole, switch off the alarm, keep one hand on the panic button. I open the door a tiny crack. No worst-case scenarios, only best. A vision manifested.

Shola.

"You're here," I say, my eyes filling with tears. What I think but don't say, because I realize it's not fair, is: *What took you so long?*

"I'm here," she echoes, and follows me inside.

. . .

We end up in the kitchen, on the high stools, where we've spent countless hours together. This is the first time we don't know what to say to each other.

"I thought you'd be at Giving Day," I say, and then mentally kick myself for wasting time. What I want to say and on repeat, forever and ever: *I'm sorry, I'm sorry, I'm sorry. You have to forgive me.* And also: *Please don't leave me behind.*

"I went, and then, I don't know, I left. I knew your mom had her thing today, so I thought I might catch you alone," she says.

"You did," I say.

"How's it going?" she asks.

"Shitty," I say, though that's the understatement of the year. *Shitty* is the word I'd use when I blew a test or had bad cramps. Surely, there must be a better way to describe how I feel. What's the word for *shitty on steroids*? What's the word for realizing even your own mom and dad think you are too stupid to function? What's the word for wondering if you deserve to live? I should ask Linda to make "synonyms for 'shitty on steroids'" flash cards.

"My parents wouldn't let me call or text or come over. They don't know I'm here," she says. "It's funny—I mean, not funny ha-ha, but ironic—because they used to be so excited that we were friends. *These are the kind of people you should be mingling with.*" Shola drops her voice low and does her best Nigerian accent, the one she always uses when she's imitating her father, and I feel a pang of hurt. Even Mr. Balogun, who stuffs me silly with jollof rice when I go to Shola's

253

apartment and sent me a virtual congratulations card with dancing hedgehogs when I got into SCC, has abandoned me.

I get it, sort of. My exile. We are judged by the company we keep. Their job is to protect Shola, just as my parents' job is to protect me. But it's not a zero-sum game, parenthood. That's what we keep forgetting.

"They're not the only ones who don't want me around. Mrs. Oh doesn't want me to come back to school. She gave me a packet of work to finish at home so I can graduate."

"Lucky," Shola whines, half joking. "School has been . . . weird without you."

"Yeah?" I ask, not fishing exactly, but I need acknowledgment that our friendship was real, that I have not made up the last six years. Maybe I was never as important to Shola as she was to me; maybe I was simply a placeholder at school until she got to go home to her real friends. Shola shakes her head, like she doesn't want to talk about it, or maybe to say, *That's not why I'm here.* She's harder to read suddenly, or maybe it's that I suddenly trust myself—or us—less.

"I can't stop thinking about the fact that all I used to want was to switch families with you. In seventh grade I'd have this recurring dream that you and I *Freaky Friday*'d. No Sunday church. No having to watch out for the Littles. No doing my homework before I could turn on a screen. In the dream, I'd walk into your mother's closet and borrow everything, and I'd be the one who got to ride horses. I mean, you had a literal pony! Do you remember that? Who has a pony?"

"He died," I say inanely, because I don't know what else

to say. I did have a pony. Well, actually, a horse. I liked the petting him part way more than the riding.

"I outgrew that in the last year or two. Even before this all happened, I knew to be ashamed of those feelings. Just because you were so rich and had everything, you guys weren't better. Or even happier actually. I knew that," Shola says, her eyes watery, but tears do not fall. Shola will not let them.

"Remember that day you and Levi told me you both had private college admissions counselors?" Shola asks.

"You were astride your favorite unicorn float. You can have it, you know." I don't tell her that recently, on one of my insomniac zombie strolls, I went outside and deflated it in the middle of the night. I was tired of looking at its jaunty horn, tired of thinking how sad it must be without Shola around to ride it. I don't tell her this, because I realize it's both insane and embarrassing.

"To put where, Chlo?" Her voice holds that slow simmer, and I feel like an idiot all over again, forever and always. Shola doesn't have a pool.

I am the monster, I think.

"I went home that day and I cried. I hadn't let myself think about it before you said it, but I must have known that you had a private counselor even if you didn't talk about it. I mean, of course you did. You paid for everything else," Shola says, and then sees my stricken face, and despite everything, she tries to spare my feelings. "No offense."

"None taken," I say. There's no point in being offended by the truth. She's right. I had tutors and specialists and advisors, long before I ever met Dr. Wilson. My mom once took me with her to see a special alternative doctor to make sure we were both pooping in the optimal position. At the time, it seemed like a totally valid use of our time and energy; now, I wonder if too much money renders you helpless. Leaves you feeling like you can't even take a crap on your own without consultation with an "expert."

Guilt fills me; I'm saturated with it, because I really see us from the outside looking in. Our brazen entitlement. How we thought the normal rules didn't apply. How we thought we had earned all of our own good fortune and manipulations.

"You always used to say that my family was weird, and I used to laugh, because we are weird, but I think what you really meant was *your family is gross and self-indulgent*. I realize we are that too," I say.

I examine us from Shola's vantage point.

Our deck was stacked, even before we stacked it some more.

The bright line of well-off and super-rich we drew between us and Aunt Candy would be meaningless to her.

I've spent the last six years feeling, if not envious of Shola, something closely related to it, believing that things came so much more easily to her. Not money, of course, but everything else: talent, brains, joy, likeability. All the things nobody could buy for me. I bet Shola's never once sat over a toilet and thought, *Am I doing this right?*

"That's not fair. I loved your family. But you betrayed me. Do you even get that? Why I'd feel that way? Personally betrayed?" Shola asks, but it's not a question. It's a rebuke. And so I don't say, *Yes, yes, I get that*, even though I do.

I listen, which is what Shola tried to teach me to do years ago when she told me I needed to examine my white privilege. *To be an ally you need to be a better listener*, she'd said. I had been too shy to say *I don't even know what an ally is.* Later, I looked it up on Google.

"Like didn't you guys realize that you were obviously screwing over people like me who worked so much harder and had so much further to go and who had earned our spots? I think you did realize that but you didn't care. You thought, *I deserve this. I deserve everything. I deserve the whole world even at everyone else's expense.* But here's the thing, Chloe: You don't. You don't deserve everything."

The feelings of shame that I've been riding for weeks overtake me again. I start to shake with it.

"I don't know what you knew or didn't know, and this is the tip of the iceberg, but it's clear you knew this part: ADHD and extra time on the SAT? Seriously, Chloe? We once played Xbox for ten hours straight. You do not have ADHD." Shola slaps her hands on the counter, and the sound reverberates through the house.

"I know." I keep my voice small, because I am small. I should be folded up and recycled. Come back as something more useful.

"And because of you, it's going to be harder for people who legitimately have a disability—"

"I know." I hold her eye contact, even though I'm crying openly and want nothing more than to disappear, to run away, to leave the rest of her words unheard.

I will stand here and hear her. I do not need to make this easy on myself.

Easy, it turns out, gets you nowhere.

Easy, it turns out, gets you facing a felony charge.

"At some point, you could have said, *No. I'm not doing this. We've finally gone too far. This is wrong.* And you didn't do that, did you?" Shola asks, and she looks at me almost hopefully. Like maybe she thinks it's possible I did try to stop it and my efforts failed. Shola wishing the best about me.

I cannot lie to my best friend.

"No, I didn't. I did nothing."

"I thought so," she says, and her face crumbles. I want to reach out my hand to touch her, I want to explain myself, and yet, I don't know how to do that. I consider saying, *I aggressively chose not to know, which isn't the same as knowing, but maybe it is; maybe it's the same thing after all.*

"I'm sorry," I say, more empty words. Useless nonsense. "For everything."

"I don't even want your apology. You know what's a horrible feeling? Realizing your best friend isn't the person you thought she was." Shola's eyes flash, and my insides tremble. I've always suspected a time would come, when her world got bigger and she had access to other, cooler people beyond Wood Valley. When she finally had more choices, no doubt she'd ask herself: *Wait, why am I friends with her again?* But not so soon, and definitely not like this.

"I've lost everything. Please, you have to forgive me. I don't know who I am—"

Shola pointedly looks around. At the oversized house, the backyard pool, the fact that I've poured her a glass of water in a thick crystal goblet. She points to our two refrigerators, one whose sole purpose is to store sparkling water in glass bottles for my mother.

"You've lost everything?" she asks incredulously.

"If you're not my friend anymore, then yeah. I've lost everything," I say, and hold her stare. She must understand that all of this is only stuff. But then I realize I'm the one who doesn't understand. It's not about the stuff—those are markers, signals, the million and one ways we let the world know where we stand. They are the flex but they are also the muscle.

After all, my mother was able to hire a literal army of lawyers to protect her.

"I'm not going to SCC, obviously. My mom's probably going to jail. Levi's whatever. Other than Isla, all that I have left that I care about is you."

"Levi's going to prom with Sophie."

"Oh." I didn't know this and yet of course I did. Levi and Sophie again, confirmed. I let this sink in. It hurts way less than I'd thought it would. A press on a minor bruise. Another recent revelation born out of this whole mess: Levi was a fun distraction, never the real thing.

The loss of Shola, though, would be a septic wound. She is my person.

Who knew first loves could be platonic? How did I not see that?

I allow myself to picture it, for a moment. An alternative future. One day making new friends, maybe not at SCC or even at college, but somewhere, a future me telling the story of me and Shola, my first real friend, my first true partner.

I hope it ends better than I fear. I hope it doesn't end at all. That it's the story I tell before she comes to visit me in my new, wholly theoretical one day grown-up life so I can say to my new friends, *I can't wait for you to meet her.*

"I miss you," I say, the tears falling again, because I already know where this is going. I am being broken up with. I can tell by the way her eyes keep slipping to the floor. I can tell by the way my heart feels sliced right down the middle, a clean incision.

"Chloe, you pretended to be half Latina on your application." I close my eyes because I can no longer look at her face. It's too painful.

This, it turns out, is the only thing we've been accused of that is technically not illegal. Immoral, grounds for rescinding my acceptance, disgusting, wrong, shameful—all of these things, yes, despite my father's belief that he's part Argentinian. But it's not the charge that will put my mother or me in prison. The bribery will.

But with Shola standing here, I realize it will be the charge that makes me lose my best friend.

I don't blame her.

There's no bouncing back from the dirty truth, no way to spin my way out of this one. I cannot morph back into the person Shola thought I was. Who she'd hoped I'd be. The one who laughed but understood when she wouldn't let me copy her homework before class.

I refuse to say *I didn't know.* I will not keep beating that meaningless drum.

"I can't do this to myself anymore. Can't keep doing this. Being friends with you, it's not . . . it's not okay for me."

"Shol," I say, my eyes still closed.

I hear but don't see her get off the stool and walk away from me.

"Shol!" I call again, but she keeps walking.

All the way out the front door, which she closes behind her, gently.

I picture her on the other side, resting her back against it.

Instead of keeping out the zombies, though, Shola's keeping them in.

And then I think about sneaky side doors, how the zombies will always get out anyway.

With the soft click of the latch, it's official.

I have lost my best friend.

CHAPTER THIRTY-EIGHT

Then

Dr. Wilson sends final confirmation that all my applications have been filed. His email is short and to the point. *In.*

That's all it says: In.

It's official. I've applied to college.

My mother takes that as permission to treat my acceptance at SCC as inevitable, as if applying is synonymous with being admitted. The last thing she was this sure of was that Brad Pitt movie that fell through.

I refuse to get my hopes up, though I secretly share her dream. I loved SCC when we visited, I love LA, and though I'd never admit this out loud to my family, I love the idea of sticking close to home.

Maybe my life doesn't have to change all that dramatically next year. Unlike Shola, who at night likes to text about all the things she's looking forward to next year—no longer sharing a room with the Littles, taking an Intro to Philosophy class, no more Wood Valley jerks giving her looks about her clothes—I still can't quite wrap my head around graduation and what comes next for me. I feel overwhelmed when I think about all the new responsibility that will be mine alone to bear—figuring out freshman requirements and dining hall cards and the social hierarchy. How do you know what books you need? What if I'm randomly assigned a roommate with questionable hygiene and a clashing color scheme?

Levi, like Shola, has already graduated in his mind. He's taken to wearing a disturbing amount of Harvard gear, and on the increasingly rare occasion when we spend time together, all he can talk about is the fall. There's no mention of us or of me visiting or even of the two of us keeping in touch when he monologues about the classes he's going to take, the famous professors he'll meet, where he'll do his year abroad, all while he has one hand up my shirt.

I get the hint. We are temporary.

Admittedly, I understand this desire to fast-forward—when a big change is coming, it's human nature to want to get there already—but lately, I find myself out of step with my friends. I want to slow down time and savor the months we have left together. Our lives up to now have been full of firsts, and suddenly, almost without warning, they seem packed with lasts.

I want to float in the pool with Shola and play beer pong at Xander's and kick back at the Koffee Kart, because soon we won't get to do any of that. These inexorable leaps forward give me whiplash. It's winter break, which means I'll blink and soon it'll be my own acceptances and rejections, prom and graduation, and then, of course, goodbye, goodbye, goodbye.

Tonight, though, I put these thoughts aside, because it's me and Levi and Shola and Axl and Simon and Mateo, that guy from Brentwood Country Day, in lounge chairs in my backyard, making one more memory while my parents are away for the weekend at that Aunt Candy fund-raiser in San Francisco my dad was so annoyed about.

We're all still here.

We drink the lukewarm beers someone nicked from their parents' fridge, and Shola puts on Oville and hooks her phone up to the speakers. Axl keeps threatening to jump into the pool.

"Let's make a pact to do this again next year. Let's all get together over winter break," I say. I'm sitting between Levi's legs, and he trails his fingers up and down the sides of my arms. *This*, I think. *Hold on to this while you can.*

"No way," Axl says, and I notice he's had both of his ears pierced with large diamond studs, a weird choice considering the rest of his style is uber-preppy, and I wonder if he did this to distinguish himself from Simon. "Once I leave, I'm leaving for good. Not coming home for break. Not coming home ever."

"Why?" I ask.

"Have you never met my mom? Once I graduate, it will be peace out, bitches." I picture Axl's mom. She has one of those generic *Real Housewives* faces you see on women around here—duck lips and taut skin and lush fake lashes as thick as brush bristles. A conscious choice to look a little weird, instead of the far more terrifying option, to God forbid look old. She also has that amateur cage fighter body that advertises its restlessness: *I don't work—I work out.*

Thick, cut shoulders and tightly wound. Minus that rumor about her calling Mrs. Oh's office to report Simon, she's always seemed perfectly nice, if a little sad.

"I may not be home for break," Shola says, and I see Mateo dart a glance at her, and I wonder if he likes Shola for real, not in a hook-up-every-couple-of-weeks-at-Xander's-parties way. I wonder if he feels about Shola like I do about Levi—that we'll take what we can get while we can get it. The thought makes me depressed for both of us.

"Of course you'll be home for break," I say, and I hear the slight aggression in my tone and try to shake it off. "You *have* to come home."

"If I'm on the East Coast, I might not be able to afford to. Those flights aren't cheap around the holidays," Shola says.

"Right." I decide later I'll offer her my frequent flyer miles or to float her the cost of the ticket, but not in front of everyone. Knowing Shola, she'll refuse. But I can't imagine saying goodbye to her until next summer. We've hung out every day for the last six years. We can't be expected to go cold turkey.

"Harvard's winter break is—" Levi says, but he doesn't get to finish his sentence, because Simon walks over, picks him up, and throws him in the pool. Everyone else spontaneously applauds.

I guess I'm not the only one who's had enough of Levi's Harvard talk.

CHAPTER THIRTY-NINE

Now

"GossipPolice says Mom and Dad are on the verge of divorce," Isla says while we eat pizza on the floor of the screening room, like we used to when we were little. This is how we'd spend every Friday night before I started at Wood Valley—Dad would pop popcorn in the old-fashioned machine and Isla and I would watch Disney movies down here.

"You know better than to listen to GossipPolice," I say, distracted. I keep hearing the soft click of Shola walking out the door. *Click, click, click*. "Who's their source?"

"Someone 'in the family's inner circle.' Probably Hudson," she says glumly, and while I wish I could tell her that's an unfair leap, I too suspect Hudson has long ago replaced the phone we stole and has been planting stories all over town for cash. Two weeks ago, in a piece also sourced to our "inner circle," GossipPolice claimed that my mother's hair was falling out because of stress over the scandal; that one, which took such clear aim at her biggest insecurity, *had* to be him.

Isla and I are watching cable news again. We've stopped expecting updates from our parents, who, when anything breaks—additional people charged, additional people pleading out—need to immediately consult with their lawyers and don't have time to give us a full download.

CNN tends to be quicker, less sugarcoated.

"Mom and Dad are fine," I say. "I mean, not fine-fine. None of this is fine. But solid. They're solid."

"Stop saying *fine* and *solid*. You're freaking me out more."

"They're not getting divorced," I say, and reach across her for a napkin.

"Holy shitballs!" Isla screams, and my heart plummets into my stomach. This is how things are: We live on high alert. There's always farther to fall. "Look!"

Isla points to the screen. The headline along the bottom reads: COLLEGE ADMISSIONS SCANDAL: POLICE WERE TIPPED OFF BY BILLIONAIRE IN LEGAL TROUBLE. A tall man walks into a courthouse holding up a leather briefcase to shield his face. Rookie move, as I'm sure they already have hundreds of other images of him all teed up to use next.

"So?" I ask. My dad likes to enumerate all the things he'd do to the guy who tipped off the feds as payback for ruining our lives.

I couldn't care less who the informant is.

I think it's pretty clear we ruined our own lives.

"That's Charles." Two pictures of Charles, Aunt Candy's husband, who we've never called Uncle even though we've known him forever, fill the screen. In the picture on the left, he's smiling with his arm around George W. Bush. In the one on the right, he's ringing a bell at the New York Stock

Exchange. In both, he looks tanned and tired, the kind of dude with manicured nails and an ulcer.

"CNN has learned that Charles Bonaparte, billionaire president and CEO of the hedge fund Napoleon, tipped off prosecutors to the college admissions scandal a year ago. Reports say that he offered the information in exchange for leniency in his own legal troubles, as he is facing charges of tax evasion and money laundering," the silver-haired reporter says. "Apparently, Bonaparte became aware of the nationwide scheme when Dr. Wilson, the mastermind behind the scandal, offered to bribe a tennis coach at Yale to help Bonaparte's son get into the university. Bonaparte claims that he turned the offer down, using Dr. Wilson only for his legitimate college admissions services, and that his son gained entry to Yale on his own merits."

"Mom's going to freak," I say, my heart sinking. "Also, 'own merits' my ass."

"Sources report that Yale is currently reviewing all transcripts and applications of students who may have been illegally admitted, and at least one student has been expelled," the reporter continues.

"No wonder Aunt Candy hasn't even called," Isla says.

"Were we set up? I mean, if he tipped them off a year ago, Aunt Candy knew exactly who Dr. Wilson was. Did she recommend him knowing that the feds were listening?" This is, of course, a silly question, because though Isla usually has all the answers, there's no way she can have this one. As I've come to learn from my mom's middle-of-the-night murmurings, it's not like Candy has the happiest of marriages. Who knows how much she knew?

As I understand it, the biggest piece of evidence the feds have against my mother is a wiretapped conversation between her and Dr. Wilson in which he manipulated her into reciting their plan out loud. My dad happened to have a meeting that day, which is the only reason he isn't facing charges too.

I decide it truly doesn't matter why Aunt Candy connected us to Dr. Wilson. That feels too much like looking for a loophole to our own culpability.

"I don't know," Isla says. "Maybe Aunt Candy didn't know."

"What does that even mean? 'Didn't know'?" I ask, and we both dissolve into giggles, and then, as the report flashes photos of my mother on the screen, we sober up.

"Poor Mom," Isla says, and I wonder if she's finally softening. "I mean, Aunt Candy is her person."

"Dad is her person. I'm her person," I say, then add as an afterthought: "*You're* her person."

Isla smirks. Okay, fine. We both know Isla is not her person. Her mini-me, maybe, but not her person.

"Maybe she has a few people. You can have a few people," she says, and that sweep of sadness whenever I think of Shola takes hold of me again.

"It's good to have backup," I say.

"I'm sorry about Shola."

"Me too. She's right, though. I don't think I'd forgive me."

"It's not like you killed anyone."

"I killed people's dreams," I say with a teary half-smile, and she nods, because it's kinda true. "It's so big, the scale of it, what it all meant, and I don't know how I didn't realize that when it was happening. I was so clueless. I should have listened to you."

My phone chimes and I see that my Signal group is active again. After they went quiet in the wake of all the plea bargaining, I found myself missing them. Beyond my sister, they're the closest thing I've had to friends since this mess began.

TheIgster: That dude deserves a beatdown. How dare he?

Slyse: Right? What a POS

PhinnyB: We were going to be found out somehow eventually. If it wasn't him, it would have been someone else

ALC: My therapist says I need to learn from this experience. That maybe this is a good thing that happened to all of us. A wakeup call

Slyse: Screw your therapist

TheIgster: I wish I could screw my therapist. She's smokin'

ALC: Ew

TheIgster: Why'd a billionaire need Dr. Wilson anyway? Why didn't he buy a freakin' building? That's what I keep telling my parents they should have done

PrettyPen: I wish I was a billionaire. I lost my LipPlump endorsement deal. My career is over

Slyse: Being an influencer is not a real career

PrettyPen: Tell that to my seven million subscribers

ALC: Who added Penny back on the thread?

PrettyPen: Up yours, bitches

CHAPTER FORTY

Then

"You got in somewhere?" Cesar asks when I walk into the Reading and Resource Center with a big gummy smile. He knows that over the last two weeks, I've been rejected from ten different schools. One by one, I've logged on to an admissions page, hopeful and expectant, and I've been met with a variation on the theme *We regret to inform you* . . . Each time, instead of marinating in my parents' disappointment, I've gotten into my car and driven to hang out with Cesar. He always greets me with the handshake we made up, which he treats as a matter of utmost importance—a complicated slap, fist-bump, foot-tap routine that ends with a tweak of each other's noses. Afterward, though it's not part of our choreography, Cesar rests his forehead in my elbow, a gesture that reminds me of Fluffernutter in its unconditional affection.

With Cesar, I don't feel like a reject.

"I did! AIU, baby!" I say. Honestly, I know very little about AIU—it wasn't on our college tour last summer—but that doesn't seem to matter so much. It's likely my only option. The only other school left to hear from is SCC, which was a long shot to begin with and now, in the wake of so many nos, seems like an impossibility. Mrs. Oh told me that Dr. Wilson's application strategy was too risky: *You can't only reach up. You need at least one safety unless you're okay with the possibility of a gap year, which come to think of it might be a great idea for you.* Since, unsurprisingly, my parents are not on team gap year—"No way," my dad said—I threw in the extra application she recommended just in case.

"Too bad you can't go to Hogwarts," Cesar says, thrusting this next volume of Harry Potter in my hand even before I have time to shrug off my backpack. "Then again, I mean, what's the point of anything if you're a Hufflepuff."

"Dude, Hufflepuffs rock." I grin at him. He's too young to take the Pottermore Sorting Hat test online, and I haven't been able to bring myself to bend J. K. Rowling's rules, not even for Cesar. As a result, he's been able to nurture the fantasy of children everywhere that he's a Gryffindor, just like Harry. Today he's wearing the Gryffindor Quidditch T-shirt I bought him.

"Where's AIU?" A shyness creeps into his voice. Like every other part of my life, my impending departure seems to sit heavy in the air, like a chore I've been putting off.

"Arizona." I get up to circle it on the dry-erase map of the United States that hangs on one wall of our favorite reading corner. We like the overstuffed chairs on this side best, because as Cesar says, they have more oomph.

"That's far." My heart tugs. I've promised to read to him over FaceTime while I'm away—we still have the rest of the series to finish—but of course it won't be the same. I've spent more hours after school here than I have anywhere else these last few years, and I'm going to miss our low-key afternoons together.

Still, I didn't expect Cesar to feel sad already.

Surprisingly, my parents have taken the news well. No tears or panic attacks or any of the *What are we going to tell people?* I expected. They haven't even called to yell at Dr. Wilson, which is what I assumed would be my dad's MO, especially after the ridiculous amount of money they donated to his charity. My mom keeps telling me to chill—that's the word she uses, *chill*—and claims SCC is my school. Says we put it on the vision board. Says she's known from the moment we stepped on campus for a visit last summer that it's where I belong. I've listened to this optimism for months, which is really just magical thinking because she doesn't want me far away. After the Week of Rejection, I'm done. In fact, I'm practically looking forward to crossing this last school off my list today so we can all move on.

I can't wait to burn that freaking vision board in our fire pit in the backyard. Make s'mores on its ashes. Maybe tonight I'll order an AIU sweatshirt online, or two, one for me and one for Cesar, a size too big so he can grow into it.

"You'll still be one of my backups, right? Even if you're in Arizona?" he asks. Our conversation in the fall feels like forever ago. According to Rita, ICE has been ramping up its raids on immigrant communities all over the country. I haven't heard of it directly impacting any of the kids at the Reading and Resource Club, though of course, it impacts them every single day in the form of a constant, low-level trauma.

I don't let myself think too much about what it must be like for Cesar's mom to move through the world so unprotected and powerless, to know that if she were to be swept up, she'd have no ability to fight back. No money for a lawyer. No way to stay with Cesar. My impression is that she'd likely be immediately deported.

I don't let myself think too much about the reasons behind all this—how she came to this country pregnant at the age I am now, under the most desperate of circumstances, fleeing not only poverty but also violence. How it was this wobbly life for them or none at all. How that's not a choice she should be punished for, but a success story to be celebrated.

I wouldn't be capable of doing what she did—what she *does*—should I have been born in El Salvador instead of Beverly Hills. She works three jobs.

I think about my parents' donation to Dr. Wilson's charity for "underprivileged children," which is so general as to mean almost nothing. I say a silent prayer that it's going to an organization that will help families like Cesar's or to somewhere like RAICES, which helps reunite families separated at the border.

"Of course. I'm always here for you, even if I'm not here-here," I say, and wonder if this is what Cesar's mom says to him, too, to make him feel better about the possibility of her being taken. Cesar once showed me the laminated card he keeps in his pocket at all times, like a security blanket. It has the telephone numbers of two distant cousins, one who lives here in Los Angeles, the other in Texas, backup plans one and two for where he'd go live should his mom be deported. It also has Rita's number, his first-grade teacher's, his grandma's back in El Salvador, and then, at the very bottom, mine. Of course, Cesar's mom has never told me outright she's undocumented—that would be too big a risk—but I've known her and Cesar for four years. It would take a leap of active ignorance for me not to understand why he carries that card in his pocket, what he means when he says *backup*. "You know that, right?"

When I think about that list—and despite my best efforts, I often do—I cry.

"Yup, and that's why I'm willing to break my No Hufflepuff rule for you," he says. He opens the book for me to start reading, but then he closes it and turns to me instead. He puts out a fist for one last bump. "Congrats, Chlo. I'm really proud of you."

"You sure you want to do this?" Shola asks after I tell her my new plan, which I devised during English 4 while Mrs. Pollack droned on about *The Picture of Dorian Gray*—another book I haven't read, this time because I have no interest in spending 320 pages with a spoiled narcissist. I want to spare myself the drama of having to watch my parents feel the sucker punch of my last rejection. I want to check my SCC application online with Shola during free period instead of waiting till later. "Your mom's going to be mad. She's told me you're going to SCC, like, no less than five times."

We're in the far corner of the library, away from prying eyes, at the computer station. Because of the giant screens, if I cry, the only person who will witness it is my best friend. Later, I'll seek out Cesar, take him for ice cream to celebrate that I'm officially going to AIU, which, according to *US News & World Report*, ranks 115th in the nation. That's pretty good.

"Exactly. She's going to be devastated. This way I don't have to see her disappointment in real time." After my rejection is confirmed, I'll send my parents a text that says *SCC a no. I'm really sorry but go AIU!* Maybe I'll throw in a sunglass-face emoji.

So far, Shola's been accepted to six schools—three UCs, Columbia, Stanford, and UPenn—and rejected by only one: Princeton. She has not yet heard from Harvard or Yale. She'll be checking SCC at the same time I am, though of course she's not nervous. For her, the only question is whether they'll give her enough scholarship money.

"On the count of three?" Shola asks.

"Okay." We navigate to the landing page, and I stumble a minute, trying to remember my password.

"One, two, three," I say, and we click. At first, when the page loads, I keep my eyes closed. I'm not ready, I decide. I can't handle another *We regret to inform you* . . . I don't want to let my parents down, by text or otherwise.

"Seriously?" Shola says, disappointment in her voice. "I got wait-listed. I thought I might get a full ride and I got wait-listed? Well, that sucks."

"Sorry, Shol," I say, but I don't look at her, because my eyes are still closed. If Shola didn't get in, obviously I didn't either. I'm tempted to click over to Instagram and never look. Turn the SCC admissions page into Schrödinger's cat, which is one thing I actually remember from physics last year. Basically, the idea is if you put a cat in a box and close it, before you open it again, the cat is both alive and dead simultaneously. If you don't know which is true, then both are true. I want to keep SCC like that—dead and alive.

But I am not a coward. I can do this. I'll go to Arizona and live happily ever after in the dry desert heat. I'll buy a large sun hat and new Tom Ford sunglasses and steal my mom's Mallorca sandals. I'll join a sorority and sip margaritas by a pool.

I open my eyes, stare at the screen. *Congratulations! On behalf of the Southern California College, it is with great pleasure that we offer you a place . . .*

Wait, what?

I read it again.

"I got in," I say, turning to Shola. She looks at me, stunned, and then, without missing a beat, pastes a giant smile on her face. I wonder if she's ever had to do that for me before, swallow her own envy, but I'm too overcome to dwell on the question.

"Oh my God, I got in." I stand up, throw my arms in the air in triumph.

"I'm so happy for you," Shola says. This is why she's my best friend. Because even at this moment, when the inexplicable forces of the universe somehow let me into SCC and not her, a clear violation of the world order and any metric of fairness, she's still gracious in defeat. She pulls me in for a giant hug. I'm crying, happy tears and a few sad ones too. I'm not going to lie—during weak moments, I fantasized about both of us getting in, Shola with a full ride, and the two of us rooming together. Me still getting to see Cesar a few times a week.

Very little actually changing.

"I don't understand. I mean, you should have gotten in too." She shakes her head, like it doesn't matter, though of course it does. I know she has mixed feelings about going to school in LA, and maybe even mixed feelings about going to school with me, but I also know a full scholarship would have really helped her family. Her mom has hinted more than once that it would be good to have her nearby to help out with the Littles. "I'm sorry."

"Not your fault," she says, and even though she's right and I'm not privy to the weird decisions of the SCC admissions committee, I still feel like somehow it is.

CHAPTER FORTY-ONE

Now

"Go get ready. You're taking me hiking," Isla says on Sunday morning. Our parents will be back later today from the hearing in Boston, so my plan was to numb myself with Xbox all day and then Postmates a belated birthday cake for my mom. This might be the first one we've ever gotten her that she'll actually eat.

The only plus side I can come up with to this whole disaster is that our house is no longer carb free.

"I think you've forgotten that hiking happens outside."

"You have to get out, Chloe. This hermit depressive thing isn't cute," Isla says. She gathers a dirty T-shirt and yoga pants from the floor of my room and throws them at me. I know my room smells, and probably so do I. Since Shola came by, I've been doing some next-level wallowing. "Get dressed."

"There are people outside, and did you know all of them have cameras in their pockets? Also, what if I run into Levi? Or Shola? What if someone tips off the paparazzi and they take a picture of me with a sweaty red face?"

"First of all, LA is a huge city, so the chances that you'll run into Levi are like literally one in a million. Also, screw him. He's kind of a conceited douche. Did I tell you he put a Harvard sticker on his locker? The *outside*. And it's Sunday morning, so you know Shola's at church with her family. So get over yourself. The paparazzi have better things to do than hunt you down. Sneakers. Hurry."

"Have you always been this bossy?" I ask.

"I'm not bossy. I have leadership skills," Isla says.

An hour later, I find myself at the top of Runyon Canyon with Isla and Fluffernutter. I'm out of breath and slick with sweat. I wear large aviator sunglasses and a baseball hat low on my forehead to go incognito. We've been hiking for an hour and I haven't noticed a single second look. I realize these are probably unnecessary precautions. It's my mom who draws attention, not me.

We collapse on a bench, and I hold Fluffernutter's leash tight. I worry about him jumping off the edge. Below us stretches this whole silly city, clusters of tall buildings and little houses and the disorganized, smoggy sprawl. LA in all its ugly, beautiful glittering mirage. I turn east to where Cesar lives, and I picture him at home with his mom, her making him a pancake breakfast; I do not think about his list, how his mom presumably crossed out my old number in Sharpie and replaced it with my new one, like I asked her to over text when I explained I'd be away from the Center for a while. How it's getting wrinkled in Cesar's pocket because I keep catching him rubbing his fingers over the edges.

"You were right," I say, taking in an extravagantly deep breath. "I needed to get out."

"Can you repeat that please? Did you say I was right?" Isla asks, pretending to gasp. "We should take a selfie to commemorate the moment."

Isla whips out her phone, and in a sudden frenzy, it beeps and vibrates in her hands. Cell service is spotty up here, so this happens sometimes: that frantic flurry of missed calls and text messages all at once.

"What is it?" I ask. I left my phone at home because I am friendless, so no one calls me but Kenny. Since it's Sunday, I figured he'd take the day off.

I scoot next to Isla to read over her shoulder, but she gets up and walks away. She paces back and forth, holding a finger to her ear so she can hear what must be multiple voice mails. Who leaves voice mails anymore?

"What's going on?" I ask again as I read her body language. Tight and overly controlled. My panic mounts, but Isla ignores me. She folds over, head between her knees. I get up and rub her back and she makes a strangled noise. I go through the list in my head, every imaginable disaster, which is silly, because lately all of the disasters have been unimaginable. "Are you okay? What's happening, Isl? Tell me."

She straightens herself, clears her throat.

"We have to go. It's Hudson." My go-to disaster, which somehow over the last few months has receded to the end of my worry list. I haven't been thinking about my half brother, and maybe in the forgetting, in the not tending to those fears, I willed the worst. "He overdosed."

• • •

We run down the mountain, dirt kicking up our legs, sweat turning it to mud, Fluffernutter barking beside us. He thinks our sudden urgency is a game, and he wags his tail with enthusiasm, like our panic is fun. As we go down the hill, desperate for full cell service, Isla chants over and over, with each step: *Be okay, be okay, be okay.*

Here's all we know: Hudson is in the emergency room at Cedars-Sinai Medical Center, which I decide means he's alive.

Both Isla and I were born at Cedars. This feels like compelling evidence that my brother cannot die there. I don't say this out loud to Isla, who would dismiss the thought the same way she dismisses my mother's vision boards (which, fair enough) and the rest of what she calls our "woo-woo crap."

I don't say this out loud because I don't want to use that word, *die.*

"You think Sage will be there?" I ask once we're in the car, speeding toward the hospital. I run a stop sign and then turn left despite the fact that it's restricted hours. Sage is Hudson's mom, my dad's ex-wife. She's a short woman with tattoos snaking up both of her arms and emphatic, jagged dyed-black bangs. She has the sort of tanned, wrinkly skin that gives the impression she's spent the last twenty years hard-living on the beach.

It's almost impossible to picture her and my father doing all the things they apparently did once upon a time: falling in love, getting married, having Hudson.

"Carrie said in her messages that she's leading a yoga retreat in Nevada. So it should be just us, until Mom and Dad get here. They're landing any minute. Carrie's going to meet us at the hospital to take Fluff home."

Isla kisses our dog's head, scratches under his ears. I wish we could take Fluffernutter with us into the waiting room. His heavy dog inhalations are comforting. As is the fact that he doesn't know how screwed up we all are, and if he does, he loves us anyway.

"This family is so screwed up," Isla says, reading my mind.

"Hud's going to be okay," I say.

"Maybe. Maybe not," Isla says.

The woman sitting behind the desk in the emergency room tells us to take a seat with barely a glance in our direction. When I ask to see Hudson, she says, "That will not be possible at this time." When I ask when someone will tell us what's going on, she holds up her palms, like she's not in charge, even though she's the one with access to a computer and a phone and a special hospital pass, which means she can go behind those swinging double doors, where presumably our half brother is.

"Is my brother even alive?" I ask. "Can you at least tell me that?"

She looks up at me and then over at Isla, and for the first time, I can see the recognition in her eyes. That we are human beings stuck in the swampiness of real life, and that we are scared. I wish I weren't wearing my hiking clothes. I pull out my jaunty ponytail, hoping that will add a year or two.

"Have a seat, sweetheart," she says. "Waiting is always the hardest part."

Is waiting the hardest part? I wonder. I don't know. In the last few weeks, while we've been waiting in a different kind of purgatory, I've thought that the in-between was what made everything so difficult. Now, I think the in-between is emotional boot camp. It's what prepares us for whatever's next.

A few kids hold their elbows at awkward angles. I see a couple of black eyes, and one person who looks like they might have the flu. A woman drenched in blood sits across from us. The nurses give her a towel to drape over the rust-colored stains, but she refuses to cover herself. Maybe she thinks that will get her seen by a doctor faster. I hope it works.

I try to pin down Hudson in my mind's eye, as if seeing him in my brain will mean he still exists somewhere in our world. I decide to think not about the Hudson I saw the last time he was at our house—hopped up and twitchy—but about the sober Hudson from two Christmases ago. He was fresh out of rehab, and he showed up shaved and with a new haircut. He'd bought Isla a book—*The Secret Garden*, I think—and me a candle from Anthropologie, and my mom and dad made such a big deal out of him remembering to bring us gifts, like he'd won the Nobel Peace Prize and not like he spent an hour picking stuff out for his sisters at the Grove, that their low expectations piled on another unnecessary layer of awkward.

Later, though, we watched a movie marathon downstairs under cashmere blankets because my mom had the screeners for the Golden Globe nominees, and Hudson didn't refer to my mother as *stepmonster* even once. For a while there, all tucked in with them like a normal family, I wondered if all the energy I wasted on worrying about my half brother could be spent on liking him instead.

"People don't always die from overdoses. Some people live and it's the wake-up call they need to get clean," Isla says. I don't ask how she knows this. If I could, I'd erase this information from her brain. I hate that my sister so casually tosses off the words *die* and *clean*. That this is the stuff she googles late at night when she can't sleep, or when she's not busy googling words like *honest services fraud* and *mail fraud* and *felony vs. misdemeanor*.

"Yeah," I say.

"He texted me yesterday. And I didn't write back. I should have written him back." She chews on the ends of her hair, like she's munching on a corn cob.

"What'd he say?" I ask.

"Nothing really. *What's up?* We talk sometimes, so . . ."

"You and Hudson talk?" This shouldn't surprise me. Isla and Hudson have always had a bond I've never quite understood. Still, for a moment, I feel excluded and sad. Why could I never figure out how to pin Hudson down?

"I mean, we text more than talk. He checks in on me. He might be a mess, but he's still our brother." I don't add in my usual disclaimer, *half brother*, because that seems wrong when we don't know if he's going to be okay. "I shouldn't have stolen his phone. He got a new one like the next day anyway."

"Aren't you mad at him?" I ask. "Because I am. At Mom too. I'm mad at the whole world."

For a second, I let the rage flow through me, and it feels empowering, as if I've been given an extra blood supply. I want to punch the wall and knock over the magazines neatly stacked on the side table with titles like *Modern Health* and *250 Easy Instant Pot Recipes.* I want to hulk out and find that random bleeding lady a freaking bed. Also a pillow.

I want to see that Hudson's okay, and then I want to pinch his side handles, like he used to do to me when we were kids, so tight they leave red marks, and then drag him to some magical rehab place he hasn't tried yet.

I want to show up at Shola's door with a frozen yogurt and two spoons and beg for forgiveness.

I want to buy Cesar ice cream and get his mom a green card.

I want to stop being such a goddamn monster.

"Addiction is a disease, Chlo. Like cancer. You wouldn't be mad at him if he had cancer."

"I know," I say. "Still."

"Waiting is not the hardest part," Isla says, and shivers, like it has occurred to her for the first time—though much more likely, it has occurred to her again, again, again—that things may not go the right way. That the reason they haven't let us see Hudson is because he is dead.

Dead, I think, which is a word that has a soft click, like a closed door. *Dead, dead, dead.*

"Not, it's not," I agree.

CHAPTER FORTY-TWO

Then

When I get home from school, the living room is full of cardinal and gold balloons, SCC colors, which are coincidentally similar to those of Gryffindor, and a giant sign hangs from the archway: CONGRATS CHLOE!

"You guys didn't have to do this," I say, even though I know my parents didn't actually go to Party City or make the sign. This is all Carrie.

"It's not every day your baby gets into SCC," my mom says, getting up from the couch, where she's highlighting a script—likely the new *My Dad, My Pops, and Me* reboot—to hug me. "We are so proud of you. I told you it was going to happen."

"I still don't believe it."

"Believe it. We know you're staying in LA, so pinky-swear that you'll have family dinner with us at least once a month."

"Mom," I say, pretending to whine, but of course I'm grinning. Los Angeles is my home, and no one is making me leave.

"I can't wait to tell everyone." My mom shimmers with

excitement, her eyes big and round and thrilled. I feel the glow too, a warmth in my belly, like I've eaten a good meal. Not pride, exactly. Satisfaction.

"Mom. Chill."

"What? It's SCC! This is a big deal. A huge deal. I'm allowed to be proud of you."

"Okay, be proud. But like, don't broadcast it."

"Whatever. When have I ever been chill?" she says, and then starts chanting, "SCC! SCC! SCC!"

"Shola got wait-listed," I say, and my mother's face closes for a minute, a studied blankness that comes in handy when she needs to play dense on TV. The calm before the punch line. Then it opens up again, a computer rebooted.

"That sucks, but hasn't she gotten in everywhere else?"

"Pretty much. She was hoping for a scholarship. It's weird, right? That I got in and she didn't?" I don't know what I want my mom to say. I used the word *weird*, but I think what I mean is *wrong*. It's wrong that I got in and Shola didn't.

"Who knows how these admissions people think? Maybe they realized there was no way she'd accept. It hurts their admissions percentages to let in someone who they know will go elsewhere. It's not like it's one for one. They don't directly compare you."

"It's still weird." Again, I use a safer word. *Weird*. Not *wrong*. How can my getting into college of my dreams be wrong?

It's not.

"Shola will be fine. You deserve this, baby. Here, I got you a present." My mom hands me a professionally wrapped box. The paper looks like an old-timey map, pretty enough to frame. I carefully open it up, and inside are two SCC sweatshirts.

"Why two?" I ask.

"One is extra small and preshrunk, to wear with jeans and stuff. The other is looser, more comfy, for hanging out at home. I also got a couple for Dad and me. I've been saving them for months."

I'm touched by her enthusiasm, if not a little disturbed by her confidence. I decide to save the extra-small for Cesar, who is going to freak that I'm staying in town.

"Thanks," I say. "For everything. You and Dad have been really supportive."

"You did it, sweetheart. Not us." She cups my cheeks and kisses me on the forehead. "Dinner at least once a month. I'm not joking."

Later that night, Shola texts.

> **Shola:** Just wanted to say again, I'm so so happy for you.

> **Me:** Thanks! I don't know what to say about you and SCC. I bet they thought you were too good for the school. They didn't want to hurt their accept percentages

> **Shola:** I'm over it. Bigger problems now. The Littles didn't get into Wood Valley. We found out today

Me: WTF

Shola: My parents are freaking out. Like full Balogun meltdown

Me: What's the backup?

Shola: There's no backup. Our local public school sucks. We hoped they'd get in because of sibling preference

Me: Siblings always get in

Shola: Apparently not when they need fin aid

Me: Seriously?

Shola: Welcome to the real world, Chlo

Me: Maybe you guys should move to a better school district?

Three dots appear, and then disappear, and then appear again.

I wish I could erase what I've just written. Of course they can't just pick up and move to a better school district. I'm an idiot.

Me: Sorry. Ignore that

But Shola doesn't write back.

• • •

Later, I get what might be my very first text from my half brother.

> **Hudson:** Heard about SCC! How much did Mom and Dad have to pay to get you in there?
>
> **Me:** Very funny
>
> **Hudson:** Kidding! Happy for you lil sis. Go Trojans!

CHAPTER FORTY-THREE

Now

When my parents finally shuffle into the emergency room waiting area, Isla and I have already been waiting for two hours and have been given no new information despite multiple attempts to break the front desk lady. I've flipped through the Instant Pot recipe magazine, even though (a) we don't own an Instant Pot, and (b) we have Cristof.

After the bloody woman passed out, she was finally moved inside, so at least one question was answered for us. How much blood do you need to lose to get through Cedars' double doors? Answer: enough to lose consciousness, apparently.

My dad storms over to the desk, while my mom runs to Isla and me and gathers us into a hug. I ignore the looks of the other people in the waiting room, who clearly recognize my mother, despite the fact that she's wearing a brand-new Red Sox baseball cap obviously bought at an airport gift shop. She has door-to-door VIP service when she travels, so I assume this was a futile attempt at anonymity for the plane ride itself.

"We don't know anything yet," she says, which is not new information but feels like it anyway, because it's coming from them and not from us. From the real adults.

"We keep asking to see him and they keep telling us to wait," I say. I don't tell her that in the meantime I learned how to make taco chicken or that the seat she takes used to be covered in blood and was wiped down with Lysol less than ten minutes ago.

I don't scream: *Is Hudson dead?*

I want to, though. I want to yell until my voice gives way.

"Come on," my dad calls, and he signals us to follow him and a nurse, who uses a magnetic pass to let us through the double doors. I have no idea how he managed to do in twenty seconds what I couldn't do in two hours, but that's so like my dad. To show up in a white button-down shirt rolled to his elbows—a tall, white, middle-aged well-off man whose clothes look professionally laundered and who sports an outrageously expensive watch—and make people listen at the mere sight of him. This nurse, a tall woman with long, thin legs and a long, thin face, like a greyhound, leads us to a room, and with an unnecessary flourish pulls open the curtains. She doesn't say *ta-da*, but I bet she thinks it, and then with her matching creepy, long, thin-fingered spider hands, she waves us in.

Hudson is lying in a bed, an oxygen tube hooked up to his nose, and though he has an IV, I can't bring myself to look at his arms, which are no doubt mottled with track marks and bruises.

He's unmistakably alive.

I feel a relief so palpable, my legs quiver. Isla bursts into tears.

"Come on, guys. It's not so bad. It's not like I'm going to jail or anything," Hudson says.

"Not funny," my dad says.

"It's a little bit funny," my mom says. "Prison, actually," she adds. She's full-on laughing, and so is Hudson, and while normally the two of them laughing together would be a happy thing—the stepmonster and her stepson, finally bonding—today, the rest of us watch in horror.

"It's not funny. Not even a little bit funny. Any of it," Isla says, and she marches right up to Hudson and gets in his face. So much for not being angry and addiction being like cancer. She's practically spitting. "You almost died. You know how scared we were? This needs to stop. Why can't you stop?"

I think, not for the first time, that we've broken my sister. That if I could, I'd swap her out, send her off to a better family, one that wouldn't test her so often. At the dinner table, instead of talking prison strategies, they could discuss molecular biology and the work of Anaïs Nin.

"Shh, it's okay. I'm okay," Hudson says, still wearing that goofy smile, like we're overreacting, though I catch a thread of nervousness. I don't know if he's worried about Isla or pondering the fact that he almost died or if he's doing calculations in his head about how quickly he can get out of this hospital and get his next fix.

For the first time, my anger mutates into compassion. I know what it's like to be your own worst enemy, to have inflicted your own deepest cuts, to let the easy way always win. To have dug yourself a hole so deep you wonder if you'll ever crawl out.

Maybe my brother and I have more in common than I realized.

"It honestly wasn't all that bad. They didn't even need to take me to the hospital. This was a precaution," he says carefully, like he's testing out a line.

"You need to stop," Isla says again, though even as the words are coming out, I can see she knows they're pointless. She's too smart to think she can reason Hudson into getting clean. We've all met with enough family therapists over the years to know at least that much. "Just stop."

My dad puts his hand on her shoulder and pulls her to him. He kisses the top of her head, then quickly wipes his eyes in hopes that the rest of us won't see him crying.

I think about all the things money can and cannot buy. A spot at SCC, but not a moral compass. Health care and rehab, but not immunity from our worst impulses. Fluency in Mandarin, but not the ability to talk honestly.

Privilege and large heaping chunks of the world, but not confidence. Or self-reflection.

And certainly not courage. No, money doesn't buy courage. In fact, if I've learned anything since the scandal, it's that the opposite is true.

Money makes you weak because it tricks you into thinking you're strong.

"I wish it worked like that, Isla," Hudson says. "I really, really do."

CHAPTER FORTY-FOUR

Then

I need a breath mint. Levi texted, *Be there in five,* and I'm pretty sure this is it, the moment I've been hoping for all year—Levi Haas is going to ask me to the prom. Of course I had red onions on my salad at lunch, even though I told the guy explicitly *please no red onions,* and I don't have time to run upstairs to the bathroom to brush my teeth again. I can't risk Isla opening the door and ruining whatever Levi has planned.

I'm nervous, which is silly. He's the one doing the asking. I only have to smile and say yes. It's not like I expect some elaborate promposal, because that isn't really a big thing at Wood Valley. Still, this is another milestone reached, which seems to be happening almost daily. First getting into college, now prom, next graduation.

Check, check, check.

Goodbye, goodbye, goodbye.

I've already picked out an array of dresses for the dance, and I make a mental note to buy a new makeup palette to test before the big night. Maybe I'll try teal eyelids. I can be brave for once.

"Dad, help!" I yell, sprinting to his office, since I know he usually keeps Altoids in there for emergencies. "I can't get asked to the prom with onion breath." I simultaneously brush my hair with one hand and put on lip gloss with the other, a brilliant effort at multitasking. I need to be prepared. I bet we'll take an after-ask selfie, and Levi will post it on Instagram with a cute caption like *She said yes*.

My dad's not in his office, though, so I push his door open and help myself. I love this room. My father has one of those oversized wooden power desks—glass-topped and studded down the legs. A brass bar stocked with fancy man bottles—bourbon and gin and even tequila—stands in one corner, and a bookcase full of leather-bound classics that only Isla reads stands in the other. An original of the Baby Hope photo hangs on the wall, though why he'd want to see that every day, no matter how much money it's worth, I don't understand. The sofa faces the desk, and when I was little and Mom was on set, Isla and I would sit tucked into its corner and draw. We preferred to be with my dad, even when he was too busy to pay attention to us, instead of in the playroom with our toys and the weekend nanny. He'd yell into the phone and scowl at his computer screen and mutter curses to himself, and it felt a lot like watching my mother on television—a glimpse at their strange alter egos, the people they morphed into when we were not around.

I rummage around in his top drawer and find only orange Tic Tacs, which my mom would say are more candy than breath mint, but beggars can't be choosers. I steal a handful, throw them in my mouth, and enjoy their sweet crunch. A red file sits loose in the drawer, and before I realize what I'm doing, I lean down to read the label.

It's neatly typed, innocuous: *Chloe College Apps.*

Isla always claims to have a sixth sense, and for the first time, I understand what she means. There's a physicality to what's happening, a cellular expectation deeper than my consciousness. Opening this folder will change everything, I realize; there'll be no going back. Still, I feel the moment's inevitability, no different from anything else inevitable— leaving home, growing up, dying.

I open the file carefully, slowly, as if how I open it will alter what's inside. At first, I can't make sense of what I see. A photograph is clipped to the top.

It's me and it's not me.

I recognize my own face, of course, from that bikini photo in Cabo, though I don't remember getting that tan on the trip. My mom is such a fascist about sun damage that she makes us all sit in the shade and wear 80 SPF. Instead of lying on a chaise lounge and throwing a peace sign at the camera, as I am in the original, in this one, I'm running, spear in hand, like an extra in *Gladiator.* I have biceps, the kind my mom has from strength training, a solid mountain range of bumps, not the kind I actually have, a slight sag from Pringles eating. My legs look longer, like an Olympian's legs, or Stretch Armstrong's.

I have no idea why they'd manipulate my picture to make it look like I'm doing warrior-princess cosplay. On second glance, I realize I have it all wrong. It's not cosplay. Not a costume, a sports outfit. Again, not the right word. A uniform.

This is a picture of me pole vaulting.

Pole vaulting?

Fake news, I think. Which I realize doesn't really make sense, but it's a phrase I hear bandied about and it seems to apply here.

I don't pole vault.

I don't even run.

This picture isn't real.

Fake news.

I flip through the pages. An essay with my name at the top, though I didn't write it, tells an elaborate love story about how I, Chloe Wynn Berringer, fell head over heels for the sport of pole vaulting after running track competitively for seven years. I'm a champion, a master, an athlete who wakes every morning before five a.m. to sprint in the refreshing morning air. I describe the spike of adrenaline and the cold clench of goose bumps as I hit my stride. Apparently, I get the same feeling when I win.

According to the essay, I'm addicted to winning. Those are the words I use—or alter-ego me uses. *Addicted to winning.*

Never mind that I don't particularly appreciate heights, nor would I ever choose to use a pole to hoist my body over a bar, a sport that sounds like an f'ed up version of limbo. I don't even like rooftop parties—I hate the idea of being solely responsible for keeping myself from falling off an edge. They make me the same kind of nervous I get when I'm stopped at a stop sign and a pedestrian walks in front of my car. How do they trust me not to let my foot slip off the brake?

I don't even trust me.

Obviously, I can't avoid driving, but I keep myself at a safe elevation. No need to throw my body around.

So Dr. Wilson did a last-minute bait and switch. Assumed SCC would prefer Pole Vaulting Chloe to Noncommittal Chloe.

I scan the basic information section, figuring at least here, they'll have hewn close to the facts. My name is again at the top of the application: *Chloe Wynn Berringer.* No typo there. My birthday is again, correct. My parents' names and occupations. Next to *Race* two boxes are checked: *Caucasian* and *Latin American.*

This must be a joke, or an honest mistake or another Aunt Candy prank, like her framed intestine. There's no way my mom and dad would have signed off on this sort of lie.

Both of my parents are white.

I am white.

I might be tan in that photo, but that's beauty bestowed by the Cabo sun.

I'm so white, I'm sure my mom played Billy Joel in the delivery room.

The doorbell rings, and I panic. I somehow forgot about Levi and prom and my real life. I close the folder and stuff it back in the drawer. I chomp on a few more orange Tic Tacs. I jump up and down a few times to stop my hands from shaking. And then I run and answer the door.

• • •

Levi carries two dozen red roses under one arm and holds up a large poster board that reads *Hey SCC girl will you go to prom with this Harvard guy?* I feel dizzy and sick as everything falls into place in my brain. All the weirdness of the fall, my mother's overconfidence, the emails, the exorbitant donations to charity.

I didn't get into SCC. The fictional character that Dr. Wilson created did.

There are too many falsehoods to wrap my brain around. The bizarre pole-vaulting essay. The fact that I'm suddenly, conveniently Latina, which is a sneaky choice, one that couldn't be dismantled by googling my family. My father's golfing perma-tan leaving the benefit of the doubt.

That photo.

I have to confront my parents. I have to call the SCC admissions office and explain, though I don't know what I can say. That they've let in the wrong person?

I've already turned down AIU.

"Chloe?" Levi asks, signaling again to his sign. "So? Will you go with me?"

I stare into his eyes, and he looks expectant, like he's sure I'll say yes. This is the look I bet he had when he sat at his computer and checked to see if he had been accepted at Harvard. The look he will carry throughout his life as he goes forth and conquers, making his parents proud. I remember our conversation from only a few months ago, though it feels like longer, about his biggest fears, how he's always so careful not to disappoint. I know now how little my parents must think of me, how incapable they assume I am, if they thought they had to resort to this.

I wonder if they are right.

"Yes, of course," I say, forcing my mouth to curve upward. Too bad I'm not an actress like my mother, who'd be able to turn the energy of the moment and blind Levi with her high-wattage smile. "I can't wait to go to prom with you."

Levi steps forward and drops the poster. He leans in for a kiss, soft and slow, and it all plays out exactly like I hoped it would before I opened that file. The ask, the yes, the kiss, as if I scripted it, or as if the fall version of me—who wanted nothing more than to be Levi's girlfriend—made this reality manifest with my own, different vision board.

"Yum. Orange Tic Tacs. My favorite," he says.

Once Levi leaves, my parents head out grim-faced for what they call an "important meeting"—maybe the reboot is in trouble?—and Isla ensconces herself in her room, no doubt reading more Dostoyevsky for fun. I put on my SCC sweatshirt, the cozy version, and stand in front of my full-length mirror. I look at my reflection and imagine myself in college: the real Chloe Wynn Berringer, not the one on my application. I imagine doing all the stuff that frightens me: Buying books and keeping up with my classes. Drinking beer at fraternity parties with people I don't know. The comfort of having my parents only twenty minutes away should I need a hand.

I think through my options. What good would alerting the admissions office do? If they can rescind your acceptance because of a slip in grades, surely they can rescind it for something like this, even if I wasn't the one who did the Photoshopping.

What's done is done, I tell myself, if anything was actually done in the first place.

After all, there are a lot of reasonable explanations for that file. It's entirely possible that that application was never submitted, that I'm telling myself a story that isn't true. That I'm making something out of nothing.

I look in the mirror again, examine my decidedly non-pole-vaulting body. I will let this go. Even if my admission is some sort of cosmic mistake or even, worst-case scenario, the result of a rogue college admissions consultant's lies, I'll make myself worthy of SCC. I'll rise to the occasion and earn my place retroactively. I'll study hard and graduate with honors. Make sure to have a full, well-rounded college experience.

I decide I didn't really see anything in my dad's drawer after all. That was a potential application or a prank, not *my* application.

Shola: Levi asked finally?!?!?

Me: He did!

Shola: Yay.

Me: So what's your position on teal eyeshadow?

Shola: DO IT

I want to ask about the Littles and where they're going to school. I want to ask if she's heard from Harvard or Yale yet. But I keep putting my foot in it lately, so I think it's better to stay quiet. I guess this is what happens as you start your goodbyes—little chasms open up to prepare you for letting go.

> **Me:** Done. Will you come over and get ready with me here before prom? We can raid my mom's accessories
>
> **Shola:** Duh

Before bed, I click over to Sephora. Order a teal eye shadow palette for prom. Since I still have some time, I decide not to pay extra for overnight shipping.

I paint my nails, alternating cardinal and gold.

I think about Levi's cheesy sign: *Hey SCC girl will you go to prom with this Harvard guy?*

That's me, I think. *SCC girl.*

I snuggle up in my sweatshirt, set my alarm for 6:15 a.m., and go to sleep.

I let go of the pit in my stomach, the slightest ache of doubt, the shame I can't quite shake.

Tomorrow will be a new day. A better one. A clean one.

I will forget.

SCC girl.

Here I come.

The next morning, before the doorbell rings, I don't hear the footsteps, or the line of men saying "On the count of three."

As I walk to the front hallway, I think of teal eyeshadow, of Levi's handmade sign, of the bright, bright future unfolding before me like a promise or a vow. I smile quietly to myself, hand on the knob.

I open the front door.

CHAPTER FORTY-FIVE

Now

"Can an entire family hit rock bottom? Asking for a friend. Who is me," my mom says. She sits at the kitchen table and eats cookie dough ice cream straight out of the gallon container. She's gained weight, and the padding suits her. Her edges seem less jagged, her face softer. She looks like what my mom might look like if she were a regular person, not an actress. Still beautiful, but more human somehow. What I'd imagine her sister might look like if she had one.

"The good thing about bottom is that the only place to go is up," my dad says, and lifts his cup of coffee and clinks with her ice cream. He looks hollowed out, his eyes watery above blue bags, his face slipped off his jawline. Last night, after Hudson was sprung from the ER, my dad took him to his apartment and packed his bags, then drove him back to rehab. Apparently, he even followed him into the bathroom and watched him pee; he was scared that Hudson might climb out the window.

"I'm only going because it's the cushy place with the

masseuses and the hiking and the chakra realignment in Malibu, not the mean boot camp in Tahoe where they check your orifices for drugs," Hudson said when my dad told him that he'd secured him a bed at a live-in treatment center and that he was going whether he was ready or not. That we weren't going to sit around and wait for him to die.

We are all done waiting.

"What's that famous expression? 'Fifth time's the charm,'" Hudson said, and we all laughed, like he was joking. And maybe he was. A little.

According to my dad, the short drive to Malibu was uneventful. Hudson stared out the window and mumbled the Serenity Prayer. My dad said he felt hopeful when they said goodbye, like maybe there was a chance he'd get Hudson back whole at the end of all of this, like something good might come from our nightmare day yesterday. Like maybe a near-death scare might be exactly the thing that he needed to be set straight. And then he caught sight of Hudson eyeing the door, as if he was going to make a run for it the second my dad turned his back and drove away.

"I don't know. What does rock bottom even mean? Things could totally get way worse, and then you'll be like, *Wait, that wasn't rock bottom, this is*. And then they could get even worse again, and then you'd be like, 'Wait, this is it?'" I say.

"Helpful, thanks, Chlo," my dad says. "I spoke to the counselor this morning and she said they're giving Huds meds to help manage the withdrawal. So for today at least, or for this hour, I'm going to be optimistic, because the alternative is unimaginable."

My mom rests her head on my dad's shoulder, kisses his cheek. Hands him the ice cream container. I don't correct my father, though *unimaginable* is the exact wrong word. I've had nightmares where we're all dressed in black at Hudson's funeral. Just yesterday, we took a test run.

Of course we can imagine it.

Just like I can now imagine my mom going to prison.

I can't stop imagining both scenarios.

"You picked out all the cookie dough," my dad says. "Maybe this is truly bottom."

"Hudson's going to be okay," my mom says. "I know it." I wonder if she actually believes this or she thinks this is what my dad needs to hear. I don't believe it—why would rehab stick on the fifth try if it didn't on the fourth?—and yet I hang on to the thought with white-knuckled desperation. Maybe my mom, like Isla, knows things the rest of us don't.

I might hate my brother, but I also love him.

"Hudson's stronger than you think, Dad," Isla says, and I notice she too is drinking coffee. When did that happen? She usually drinks milk in the morning, a tall, cold, sweating glass, like a toddler. "He looked me in the eye yesterday when we said goodbye, which is the first time he's done that since I don't know when. Maybe two Christmases ago? That has to mean something."

"I hope so," my dad says, and grips my mom's hands. When I see them locked like that, I let my usual fury turn to warmth, an unexpected twist in my gut.

Maybe we're all stronger than we think.

Maybe there are worse places to be than hitting bottom with the people you love-hate.

Maybe monsters can give up their monsterhood.

"When are the lawyers and Paloma coming back?" I ask. My parents have returned from Boston, and I assume their new entourage will soon follow. The kitchen will again smell like tuna sandwiches and cologne. The dining room will give off that anxious hum of a command center.

"They're not," my mom says, looking around as if surprised not to see them here with us. "Actually, we have a lot to talk about. Isla, would you be able to take tomorrow morning off from school? Would that be okay, honey?"

I look over at Isla, but I can't read her face. My mom has never asked our permission for anything, has never said the words *Would that be okay, honey?* Not even that time she flashed that picture of me in my Halloween costume in eighth grade on the *Tonight Show*—even though I was dressed as a carrot—or when she tweeted that I had my first crush.

"I guess," Isla says.

"And you can be here too, Chlo? Tomorrow morning?" my mom asks.

"I'll have to clear my very busy social calendar," I say. "But I think it can be arranged."

"Thank you. Thank you so much," she says, with real gratitude, not the sitcom variety, and that's when I get scared.

For the first time, I call a meeting with Kenny. I decide it's unlikely that I'll run into Levi or Shola or any of my classmates in a high-rise in Century City, so we meet in his office. Also, Isla, as usual, is right: I need to get out more, even if it's to have a chat with my lawyer. Later, if I'm sure there are no paparazzi following me, I'm going to check in on Cesar.

I pace in front of his couch, an expansive view of Los Angeles laid out behind me like a glittery net, and talk. I'm here to tell Kenny my story, whether he wants to hear it or not. I'm done with the waiting on every front.

I start with studying for the SAT the morning of the *Marie Claire* interview and don't stop until I reach the moment when the FBI knocked on our front door. I tell him how I thought I would be met by a box from Sephora, not men with guns. How Levi became my boyfriend and then my prom date, and how, like everything else, that fell apart. I tell him I miss Shola.

Unnecessary details from a legal perspective, maybe, but essential to me. I need him to understand how it felt, for even a moment, to be *SCC girl*. How it feels to have lost my best friend.

He takes notes, stopping me every once in a while when he thinks I'm dipping into dangerous territory. The weird emails and the SATs and the overheard phone call. I guess he's worried I'll incriminate myself, but I don't care. I continue despite his warnings.

Even villains are allowed nuance.

I learned that in English 4.

I think of Hudson in his hospital bed yesterday, how much courage it must have taken him to half smile and say "Fifth time's the charm." He didn't lie or pretend he didn't have a problem or make promises he isn't sure he can keep. Instead, he promised to try his best.

I've never tried my best. It's time to start.

When I finish my story with its grand finale, my big confession—I saw the application in my dad's office and made the decision to forget about it—Kenny goes quiet. I finally sit down in one of the big club chairs facing his desk, breathless, and my leg shakes up and down. My mother is not here to comment, yet I hear her in my mind like I always hear my parents' voices, so I uncross my legs and hold still.

I wonder if that's one definition of growing up—replacing your parents' voices in your head with your own. I wonder if I'll one day get there.

I check out his office. The walls are decorated with black-and-white photographs of old Hollywood stars: Marilyn Monroe. Rita Hayworth. Marlene Dietrich. I hear Madonna in my head—*Rita Hayworth gave good face*—and I think about my mother. How much harder giving good face is than it looks.

I wait for his verdict.

"Remember a few weeks ago I asked Siri about the origin of the word *capisce*?" Kenny asks, resting his chin on steepled fingers. He looks professorial today, in a fashionable beige cardigan with leather buttons and suede elbow patches. Exactly what I'd imagine my English 101 teacher would look like at SCC. "Well, I googled it, and it turns out it comes from the Italian *capisci*, which means 'to understand,' which itself comes from the Latin *capers*, which means 'to seize, grasp, take.' I love that. The idea of understanding being linked to the idea of taking something. We seize knowledge when we understand. Interesting on so many levels, right?"

I'm not sure whether I find this interesting. I didn't come

312

here for a vocab lesson; that was Linda's job. What I want to know is if he thinks I will or should be charged with a felony.

I nod anyway, hoping that speeds things along.

"Legally speaking, you didn't understand," Kenny says. "No capisce. Not really. You might have had a sense that not all was kosher, but you can't be charged for that. A strange SAT experience and an out-of-context email and call do not make a criminal case for fraud." A high-pitched noise escapes my throat. A strangled sigh, an exhalation of relief. "I think the US attorney's office was posturing even more than I realized."

"But what about the fact that I saw the file and decided not to say anything?" I ask, because that's the part that has been hardest to swallow. I might have told Isla that I didn't know, but that was a technicality. I didn't know-know, until finally, I did.

I knew.

"Nope. The crime had already been committed. Ethically speaking, you should have said something then, but legally it's a different story. Either way, you didn't have a chance, because the raid happened literally the next day," he says.

"So I'm in the clear, legally speaking?"

"Yes. Based on what you've told me, yes. But clients lie to me and to themselves all the time."

"I might have been aggressively oblivious, but I'm not lying," I say.

"Did you know I have kids?" Kenny asks, apropos of nothing. I'm surprised. His cell phone lock screen is a generic picture—a fishing boat in the middle of a bright blue sea.

My dad's, on the other hand, is a picture of our family from about thirteen years ago—me, Hudson, and Isla at Disneyland. Hudson, in metal braces and the oily, pimply throes of puberty, is squished up against Mickey Mouse. Though it's clear he doesn't want to have his photo taken, he's smiling anyway, even matching Mickey's thumbs-up. I figured the fishing boat meant Kenny lived alone. "Two boys, actually. Both went to UPenn and UPenn Law. Really great, smart kids."

"How old are they?" I'm curious about Kenny. I've shared my deepest secrets, as if he were my therapist, not my lawyer, and I know so little about him. He hands me the photo from his desk and I see two young men who look a lot like Axl and Simon: white, healthy, polo-shirted. I recognize our country club in the background. I wonder if we've ever been there at the same time—maybe the Fourth of July barbecue or the Easter egg roll. I wonder if when this is all over, or when I return to my old life, I will see Kenny there, drinking a martini, his tall, healthy, smart Penn boys besides him.

"Twenty-two and twenty-four. And until your case, I hadn't really thought about all the ways my kids had a leg up. That's not to say I'm not proud of them—I am, very—but I paid for counselors and tutors and summer programs and camps and club soccer and private school, and they're legacies, of course, on both sides actually." He points to two degrees on the wall from the University of Pennsylvania, one from the college of arts and sciences and the other from the law school. "I didn't buy a building, probably because I couldn't afford one, but I bought into the system. I still do. Every day. And lately I don't know what I think about that."

"Yeah," I say, and feel tears well up in my eyes.

"I like you, Chloe. And I hope maybe one day you find your way into college on your own. In the meantime, I hope you take a minute to think about the Latin *capers*, 'to seize, grasp, take.' Remember, knowledge is power. An important part of growing up is letting yourself see the world around you as it truly is, even if you don't like what you see or your own complicity in it."

"You're talking about knowing without knowing," I say, because I am not one of Kenny's kids; I'm a mediocre student who likes to have things spelled out.

"Yep. Though our crimes are different—and to be clear, I mean crimes in a moral sense, not a legal one, of course—we both have a lot of thinking to do," Kenny says. "We've both been aggressively oblivious, as you so eloquently put it."

A giggle bubbles up in the back of my throat. I wish I could call Shola. She'd find it hilarious that my mom's felonies have had the unintended consequence of making my lawyer woke.

On second thought, maybe she wouldn't find it funny at all. Maybe she'd wonder why it's taken us all so long to open our eyes.

Again, she's three steps ahead of me. She knows the answer to that too.

To be fair, so do I.

CHAPTER FORTY-SIX

Now

The next morning, my parents march into my room with the sort of militant urgency they usually reserve for special occasions, like movie premieres or pop-up shop appearances. I'm still in bed, the first hour of my day reserved for my new masochistic hobby: scrolling Shola's and Levi's Instagram feeds. I've watched their honor society speeches, seen tiny bits of the fencing farewell lunch, celebrated Shola's send-off from the newspaper, even vicariously shopped for a prom dress with Sophie, Levi's date. She modeled six different dresses from the Bloomingdale's dressing room for Instagram live and then let people vote.

I preferred the red one, though I kept that opinion to myself.

"Get ready, Chloe. The outfit you need to wear is on the back of the door. I don't think you'll be on camera, but it's always good to be prepared, sweet pea," my mom says. Her hair has been blown out, again in the new style—straight and simple and curled under—and she's wearing a boring black sheath dress, understated jewelry. I wonder where it all came from. My mom's stylist doesn't usually do conservative, and I imagine it took all her willpower not to attack the dress with scissors and make a long leg slit and a rib-cage keyhole.

"Wait, what?" I ask.

"Keep up, honey. The film crew will be here in an hour," my dad says. He's freshly showered and wearing one of his sharp suits, though he too compromised—with who? Paloma?—on the tie and handkerchief. Both are a solid pale blue I've never seen before. He's been forced to forgo his usual loud patterns.

"What film crew?" I ask.

"Duh, *20/20*," Isla says, coming in behind my parents. She's wearing a dress also, but hers is overly girlish—pink gingham with flutter sleeves. She mock-curtsies and makes a silly face.

"Wow," I say.

"Yeah. Don't get too excited. Yours matches," Isla says.

"We wanted *The View*, but they make you go to them," my mom says, unconcerned about the fact that Isla and I will be dressed like twinsie toddler royalty. "Also, those ladies can get a little mean. I wanted the set to be our home, to show we are real people," my mom says. "That we are a real family."

"Show who?" I ask.

"The whole goddamn world," my mom says.

By the time I go downstairs, our entire living room has been taken over by men and women with walkie-talkies hooked to belts. Furniture has been moved to the side to make room for cameras and boom microphones, and the floor is zig-zagged with taped-down wires. It's similar to the invasion of the lawyers, except this time, the energy is frantic instead of frustrated. Also, I don't see any sandwiches or curly lettuce droppings.

The anchorperson, Brittany Brady, stands off to one side while a woman powders her face and a man lint-rolls down her suit. A third person tapes a mic to her lapel.

In the corner, Paloma talks with a dark-haired woman who reminds me of Hudson's mom—same blunt bangs and grim smile. They seem deep in conversation, unaware of the commotion around them.

"She's the producer, I think," Isla says, gesturing over to them. "I'd bet they're going over the terms of the interview."

"Do you know what's going on? What's the point of all of this?" I ask.

"I assume damage control? So Mom can spin her story? Seems like a risky strategy to me," Isla says.

"I spoke to my lawyer yesterday. I think I'm at least in the clear, legally speaking," I say. "For real."

"Thank God," Isla says, and grabs me in a quick hug. We've recently become sisters who touch.

I thought I'd feel real relief from this news. Instead, the shame sits ever-present, like a gravitational force. I let my mind wander to Mrs. Oh's definition of me being *fine*, a thing I do often now, the way you'd wiggle a loose tooth. I tell myself that I'll figure out one day how to live a *long and authentically good life*, like she promised.

Isla and I look back out at the set, which isn't a set but our house. The doubling of my mom's professional life and our personal life feels weird, though not altogether unfamiliar.

"I'm nervous. I don't think Mom realizes how much people hate her. She's so used to being Missy, right? I don't think she gets that this could be a really tough interview," Isla says.

Our mother stands off to the side with my dad. They make such a striking couple, even with both of them at their most toned-down. They're holding hands, and my mother is nodding. I bet Dad is giving her a pep talk.

"She knows," I say. "Look, she's nervous."

My unflappable mother seems shaken and pale, the same way she looked when she was walking into the ER to see Hudson. Like she knew it could be the worst-case scenario.

"Maybe," Isla says. "By the way, I haven't told Mom and Dad yet, but I'm not going back to Wood Valley next year. I've registered myself for Beverly Hills High."

"Public school," I say, using my mother's best scandalized voice, the one she would use on *My Dad, My Pops, and Me* whenever her fictional kid did something wrong. Isla laughs.

"I know, right? They're going to freak."

"They'll get over it," I say, and then before Isla can respond, my mom is ushered over to the couch, and the interviewer takes a seat across from her, and we are silenced by someone shouting "Live in ten," and then the countdown begins.

I slip my hand into Isla's as the cameras roll.

My mother looks small under the overhead lights, and she blinks a few times up at Brittany Brady, who seems taller because of her bigger hair. A swoosh of blond swings across her forehead like a wave.

"I imagine this isn't easy for you," Brittany says, with a faux-empathetic tilt of her head and an attempted knitting of brows, which doesn't quite work, presumably because of injectables. "Just a few months ago you were gearing up to star in the *My Dad, My Pops, and Me* reboot, and now you're facing multiple felony charges and a possible forty years in prison."

My mom lets out a gurgle-cough. It was, of course, the mention of forty years. That gets me every time too.

"How does it feel?" Brittany asks.

"I actually . . . I have something I want to share. I know this is supposed to be an interview, and I'll answer any questions you have, I promise, but I'd like to read this first if that's okay?"

"Sure," Brittany says, shooting a quick glance at her producer, who nods, like *go with it*. We are on live television, so I'm not sure Brittany has much of a choice anyway.

My mother takes out a piece of paper that she's been sitting on and carefully unfolds it.

"I was going to speak without reading, but I'm . . . I'm too nervous," my mom says, and my entire body thrums with the tension. I've watched my mother being interviewed hundreds of times throughout my life, and always, when in front of a camera, she transforms into the sparkliest, warmest version of herself, and every time there's a cognitive dissonance and I think, *Who is that?*

Today, though, my mom seems her true self, unsure and

tired and exposed. She might as well be wearing her Wood Valley sweats.

"First of all, I want to apologize to both of my daughters, neither of whom had anything to do with this. This is one hundred percent my fault, and I want to—need to—take full responsibility for my actions. I'm so sorry, girls." My mom looks at Isla and me off to the side, not at Brittany or even at the cameras. This apology—at least this part of it—is for us and us only.

"Last fall, I made the biggest mistake of my life." My mom sets her jaw and turns her attention back to the lens. "As a result, I will be pleading guilty to the charges against me."

Isla squeezes my hand and I squeeze back, and we lean against each other, shoulder to shoulder. We're both trembling, equal parts relief and fear.

Paloma, on the other hand, not thrilled with this turn of events—apparently my mom did not fill her in beforehand—attempts to convince the producer to cut to commercial. The producer grins and shakes her head. This makes for good television, if not a great PR strategy.

My mom, under the lights, honest and raw, is riveting.

"I love my daughters more than you can possibly imagine, and as a parent, it is my job to be a role model. I have obviously failed in that regard. I'm so ashamed of my dishonest behavior, and I don't know how I will make it up to them or to all the students out there who worked hard and didn't try to cheat the system. I promise you this, though: I will spend the rest of my life trying." My mom folds her paper, swats at the tears falling down her face, and looks up at Brittany

Brady, who's taken utterly off guard. She was prepped for a different sort of interview, something in keeping with the quotes Paloma's team has been leaking to the press and attributing to a "longtime friend of the family": my mother insists on her innocence, she believes this will all blow over soon, the only real criminal here is Dr. Wilson.

"I assume you realize that by pleading guilty you will likely be facing jail time," Brittany says, which isn't a question, but she pauses for an answer anyway. Paloma takes the break to try to force her way onto the set, but my dad shakes his head at her. She hesitates, then stands down.

"Yes, but it's not 'likely'—it's definitely," my mom says. "And it's prison, actually, not jail."

"As you know, a lot of the other people swept up in this scandal pled guilty a month ago, and presumably had you done so then and taken immediate responsibility, you'd have received a more favorable sentence. So why the change of heart today? Just a few weeks ago, you vowed to fight the charges."

"My girls have always been my number one concern. I don't always do things right, obviously." My mom nervously clears her throat. "But when this all happened, I felt like I couldn't leave them. I couldn't go to prison and not be here to support them in the aftermath of this mess I had made. That seemed more important than anything else. Being with my daughters."

My mom's voice cracks, and she catches my eye. I give her a teary thumbs-up.

"So I refused to consider the possibility of a guilty plea.

Even if it was the right thing to do, it felt like the wrong thing, you know? But we had a family emergency recently, and I guess it was a wake-up call for me. As parents, we realize that no matter how hard we try, no matter how fiercely we love our children, we're going to screw it all up somehow. I have the distinct pleasure of knowing, at least in one way, exactly where I went wrong. It turns out my job as a mom is not to shield my children from the hard things, because life is life, and as much as it hurts me to see their disappointments, as much as I'd like to shield them from all the struggles I went through, I can't do that. Instead, I realized I need to start modeling courage and strength. By pleading guilty, I hope to show them that I believe in taking responsibility for my mistakes. And eventually I hope to earn their forgiveness."

She's fully crying, wet tears leaving tracks of mascara down her face, an image that I already know will transform her again from a human being into a meme. My mom has been doing this long enough that she knows it too—and not only because Paloma is obviously freaking out behind the cameraman.

"I know I've also let down my fans, and I hope to one day earn back their trust."

I have no idea how this apology will go over, though my guess is not well. I can't parse it in the ways Twitter will soon—I can't break it down piece by piece, dissect all the privilege baked into each sentence, whether she'll move from public enemy number one to laughingstock. It doesn't matter, though. I'm pretty sure my mother is beyond caring.

"Also, while I'm here telling the whole truth, you should know I'm fifty years old. Half a freaking century. The Internet says I'm forty-five. That's a lie."

I hear Paloma audibly gasp: *No!* Isla lets out a puff of air, a laugh-cry, and we are squeezing each other's hands so tightly it hurts.

"Until recently, I hadn't eaten a carb in something like fifteen years, and I get Botox and Restylane and I had cheek implants, because you can't be skinny and have cheeks. You can't. I think that's it. This is going to sound absurd, but I also don't sweat because my dermatologist took care of that, and so when I sleep, which is pretty much never, I have nightmares I'll be telling the truth but no one will believe me because I'm not sweating. Ironic, right?"

Brittany Brady stares at her, dumbfounded. My mom keeps going. She is having a full meltdown on live television.

"One last thing: there's a topless photo of me floating around out there that I paid to have taken down from the Internet. But I'm not ashamed of that photo. I'm ashamed that the world thinks I should be ashamed of it," my mom says.

This is it, I think as my mom wipes at her face, and we weep and laugh and clap with abandon from the sidelines, Isla and I in our ridiculous matching pink gingham. I guess you do know when you hit it.

This is bottom.

How glorious it is to finally look up.

CHAPTER FORTY-SEVEN

Now

Later, after they all leave—the cameras and Brittany Brady and a livid Paloma, who kept saying over and over, "Did you have to mention the cheek implants? Cheek implants are not a crime!"—we sit outside at the big wooden table near the fire pit, a giant pizza between us like a peace offering. My dad puts on some low music on the speakers, possibly because it's a lovely thing, having music piped into your backyard, but more likely to protect our privacy.

After my mother's appearance today, though, who cares what the neighbors hear? We have nothing left to hide.

My parents have both poured themselves generous glasses of wine, and though sometimes they let me have my own small smidge, today they seem scandalized when I ask.

"Okay, so yeah. Let's talk. The things I *did*—" my mom starts.

"We did," my dad interrupts. "Just because I'm not on the tape doesn't mean I wasn't part of this. I hate that you have to be the one . . . I hate it. The things *we did*."

"I'm sorry that we paid someone to correct your SATs and that we bribed your way into SCC. I'm spelling it out because I think that's part of apologizing. Not being queasy about what you did wrong," my mom says. My guess is she consulted an expert, a child psychologist, maybe, about how best to approach this with us. I'd be annoyed except I think she's right. I like hearing it spelled out. None of us being allowed to flinch.

"I'm sorry too," my dad says. "For everything. I'm also sorry for not being on that tape, and that your mom has to shoulder all the blame alone."

"You did get fired," my mom says.

"Temporarily," my dad says. He's pretty sure that as soon as this all blows over, his company will hire him again. Money is more important than morality in the venture-capital business.

I reflexively want to say *it's okay* when my parents apologize, which is what I always say when someone apologizes to me, but obviously this time, it's not okay. It's not okay at all.

We will be, though, I think.

"The prosecutor said that they'll recommend one year in prison. I could get more, and I could get less, depending on the judge. And they'd agree not to prosecute Dad or you, Chlo, though from what your lawyer told my lawyer, you're in the clear anyway. But in all likelihood it will be at least a year, which is, I mean, putting aside the fact that I'll spend that year in prison, not the Four Seasons Maui, is a scary long period of time. One night in prison is scary. But that's not the part that freaks me out the most—" She stops, her voice thick with emotion. "I only have a limited time with you

326

girls before you're off doing whatever you'll be doing with your lives. . . ."

She's careful not to mention college, our personal land mine.

"It feels unfair, like I'm being punished too much, that I will have to lose an entire year with you. But maybe it's not; maybe it's what I deserve. God knows people go through a whole lot worse, but still. You're my babies. I don't want to leave you."

"We're not babies," I say. "Dad's here. I'll be here to help Isla, at least until you get home."

"I don't need help. I'm sixteen," Isla says.

"Sixteen- and seventeen-year-olds still need their moms," my mother says.

"Carrie can be my new mom," Isla says, breaking into a big, sly grin. How come I didn't realize until recently that Isla was hilarious? It's weird how sometimes people can be so close and yet you can't see them clearly at all.

"Don't think I haven't worried about your dad running off with Carrie as soon as I'm gone," my mom says.

"Nah, Carrie's not my type. Brittany Brady, on the other hand—" my dad jokes.

"You're not dying. You're going away for a little while," I say. "You're still our mom."

"Is that the euphemism we're going to use? 'Going away for a little while'? Not bad," my dad says.

"What's going to happen to you, Chloe?" my mom asks, in that same voice I imitated for Isla earlier today when I said *public school*.

Isla grabs my hand under the table and squeezes it to

keep from laughing. Of course, we realize this is serious, this isn't my mom's usual melodrama, which makes it all the funnier. If your life is going to take a turn for the surreal, you might as well enjoy it.

"I'm going to be fine, Mom. Look at me. I'm already fine," I say. I realize that's the truth, mostly. I'm heartbroken about my friendship with Shola, and I'm terrified for my future, but if I'm honest, I was terrified for my future before this all happened anyway.

"It's seems cruel that I'll have to give up delicious things like pizza and ice cream just when I've rediscovered them," my mom says.

"We should call that prison guy. Ask if they have pizza in the big house," Isla says.

"Do you guys have any questions for me? About all this? That's what the therapist we talked to said we should do." *Bingo*, I think. "Let's open this up to questions."

Isla gives me a side-eye, obviously thinking the same thing I am: *No expert left unconsulted in this family.*

"I mean, everything I said on *20/20* was true, but you might have your own thoughts."

"Why?" I ask.

"Why what?" my mom asks. "The cheek implants? As I was saying, with aging in particular, you can get a little hollowed out."

"No! Why did you do this, all of this, any of this? I would have gotten into college, maybe not SCC, but somewhere, without you committing a felony. Why did you do this to us?" I ask, and I realize once the question is out that this is the part that I still can't quite understand, no matter how many times I turn it over in my mind. I have a trust fund. It's not like I was going to starve if I went to AIU.

"You're going to find this ironic, but you know what hooked me with Dr. Wilson? Not only finding the easy way for you into school, Chlo, that perfect side door, because that of course was part of it, I'm not going to lie. I've grown a little too used to being able to buy what I want without repercussions. I've worked my ass off all these years and figured you should get the benefit of that. But what really got me is that he told me that everyone else was doing it. I'm fifty years old, and that's what sold me: *All the cool kids are doing it*," my mom says. "I thought if I didn't, you'd be left behind. I thought—and this is ridiculous in retrospect—I thought it meant I was a *good* mom."

"That's not why I was in," my dad confesses, and his voice gets thick. "Honestly, for me it was as simple as if I can do this for you, why wouldn't I? It seemed like a no-brainer. My parents basically left me to fend for myself. I was practically feral. I fought so hard to get here, and what for? So I can give you girls the whole world. You do everything you can for your kids. It didn't even occur to me to *not* do it. It didn't occur to me that we could get caught."

"No, you don't do everything for your kids," Isla says.

"You're right." My dad has a wry look on his face, the same one he always gets when Isla astounds him. "You don't. Not everything."

"Do you think I'm stupid?" I ask, and as soon as the question slips out, I realize there it is, my biggest fear laid bare for all to see. My mom is going to prison because she thought I was too stupid to get into college on my own. "Is that why you did this really?"

"Oh, honey, no, of course not," my mom says. "We wanted things to be easier for you. School hasn't been easy. That doesn't mean you're stupid."

"Chlo. No. Never," my dad says.

"I mean, listen, you aren't the brightest bulb in the sea," Isla says, and throws her arm around my shoulders.

"That's a mixed metaphor," I say.

"It's time we all put on our big-girl panties around here and speak the truth," Isla says, and I wait for my mom to step in, which is what she usually does when Isla's about to get a little too real. "Chloe, you don't deserve to go to SCC. That doesn't mean you're stupid; it means you didn't care as much or try as hard as me. Because one day, I'm going to Harvard, like Shola."

"Shola's going to Harvard? Oh my God, that's amazing," I say. I'd been scouting Shola's feed hoping for a clue as to where she'd be next year, and in true Shola fashion, she hadn't dropped any hints. She's not like Levi. She doesn't need to brag.

I feel joy and grief in almost equal measure.

I wish I could tell her how happy I am for her. How I can't wait to watch from afar as she takes on the world. How even though I lost her, I'll always be proud of the fact that, for a while, at least, she chose me as a friend.

"Yup," Isla says, smiling.

"Good for Shola," my dad says, though I can't tell if he really means it.

EPILOGUE

Fourteen months later

Four duffel bags sit by the front door, stuffed to capacity, though this is only half of it. A bunch of boxes were shipped to the dorms last week. We looked at pictures online, and the rooms looks dollhouse-sized, so I'm not sure how this will work. The roommate, who based on her texts gave off no serial killer vibes, is from Wichita, Kansas, like Dorothy, and we've decided she'll hopefully be traveling a little lighter.

Apparently, you can take the girl out of Beverly Hills, but you can't take Beverly Hills out of the girl.

We've rehearsed this moment in our heads for months— or at least, I have—but now that it's here, like with all the big life stuff, I find I'm unprepared. You'd think I'd be used to it after the year we've had. When my mom surrendered, which was prearranged with the marshal service well in advance, I still felt like grabbing her ankles and begging her not to go. Instead, I stood dry-eyed and joked that I'd already started hoarding all of the ice cream in Los Angeles for when she comes home.

Only later, once she was gone, did I cry.

My ability to hold it together felt like progress, though. A giant step toward adulthood. Like the other day, when I made my own dentist appointment. *On the phone.*

I guess sometimes we grow up, despite ourselves.

With this departure, though, the calculus is different. We're all thrilled—celebrated it, in fact, all last spring, with another balloon arch and even a cake. This time, we're watching a natural, earned progression, what is supposed to happen in the normal course of things. The built-in goodbye at the end of the childhood. That final wave and then the no looking back before independence.

Still. The tears come, so many I don't even try to stop them. Instead, I busy myself with details. I double-check the luggage, make sure each piece has a tag with a label and a telephone number, in case it gets lost. I run upstairs and grab *Crime and Punishment* and slip it into a bag.

And then it's time. No more stalling.

My dad, Hudson, Isla, and I stand awkwardly at the door. Mom should be here for this, but that goodbye was said already, on one of our prison visits. I tell myself stories to make her constant absence feel better—that she's on a yoga retreat, or away filming; that she'll be home soon. At least that latter one is likely true. Mr. Spence said he thought her sentence of fourteen months, of which she's already served six, will likely be reduced to eight on the grounds of good behavior.

Two more months is nothing. A summer of sleepaway camp. As she says, it's just enough time to finish the memoir she's been writing between her shifts in the laundry room.

A blink and she'll be back.

But here's the thing with this goodbye: This one is permanent.

Isla won't be back, not for real. My sister and I will likely never live under the same roof again.

I look down at my KALE sweatshirt, which I bought as a gag, knowing that Isla would be wearing her YALE one today for the flight east. She's refused to let any of us come with her, not even to the airport, because she says that will only make it harder. That this is the start—this moment—and she wants to prove to herself that she's ready to go it alone from here.

I understand. If we came, there'd be more of that waiting that we've grown too used to.

It's time for her to go.

She hugs my dad, and then Hudson, who got his one-year chip in June and has moved into the guesthouse for a while. I still worry about him—not sure how many chips he'll need for that to go away—but I've also started allowing myself to like him again. She scoops up Fluffernutter, kisses him on his head, murmurs something in his ear I can't hear.

When it's my turn, Isla stands in front of me; the expression on her face the mirror of mine: a smile through tears. She puts her hands on my shoulders, like she's the big sister about to dispense advice, not the other way around. I beat her to it, though, and start talking first.

"I love you and I'm so proud of you and I'm going to come visit soon whether you like it or not and, holy crap, Yale!" I say, because I'm swollen with pride for my sister, who did it, despite our parents, and also, of course, in part, because of them.

She tackle-hugs me.

"I love you too. Be good, okay?"

"I'm always good," I say. Isla laughs and hugs me again and we sway that way for a few minutes, a back-and-forth rock, until she pulls away. I know my sister well, especially after all the time we've spent together this past year, and I watch as she begins to retreat. I can tell she's moved on from goodbyes. She's thinking about her Uber, and how long it should take to get to LAX during rush hour, and maybe texting her roommate, who got to New Haven already and claimed the left bed. I wonder if this is how things will be now that she's leaving—if our entire adulthood will be one long goodbye to each other.

I've made plans to hang out with Cesar this afternoon, to keep me from wallowing. I work at the RRC thirty-five hours a week. I spend the mornings helping Rita with the administrative stuff, all of which counts toward college credit at Santa Monica Community College. This internship I got no doubt because of my parents' large donation last year. This is something I try not to think too much about and instead simply appreciate and earn with hard work. In the afternoons, I stick to my old schedule, reading with Cesar.

I'm taking three classes per semester, all of which I'm currently acing. Who knew how much it helps to do all the reading? And next month, whether I'm ready or not, I'll start the college admissions process all over again. This time, Mrs. Oh is helping me draw up a whole new list, one that does not include SCC. I no longer care about the *US News & World Report* rankings or name recognition. I simply want a school with a strong social work program.

I haven't seen or heard from Levi or Shola since they left for Harvard, though I regularly stalk Shola on Instagram. She often posts pictures or videos, and Levi occasionally makes an appearance—the two them studying in the library or watching the Head of the Charles Regatta. From her feed, her friends seem less Wood Valley and more hipster cool, a crowd that is infinitely more diverse than the one we had in high school.

I tell myself my lurking in her life isn't creepy, because I am cheering her on. I liked knowing that last summer she found a paid internship with Alexandria Ocasio-Cortez, that she got an A in that Intro to Philosophy class she was so excited about, that she has a new cold-brew addiction. I like knowing about her life, even if I don't deserve to be a part of it.

After my mom pled guilty and I was free to talk about had happened, I sent her long apology letters, by email, detailing what I knew and when, as if the technicalities mattered.

And then I realized they didn't, not really.

There's no version of my story in which I am not a villain.

This is something we talk about often in our Signal group, which has been whittled down to only a few of us, those who are willing to wrestle out loud with our guilt.

In happy news, Isla told me that the Littles got into Wood Valley after all. The school doubled their financial aid offerings last year as part of an image rehabilitation effort in the wake of the scandal, and they found their way off the waiting list.

Maybe Wood Valley hired Paloma, who my mom let go shortly after her plea and who I find myself missing on occasion, if only because sometimes it's nice to have someone to tell you what to do.

Late at night, when I think about the future, *my future*, the panic still comes like a hand over my mouth. To help, I think about Mrs. Oh, and her definition of the word *fine*, how it insists that I carry my past so that I can learn to serve myself and the world better.

I think I'm getting there.

When I remember the old Chloe, the pre-scandal Chloe, I feel itchy and uncomfortable, like she's an old acquaintance I once knew but no longer really like or want to hang out with, which may be exactly how Shola feels about me.

I am an entire person molted.

I prefer the new me, the almost-but-not-quite-fine me. The one made brave and honest from being carved out of the carcass of a monster.

Tomorrow, Dad and I are driving down to see Mom. Because the Federal Bureau of Prisons doesn't allow you to bring gifts to visiting hours, I'll have collected my stories for her. I gather all the details about this Isla goodbye—how she was brave and excited and ready. How at work, I found a new grant for the RRC to apply for that could help increase capacity and provide daily snacks and milk. That I taught Cesar his multiplication tables up to twelve. That Kenny's son Emmet, who recently graduated from Penn Law and joined Kenny's firm as a first-year associate, though he wanted to go into public interest work, has offered to represent Cesar's mom pro bono. She might be better off remaining undocumented than risking deportation with an asylum claim, but I like the idea of her having someone on call if the worst comes to pass. Even grown-ups need a laminated card to carry around in their pocket sometimes.

I'll share the details of my life with my mom, honestly, like they're a college admissions essay—the unfiltered story of Chloe Wynn Berringer that Mrs. Oh asked me for so long ago.

This time, I'll simply tell the truth.

Isla walks out into the sunlight, bags thrown over her shoulders.

I feel like clapping with joy and heartbreak. This walk to the Uber is her taking her final bow. She tosses me one last smile over her shoulder.

Love you, I mouth, and take a picture in my mind for my mom.

When Isla goes, she leaves the front door wide open behind her.

AUTHOR'S NOTE

When the college admissions scandal broke and was splashed all over the news and social media, I became obsessed. The material was endlessly juicy: *The greed. The entitlement.* And of course: *the nerve.* Yet that wasn't the part of the picture (or the only part) that fascinated me. Underneath, I felt that the scandal was a story about teenagers and their parents, about *families*, about how the expectations of one generation shape the next. In other words, the stuff of novels.

Reading fiction is often an act of empathy—as is writing it. This scandal set my imagination on fire. I was already almost a year into writing a new novel, but I found myself constantly (inconveniently) thinking about a new character, Chloe Berringer, who one morning opens her front door expecting UPS but instead finds the FBI there to arrest her mother.

I began to cheat (yes, cheat) on my other novel, writing character sketches and thinking through the arc of this new idea. Does Chloe go to Wood Valley, the fictional high school where my YA debut, *Tell Me Three Things*, is set? (Spoiler alert: She does.) How does it feel for her to realize her parents have so little faith in her that they resort to fraud to make sure she gets admitted to the college of her choice? How much did Chloe know and when did she know it? What does it mean to examine our own culpability and privilege? Soon I abandoned my more-than-halfway-finished work in progress and started writing *Admission* instead.

This book is 100 percent a work of fiction, and the characters are all born from my imagination, not from real people in the real world. I do not know anyone involved in the scandal, nor did I do any investigative reporting. And though there are a bunch of characters in that half-written novel on my laptop that are probably furious with me for abandoning them, I'm still so glad that Chloe took hold of my imagination and demanded I tell her story. After reading *Admission*, I hope you are too.

ACKNOWLEDGMENTS

First and foremost, I'd like to thank every single person who has ever bought, borrowed, or recommended a book with my name on the cover. I am deeply, eternally grateful. There are a whole lot of novels in the world to pick from. I'm so honored you took a leap of faith and found your way to one of mine.

Forever thank-yous to Susan Kamil and Elaine Koster, the two women who are responsible for starting my career. I miss them both dearly.

Giant high five and thank-you to Jenn Joel and Beverly Horowitz. Fist bump/prayer emoji hands to Jillian Vandall. You guys rock.

All my gratitude to the wonderful people at Random House Children's Books: Barbara Marcus, John Adamo, Dominique Cimina, Kate Keating, Elizabeth Ward, Kelly McGauley, Hannah Black, Neil Swaab and Alison Impey, Adrienne Waintraub, Kristin Schulz and the School and Library team, Rebecca Gudelis, Colleen Fellingham, Nathan Kinney, Tamar Schwartz, and a million other awesome people who I will kick myself for not mentioning as soon as this goes to print. I'm deeply grateful to the international rights team at ICM and Curtis Brown, and in particular, Roxanne Edouard. Thanks also to Tia Ikemoto; the Hatchery, for providing me a writing home so close to home; and the Fiction Writers Co-op, for your water cooler magic. A special shout-out to Jennifer Mathieu, who answered a Facebook pun call and named Chloe's yoga studio 9021-OM. A special thank-you to Andrea Peskind Katz for all of her insight, thoughts, and time.

Thank you always to the amazing Lola Wusu, Charlotte Huang, my college crew, and the rest of my amazing village. You all know who you are.

Big love to my amazing family: Dad, Josh, Leia, Jamesy, and of course, the Flore clan. Special thank-you to my mom, Elizabeth, who is loved and remembered every single day.

And finally, thank you to Indy and Elili and Luca, my snugglebugs and my favorite people in the whole wide world. ILYTTMABABAI.

ABOUT THE AUTHOR

JULIE BUXBAUM is the *New York Times* bestselling author of the young adult novels *Hope and Other Punch Lines, What to Say Next,* and *Tell Me Three Things.* She also wrote the critically acclaimed *The Opposite of Love* and *After You.* She lives in Los Angeles with her husband and two children. You can find her procrastinating on social at @juliebux (Twitter) and @juliebuxbaum (Insta).

JulieBuxbaum.com